POKÉMON™

THE COMPLETE POKÉMON POCKET GUIDE

D1176169

#001–442
Bulbasaur to Spiritomb

A two-volume set that includes all 898 Pokémon!

All 898 Pokémon! *The Complete Pokémon Pocket Guide* consists of two volumes. This is volume 1, where you can learn about 442 Pokémon, from Bulbasaur to Spiritomb.

 TABLE OF CONTENTS

The Pokémon with Pokédex numbers 443–898 can all be found in volume 2.

This series recognizes Pokémon up to Generation 8, Pokémon: Sword & Shield.

GIGANTAMAX, MEGA EVOLUTION, AND PRIMAL REVERSION POKÉMON

*The Mega Evolution and Primal Reversion forms are on the pages after the original forms.

HOW TO READ THE POKÉMON POCKET GUIDE

This guide is in Pokédex order, so you'll be able to find the Pokémon you're looking for with ease. Check out how you should read this guide!

CATEGORY

A Pokémon's unique characteristic.

POKÉDEX NUMBER

The numerical listing of a Pokémon.

TYPE

There are 18 types in all. Some Pokémon have two types. Type effectiveness is very important in a battle.

ABILITY

A special ability that each Pokémon has that is useful in battle. If there are two abilities that a type of Pokémon can use, then each individual Pokémon will only be able to use one of those abilities.

SIZE

The height and weight of a Pokémon.

DESCRIPTION

The Pokémon's detailed description.

EVOLUTION

A Pokémon may evolve under certain conditions, at which point its name and form will change. The name written in red is the Pokémon being explained on this page, so you can easily see what the Pokémon looks like before and after it evolves.

POKÉDEX NUMBERING

The numerical section of the Pokémon within this guide.

NAME

The Pokémon's name.

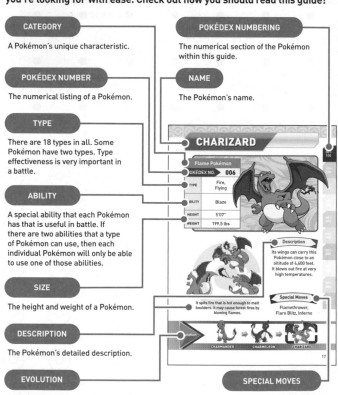

CHARIZARD

Flame Pokémon
POKÉDEX NO. **006**
TYPE — Fire, Flying
ABILITY — Blaze
HEIGHT — 5'07"
WEIGHT — 199.5 lbs

Description

Its wings can carry this Pokémon close to an altitude of 4,600 feet. It blows out fire at very high temperatures.

It spits fire that is hot enough to melt boulders. It may cause forest fires by blowing flames.

Special Moves

Flamethrower, Flare Blitz, Inferno

Evolution

CHARMANDER → CHARMELEON → CHARIZARD

17

SPECIAL MOVES

Moves that this Pokémon will learn. It may learn many other moves too.

REGIONAL FORMS

Some regions like Galar and Alola have Pokémon with regional forms who have the same name but look different and have different features. These Pokémon will say "___ Form" below their names.

GALARIAN FORM

Pokémon who have changed to adapt to the Galar region. "Galarian Form" will appear below their name.

ALOLAN FORM

Pokémon who have changed to adapt to the Alola region. "Alolan Form" will appear below their name.

CORSOLA
GALARIAN FORM

Coral Pokémon

POKÉDEX NO.	**222**
TYPE	Ghost
ABILITY	Weak Armor
HEIGHT	2'00"
WEIGHT	1.1 lbs

Description

Watch your step when wandering areas oceans once covered. What looks like a stone could be this Pokémon, and it will curse you if you kick it.

Special Moves

Night Shade, Strength Sap, Curse

Sudden climate change wiped out this ancient kind of Corsola. This Pokémon absorbs others' life force through its branches.

Evolution

CORSOLA GALARIAN FORM → CURSOLA

294

DUGTRIO
ALOLAN FORM

001-100

The three of them get along very well. Through their formidable teamwork, they defeat powerful opponents.

Mole Pokémon

POKÉDEX NO.	**051**
TYPE	Ground, Steel
ABILITY	Sand Veil, Tangling Hair
HEIGHT	2'04"
WEIGHT	146.8 lbs

Description

Their beautiful, metallic whiskers create a sort of protective helmet on their heads, and they also function as highly precise sensors.

Special Moves

Iron Head, Night Slash, Tri Attack

Evolution

DIGLETT ALOLAN FORM → DUGTRIO ALOLAN FORM

81

GIGANTAMAX POKÉMON

BLASTOISE
GIGANTAMAX FORM

Water fired from this Pokémon's central main cannon has enough power to blast a hole into a mountain.

BLASTOISE

Shellfish Pokémon	
POKÉDEX NO.	**009**
TYPE	Water
ABILITY	Torrent
HEIGHT	82'00"+
WEIGHT	??? lbs

Description

It's not very good at precision shooting. When attacking, it just fires its 31 cannons over and over and over.

Special Moves

G-Max Cannonade

24

"Gigantamax" is the phenomenon of the Pokémon growing in size and changing form. It is a unique phenomenon that only occurs in certain areas of Galar. So far, 32 Pokémon have been discovered that can Gigantamax.

It can use G-Max Moves!
A very powerful move that only Gigantamax Pokémon can use.

Its form and size change!

It is so huge that its weight is unknown. Its type and ability remain the same.

BLASTOISE
(GIGANTAMAX FORM)

BLASTOISE

MEGA EVOLVED POKÉMON

MEGA SCEPTILE

SCEPTILE

It agilely leaps about the jungle and uses the sharp leaves on its arms to strike its prey.

Forest Pokémon	
POKÉDEX NO.	254
TYPE	Grass, Dragon
ABILITY	Lightning Rod
HEIGHT	6'03"
WEIGHT	121.7 lbs

Description
The leaves that grow on its arms can slice down thick trees. It is without peer in jungle combat.

Special Moves
Leaf Storm, Leaf Blade, X-Scissor

Mega Evolution is a phenomenon of the Pokémon evolving during a battle to wield incredible power. Its type, height, and weight may change, so you might want to compare them with the original Pokémon. So far, 48 Pokémon have been discovered to be able to Mega Evolve.

MEGA SCEPTILE

When a Pokémon Mega Evolves, its form and stats change!

Its attack and speed will increase, making it become even more powerful in battle. The abilities of some Pokémon will change too.

SCEPTILE

PRIMAL REVERSION

Primal Reversion is the phenomenon of a Pokémon turning back into its ancient form to regain its true power. Only two Pokémon, Groudon and Kyogre, are capable of Primal Reversion.

*The Mega Evolution and Primal Reversion forms are on the pages after the original forms.

PRIMAL GROUDON

GROUDON

Said to have expanded the lands by super-evaporating water with raging heat. It battled Kyogre over natural energy.

Continent Pokémon	
POKÉDEX NO.	383
TYPE	Ground, Fire
ABILITY	Desolate Land
HEIGHT	16'05"
WEIGHT	2204.0 lbs

Description
Through Primal Reversion and with nature's full power, it will take back its true form. It can cause magma to erupt and expose the landmass of the world.

Special Moves
Precipice Blades, Heat Wave, Earth Power

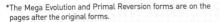

7

Type effectiveness is very important in a Pokémon battle. The effectiveness of a move will change depending on the type of the move used by the Pokémon and the type of the Pokémon defending itself from the attack. Check the chart below and memorize the type effectiveness!

MOVE/TYPE EFFECTIVENESS CHART

TYPE OF POKÉMON MOVE USED BY THE ATTACKER	Normal	Fire	Water	Electric	Grass	Ice	Fighting	Poison	Ground	Flying	Psychic	Bug	Rock	Ghost	Dragon	Dark	Steel	Fairy
Normal													▲	×			▲	
Fire		▲	▲		●	●						●	▲		▲		●	
Water		●	▲		▲				●				●		▲			
Electric			●	▲	▲				×	●					▲			
Grass		▲	●		▲			▲	●	▲		▲	●		▲		▲	
Ice		▲	▲		●	▲			●	●					●		▲	
Fighting	●					●		▲		▲	▲	▲	●	×		●	●	▲
Poison					●			▲	▲				▲	▲			×	●
Ground		●		●	▲			●		×		▲	●				●	
Flying				▲	●		●					●	▲				▲	
Psychic							●	●			▲					×	▲	
Bug		▲			●		▲	▲		▲	●			▲		●	▲	▲
Rock		●				●	▲		▲	●		●					▲	
Ghost	×										●			●		▲		
Dragon															●		▲	×
Dark							▲				●			●		▲		▲
Steel		▲	▲	▲		●							●				▲	●
Fairy		▲					●	▲							●	●	▲	

TYPE OF POKÉMON DEFENDING

MARK DESCRIPTIONS

- ● Super Effective
- ▲ Not Very Effective
- × No Effect
- ☐ Normal Effect

AIM FOR "SUPER EFFECTIVE"!

Learn the combinations for a "Super Effective" attack! For example, Grookey excels in Grass-type moves, so it is strong against Squirtle, which is a Water-type Pokémon. But Grookey is weak against Torchic's Fire-type move.

GROOKEY
GRASS TYPE

Fire-type moves are **Super Effective!**

Grass-type moves are **Super Effective!**

Water-type moves are **Super Effective!**

TORCHIC FIRE TYPE

SQUIRTLE WATER TYPE

BULBASAUR

Seed Pokémon	
POKÉDEX NO.	**001**
TYPE	Grass, Poison
ABILITY	Overgrow
HEIGHT	2'04"
WEIGHT	15.2 lbs

Description

There is a plant seed on its back right from the day this Pokémon is born. The seed slowly grows larger.

While it is young, it uses the nutrients that are stored in the seed on its back in order to grow.

Special Moves

Poison Powder, Growth, Razor Leaf

Evolution

BULBASAUR IVYSAUR VENUSAUR

IVYSAUR

Seed Pokémon

POKÉDEX NO.	002
TYPE	Grass, Poison
ABILITY	Overgrow
HEIGHT	3'03"
WEIGHT	28.7 lbs

Description

When the bulb on its back grows large, it appears to lose the Ability to stand on its hind legs.

Exposure to sunlight adds to its strength. Sunlight also makes the bud on its back grow larger.

Special Moves

Sleep Powder, Sweet Scent, Seed Bomb

Evolution

BULBASAUR → IVYSAUR → VENUSAUR

VENUSAUR

Seed Pokémon	
POKÉDEX NO.	**003**
TYPE	Grass, Poison
ABILITY	Overgrow
HEIGHT	6'07"
WEIGHT	220.5 lbs

A bewitching aroma wafts from its flower. The fragrance becalms those engaged in battle.

Description

Its plant blooms when it is absorbing solar energy. It stays on the move to seek sunlight.

Special Moves

Solar Beam, Petal Blizzard, Take Down

Evolution

BULBASAUR → IVYSAUR → VENUSAUR

12

VENUSAUR

GIGANTAMAX FORM

Huge amounts of pollen burst from it with the force of a volcanic eruption. Breathing in too much of the pollen can cause fainting.

VENUSAUR

001-100

101-200

201-300

401-442

443-500

501-600

701-800

801-898

Seed Pokémon	
POKÉDEX NO.	**003**
TYPE	Grass, Poison
ABILITY	Overgrow
HEIGHT	78'09"+
WEIGHT	??? lbs

Description

In battle, this Pokémon swings around two thick vines. If these vines slammed into a 10-story building, they could easily topple it.

Special Moves

G-Max Vine Lash

MEGA VENUSAUR

By spreading the broad petals of its flower and catching the sun's rays, it fills its body with power.

VENUSAUR

Seed Pokémon	
POKÉDEX NO.	**003**
TYPE	Grass, Poison
ABILITY	Thick Fat
HEIGHT	7'10"
WEIGHT	342.8 lbs

Description

In order to support its flower, which has grown larger due to Mega Evolution, its back and legs have become stronger.

Special Moves

Petal Blizzard, Solar Beam, Double-Edge

CHARMANDER

Lizard Pokémon	
POKÉDEX NO.	**004**
TYPE	Fire
ABILITY	Blaze
HEIGHT	2'00"
WEIGHT	18.7 lbs

101-200

201-300

401-442

443-500

501-600

701-600

801-898

It has a preference for hot things. When it rains, steam is said to spout from the tip of its tail.

Description

From the time it is born, a flame burns at the tip of its tail. Its life would end if the flame were to go out.

Special Moves

Scratch, Growl, Ember, Smokescreen

Evolution

CHARMANDER → CHARMELEON → CHARIZARD

CHARMELEON

Flame Pokémon

POKÉDEX NO.	005
TYPE	Fire
ABILITY	Blaze
HEIGHT	3'07"
WEIGHT	41.9 lbs

Description

It has a barbaric nature. In battle, it whips its fiery tail around and slashes away with sharp claws.

If it becomes agitated during battle, it spouts intense flames, incinerating its surroundings.

Special Moves

Fire Fang, Fire Spin, Scary Face

Evolution

CHARMANDER   CHARMELEON   CHARIZARD

CHARIZARD

001-100
101-200
401-442
501-600
701-800
801-898

Flame Pokémon	
POKÉDEX NO.	**006**
TYPE	Fire, Flying
ABILITY	Blaze
HEIGHT	5'07"
WEIGHT	199.5 lbs

Description

Its wings can carry this Pokémon close to an altitude of 4,600 feet. It blows out fire at very high temperatures.

It spits fire that is hot enough to melt boulders. It may cause forest fires by blowing flames.

Special Moves

Flamethrower, Flare Blitz, Inferno

Evolution

CHARMANDER   CHARMELEON   CHARIZARD

17

CHARIZARD

GIGANTAMAX FORM

CHARIZARD

The flame inside its body burns hotter than 3,600 degrees Fahrenheit. When Charizard roars, that temperature climbs even higher.

Flame Pokémon	
POKÉDEX NO.	**006**
TYPE	Fire, Flying
ABILITY	Blaze
HEIGHT	91'10"+
WEIGHT	??? lbs

Description

This colossal, flame-winged figure of a Charizard was brought about by Gigantamax energy.

Special Moves

G-Max Wildfire

MEGA CHARIZARD X

001-100
101-200
201-300
401-442
443-500
501-600
701-800
801-898

If Charizard becomes furious, the flame at the tip of its tail flares up in a whitish-blue color.

CHARIZARD

Flame Pokémon	
POKÉDEX NO.	**006**
TYPE	Fire, Dragon
ABILITY	Tough Claws
HEIGHT	5'07"
WEIGHT	243.6 lbs

Description

The overwhelming power that fills its entire body causes it to turn black and creates intense blue flames.

Special Moves

Dragon Claw, Dragon Rage, Flamethrower

MEGA CHARIZARD Y

It uses its wings to fly high. The temperature of its fire increases as it gains experience in battle.

CHARIZARD

Flame Pokémon

POKÉDEX NO.	006
TYPE	Fire, Flying
ABILITY	Drought
HEIGHT	5'07"
WEIGHT	221.6 lbs

Description

Its bond with its Trainer is the source of its power. It boasts speed and maneuverability greater than that of a jet fighter.

Special Moves

Flame Burst, Flare Blitz, Flamethrower

SQUIRTLE

Tiny Turtle Pokémon

POKÉDEX NO.	007

TYPE	Water
ABILITY	Torrent
HEIGHT	1'08"
WEIGHT	19.8 lbs

101-200

201-300

401-442

443-500

501-600

701-800

801-898

When it retracts its long neck into its shell, it squirts out water with vigorous force.

Description

When it feels threatened, it draws its limbs inside its shell and sprays water from its mouth.

Special Moves

Tackle, Iron Defense, Water Gun

Evolution

SQUIRTLE → WARTORTLE → BLASTOISE

21

WARTORTLE

Turtle Pokémon	
POKÉDEX NO.	**008**
TYPE	Water
ABILITY	Torrent
HEIGHT	3'03"
WEIGHT	49.6 lbs

Description

It is recognized as a symbol of longevity. If its shell has algae on it, that Wartortle is very old.

Special Moves

Water Pulse, Rain Dance, Rapid Spin

It cleverly controls its furry ears and tail to maintain its balance while swimming.

Evolution

SQUIRTLE → WARTORTLE → BLASTOISE

BLASTOISE

Shellfish Pokémon

POKÉDEX NO.	**009**
TYPE	Water
ABILITY	Torrent
HEIGHT	5'03"
WEIGHT	188.5 lbs

001-100

101-200

201-300

401-442

443-500

501-600

701-800

801-898

Description

It crushes its foe under its heavy body to cause fainting. In a pinch, it will withdraw inside its shell.

The rocket cannons on its shell fire jets of water capable of punching holes through thick steel.

Special Moves

Hydro Pump, Bite, Flash Cannon

Evolution

SQUIRTLE → WARTORTLE → BLASTOISE

BLASTOISE

GIGANTAMAX FORM

Water fired from this Pokémon's central main cannon has enough power to blast a hole into a mountain.

BLASTOISE

Shellfish Pokémon	
POKÉDEX NO.	**009**
TYPE	Water
ABILITY	Torrent
HEIGHT	82'00"+
WEIGHT	??? lbs

Description

It's not very good at precision shooting. When attacking, it just fires its 31 cannons over and over and over.

Special Moves

G-Max Cannonade

MEGA BLASTOISE

001-
100

101-
200

201-
300

401-
442

443-
500

501-
600

701-
800

801-
898

BLASTOISE

It deliberately makes itself heavy so it can withstand the recoil of the water jets it fires.

Shellfish Pokémon	
POKÉDEX NO.	**009**
TYPE	Water
ABILITY	Mega Launcher
HEIGHT	5'03"
WEIGHT	222.9 lbs

Description

The cannon on its back is as powerful as a tank gun. Its tough legs and back enable it to withstand the recoil from firing the cannon.

Special Moves

Hydro Pump, Skull Bash, Aqua Tail

25

CATERPIE

For protection, it releases a horrible stench from the antennae on its head to drive away enemies.

Worm Pokémon	
POKÉDEX NO.	**010**
TYPE	Bug
ABILITY	Shield Dust
HEIGHT	1'00"
WEIGHT	6.4 lbs

Description

Its short feet are tipped with suction pads that enable it to tirelessly climb slopes and walls.

Special Moves

Tackle, String Shot, Bug Bite

Evolution

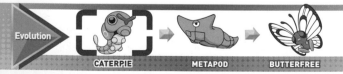

CATERPIE → METAPOD → BUTTERFREE

METAPOD

001-100

101-200

201-300

401-442

443-500

501-600

701-800

801-898

Even though it is encased in a sturdy shell, the body inside is tender. It can't withstand a harsh attack.

Cocoon Pokémon	
POKÉDEX NO.	**011**
TYPE	Bug
ABILITY	Shed Skin
HEIGHT	2'04"
WEIGHT	21.8 lbs

Description

It is waiting for the moment to evolve. At this stage, it can only harden, so it remains motionless to avoid attacks.

Special Moves

Harden

Evolution

CATERPIE

METAPOD

BUTTERFREE

BUTTERFREE

Butterfly Pokémon

POKÉDEX NO.	012

TYPE	Bug, Flying
ABILITY	Compound Eyes
HEIGHT	3'07"
WEIGHT	70.5 lbs

Description

It collects honey every day. It rubs honey onto the hairs on its legs to carry it back to its nest.

In battle, it flaps its wings at great speed to release highly toxic dust into the air.

Special Moves

Air Slash, Poison Powder, Quiver Dance

Evolution

CATERPIE → METAPOD → BUTTERFREE

BUTTERFREE

GIGANTAMAX FORM

Once it has opponents trapped in a tornado that could blow away a 10-ton truck, it finishes them off with its poisonous scales.

001-100

101-200

201-300

401-442

443-500

501-600

701-800

801-898

BUTTERFREE

Butterfly Pokémon	
POKÉDEX NO.	**012**
TYPE	Bug, Flying
ABILITY	Compound Eyes
HEIGHT	55'09"+
WEIGHT	??? lbs

Description

Crystalized Gigantamax energy makes up this Pokémon's blindingly bright and highly toxic scales.

Special Moves

G-Max Befuddle

29

WEEDLE

Beware of the sharp stinger on its head. It hides in grass and bushes, where it eats leaves.

Hairy Bug Pokémon	
POKÉDEX NO.	**013**
TYPE	Bug, Poison
ABILITY	Shield Dust
HEIGHT	1'00"
WEIGHT	7.1 lbs

Description

Weedle has extremely acute senses. It is capable of distinguishing its favorite kinds of leaves from those it dislikes just by sniffing with its big, red proboscis (nose).

Special Moves

String Shot, Poison Sting, Bug Bite

Evolution

WEEDLE → KAKUNA → BEEDRILL

KAKUNA

001-100

101-200

201-300

401-442

463-500

501-600

701-800

801-898

Able to move only slightly. When in danger, it may stick out its stinger and poison its enemy.

Cocoon Pokémon	
POKÉDEX NO.	**014**
TYPE	Bug, Poison
ABILITY	Shed Skin
HEIGHT	2'00"
WEIGHT	22.0 lbs

Description

Kakuna remains virtually immobile as it clings to a tree. However, on the inside, it is extremely busy as it prepares for its coming evolution. This is evident from how hot its shell becomes to the touch.

Special Moves

Harden

Evolution

WEEDLE → KAKUNA → BEEDRILL

BEEDRILL

It has three poisonous stingers on its forelegs and its tail. They are used to jab its enemy repeatedly.

Poison Bee Pokémon

POKÉDEX NO.	015
TYPE	Bug, Poison
ABILITY	Swarm
HEIGHT	3'03"
WEIGHT	65.0 lbs

Description

Beedrill is extremely territorial. No one should ever approach its nest—this is for their own safety. If angered, Beedrill will attack in a furious swarm.

Special Moves

Fury Attack, Twineedle, Pin Missile

Evolution

WEEDLE   KAKUNA   BEEDRILL

MEGA BEEDRILL

001-100
101-200
201-300
401-442
443-500
501-600
701-800
801-898

BEEDRILL

It can take down any opponent with its powerful poison stingers. It sometimes attacks in swarms.

Poison Bee Pokémon	
POKÉDEX NO.	**015**
TYPE	Bug, Poison
ABILITY	Adaptability
HEIGHT	4'07"
WEIGHT	89.3 lbs

Description

Its legs have become poison stingers. It stabs its prey repeatedly with the stingers on its limbs, dealing the final blow with the stinger on its rear.

Special Moves

Venoshock, Twineedle, Agility

PIDGEY

Very docile. If attacked, it will often kick up sand to protect itself rather than fight back.

Tiny Bird Pokémon	
POKÉDEX NO.	**016**
TYPE	Normal, Flying
ABILITY	Keen Eye, Tangled Feet
HEIGHT	1'00"
WEIGHT	4.0 lbs

Description

Pidgey has an extremely sharp sense of direction. It is capable of unerringly returning home to its nest, however far it may be from its familiar surroundings.

Special Moves

Tackle, Gust, Sand Attack

Evolution

PIDGEY → PIDGEOTTO → PIDGEOT

PIDGEOTTO

Bird Pokémon

POKÉDEX NO.	**017**
TYPE	Normal, Flying
ABILITY	Keen Eye, Tangled Feet
HEIGHT	3'07"
WEIGHT	66.1 lbs

This Pokémon is full of vitality. It constantly flies around its large territory in search of prey.

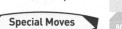

Description

Pidgeotto claims a large area as its own territory. This Pokémon flies around patrolling its living space. If its territory is violated, it shows no mercy in thoroughly punishing the foe with its sharp claws.

Special Moves

Wing Attack, Whirlwind, Quick Attack

Evolution

 → →

PIDGEY   PIDGEOTTO   PIDGEOT

001-100
101-200
201-300
401-442
443-500
501-600
701-800
801-898

PIDGEOT

This Pokémon flies at Mach* 2 speed, seeking prey. Its large talons are feared as wicked weapons.

Bird Pokémon

POKÉDEX NO.	**018**
TYPE	Normal, Flying
ABILITY	Keen Eye, Tangled Feet
HEIGHT	4'11"
WEIGHT	87.1 lbs

Description

This Pokémon has a dazzling plumage of beautifully glossy feathers. Many Trainers are captivated by the striking beauty of the feathers on its head, compelling them to choose Pidgeot as their Pokémon.

Special Moves

Air Slash, Agility, Hurricane

Evolution

PIDGEY → PIDGEOTTO → PIDGEOT

*Mach: A measurement of speed. Mach 1 is the same speed as sound, at 1,125 feet per second.

MEGA PIDGEOT

001-
100

101-
200

201-
300

401-
442

443-
500

501-
600

701-
800

801-
898

Its outstanding vision allows it to spot splashing Magikarp,* even while flying at 3,300 feet.

PIDGEOT

Bird Pokémon	
POKÉDEX NO.	**018**
TYPE	Flying, Normal
ABILITY	No Guard
HEIGHT	7'03"
WEIGHT	111.3 lbs

Description

With its muscular strength now greatly increased, it can fly continuously for two weeks without resting.

Special Moves

Feather Dance, Mirror Move, Air Slash

*Magikarp: A Pokémon you'll find on page 185.

RATTATA

Mouse Pokémon	
POKÉDEX NO.	**019**
TYPE	Normal
ABILITY	Run Away, Guts
HEIGHT	1'00"
WEIGHT	7.7 lbs

This Pokémon is common but hazardous. Its sharp incisors can easily cut right through hard wood.

Description

Will chew on anything with its fangs. If you see one, it is certain that 40 more live in the area.

Special Moves

Crunch, Quick Attack, Sucker Punch

Evolution

  →

RATTATA → RATICATE

RATTATA

ALOLAN FORM

001-100

101-200

201-300

401-442

443-500

501-600

701-800

801-898

Its whiskers provide it with a keen sense of smell, enabling it to pick up the scent of hidden food and locate it instantly.

Mouse Pokémon	
POKÉDEX NO.	**019**
TYPE	Dark
ABILITY	Gluttony, Hustle
HEIGHT	1'00"
WEIGHT	8.4 lbs

Description

It shows no interest in anything that isn't fresh. If you take it shopping with you, it will help you pick out ingredients.

Special Moves

Quick Attack, Assurance, Double-Edge

Evolution

RATTATA
(ALOLAN FORM)

RATICATE
(ALOLAN FORM)

RATICATE

Mouse Pokémon

POKÉDEX NO.	**020**
TYPE	Normal
ABILITY	Run Away, Guts
HEIGHT	2'04"
WEIGHT	40.8 lbs

Its hind feet are webbed. They act as flippers, so it can swim in rivers and hunt for prey.

Description

Its whiskers are essential for maintaining its balance. No matter how friendly you are, it will get angry and bite you if you touch its whiskers.

Special Moves

Super Fang, Hyper Fang, Pursuit

Evolution

RATTATA → RATICATE

RATICATE

ALOLAN FORM

It makes its Rattata underlings gather food for it, dining solely on the most nutritious and delicious fare.

101-200

201-300

401-442

443-500

501-600

701-800

801-898

Mouse Pokémon	
POKÉDEX NO.	**020**
TYPE	Dark
ABILITY	Gluttony, Hustle
HEIGHT	2'04"
WEIGHT	56.2 lbs

Description

It has an incredibly greedy personality. Its nest is filled with so much food gathered by Rattata under its direction that it can't possibly eat it all.

Special Moves

Crunch, Swords Dance, Double-Edge

Evolution

RATTATA
(ALOLAN FORM)

RATICATE
(ALOLAN FORM)

SPEAROW

Inept at flying high. However, it can fly around very fast to protect its territory.

Tiny Bird Pokémon	
POKÉDEX NO.	**021**
TYPE	Normal, Flying
ABILITY	Keen Eye
HEIGHT	1'00"
WEIGHT	4.4 lbs

Description

Its reckless nature leads it to stand up to others—even large Pokémon—if it has to protect its territory.

Special Moves

Peck, Agility, Aerial Ace

Evolution

SPEAROW → FEAROW

FEAROW

001-100
101-200
201-300
401-442
443-500
501-600
701-800
801-898

A Pokémon that dates back many years. If it senses danger, it flies high and away, instantly.

Beak Pokémon	
POKÉDEX NO.	**022**
TYPE	Normal, Flying
ABILITY	Keen Eye
HEIGHT	3'11"
WEIGHT	83.8 lbs

Description

Carrying food through Fearow's territory is dangerous. It will snatch the food away from you in a flash!

Special Moves

Drill Run, Drill Peck, Pursuit

Evolution

SPEAROW

FEAROW

EKANS

Snake Pokémon

POKÉDEX NO.	023
TYPE	Poison
ABILITY	Shed Skin, Intimidate
HEIGHT	6'07"
WEIGHT	15.2 lbs

Description

The older it gets, the longer it grows. At night, it wraps its long body around tree branches to rest.

By dislocating its jaw, it can swallow prey larger than itself. After a meal, it curls up and rests.

Special Moves

Leer, Wrap, Gunk Shot

Evolution

EKANS → ARBOK

ARBOK

The frightening patterns on its belly have been studied. Six variations have been confirmed.

101-200

201-300

401-442

443-500

501-600

701-800

801-898

Cobra Pokémon

POKÉDEX NO.	024
TYPE	Poison
ABILITY	Shed Skin, Intimidate
HEIGHT	11'06"
WEIGHT	143.3 lbs

Description

After stunning its opponents with the pattern on its stomach, it quickly wraps them up in its body and waits for them to stop moving.

Special Moves

Coil, Glare, Sludge Bomb

Evolution

EKANS

ARBOK

PIKACHU

When several of these Pokémon gather, their electricity can build and cause lightning storms.

Mouse Pokémon	
POKÉDEX NO.	**025**
TYPE	Electric
ABILITY	Static
HEIGHT	1'04"
WEIGHT	13.2 lbs

Description

When it is angered, it immediately discharges the energy stored in the pouches in its cheeks.

Special Moves

Thunder Shock, Thunderbolt, Thunder

Evolution

PICHU → PIKACHU → RAICHU / RAICHU (ALOLAN FORM)

001-
100

101-
200

201-
300

401-
442

443-
500

501-
600

701-
800

801-
898

MALE

FEMALE

The shapes of a male and female Pikachu's tail are different.

PIKACHU

PIKACHU

When it smashes its opponents with its bolt-shaped tail, it delivers a surge of electricity equivalent to a lightning strike.

Mouse Pokémon

POKÉDEX NO.	025
TYPE	Electric
ABILITY	Static
HEIGHT	68'11"+
WEIGHT	??? lbs

Description

Its Gigantamax power expands, forming its supersized body and towering tail.

Special Moves

G-Max Volt Crash

RAICHU

001–100
101–200
201–300
401–442
443–500
501–600
701–800
801–898

Mouse Pokémon	
POKÉDEX NO.	**026**
TYPE	Electric
ABILITY	Static
HEIGHT	2'07"
WEIGHT	66.1 lbs

Description

Its long tail serves as a ground to protect itself from its own high-voltage power.

If its electric pouches run empty, it raises its tail to gather electricity from the atmosphere.

Special Moves

Thunder Punch, Electro Ball, Spark

Evolution

 PICHU **PIKACHU** **RAICHU**

RAICHU

ALOLAN FORM

	Mouse Pokémon	
POKÉDEX NO.	**026**	
TYPE	Electric, Psychic	
ABILITY	Surge Surfer	
HEIGHT	2'04"	
WEIGHT	46.3 lbs	

It's believed that the weather, climate, and food of the Alola region all play a part in causing Pikachu to evolve into this form of Raichu.

Description

This Pokémon rides on its tail while it uses its psychic powers to levitate. It attacks with star-shaped thunderbolts.

Special Moves

Psychic, Agility, Thunder

Evolution

PICHU ➡ PIKACHU ➡ RAICHU (ALOLAN FORM)

SANDSHREW

001-
100

101-
200

201-
300

401-
442

443-
500

501-
600

701-
800

801-
898

Mouse Pokémon	
POKÉDEX NO.	**027**
TYPE	Ground
ABILITY	Sand Veil
HEIGHT	2'00"
WEIGHT	26.5 lbs

Description

It burrows into the ground to create its nest. If hard stones impede its tunneling, it uses its sharp claws to shatter them and then carries on digging.

It loves to bathe in the grit of dry, sandy areas. By sand bathing, the Pokémon rids itself of dirt and moisture clinging to its body.

Special Moves

Dig, Defense Curl, Swift

Evolution

  ➡

SANDSHREW   SANDSLASH

SANDSHREW

ALOLAN FORM

Mouse Pokémon

POKÉDEX NO.	027

TYPE	Ice, Steel
ABILITY	Snow Cloak
HEIGHT	2'04"
WEIGHT	88.2 lbs

Description

Life on mountains covered with deep snow has granted this Pokémon a body of ice that's as hard as steel.

It lives in snowy mountains on southern islands. When a blizzard rolls in, this Pokémon hunkers down in the snow to avoid getting blown away.

Special Moves

Hail, Metal Claw, Fury Swipes

Evolution

 →

SANDSHREW
[ALOLAN FORM]

SANDSLASH
[ALOLAN FORM]

SANDSLASH

001-100
101-200
201-300
401-442
443-500
501-600
701-800
801-898

Mouse Pokémon	
POKÉDEX NO.	028
TYPE	Ground
ABILITY	Sand Veil
HEIGHT	3'03"
WEIGHT	65.0 lbs

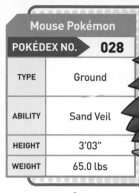

The drier the area Sandslash lives in, the harder and smoother the Pokémon's spikes will feel when touched.

Description

It climbs trees by hooking on with its sharp claws. Sandslash shares the berries it gathers, dropping them down to Sandshrew waiting below the tree.

Special Moves

Fury Swipes, Sand Tomb, Fury Cutter

Evolution

SANDSHREW → SANDSLASH

SANDSLASH

ALOLAN FORM

Many people climb snowy mountains, hoping to see the icy spikes of these Pokémon glistening in the light of dawn.

Mouse Pokémon	
POKÉDEX NO.	**028**
TYPE	Ice, Steel
ABILITY	Snow Cloak
HEIGHT	3'11"
WEIGHT	121.3 lbs

Description

It uses large, hooked claws to cut a path through deep snow as it runs. On snowy mountains, this Sandslash is faster than any other Pokémon.

Special Moves

Blizzard, Icicle Crash, Metal Burst

Evolution

SANDSHREW
(ALOLAN FORM)

SANDSLASH
(ALOLAN FORM)

NIDORAN♀

001-100
101-200
201-300
401-442
443-500
501-600
701-800
801-898

Females are more sensitive to smells than males. While foraging, they'll use their whiskers to check wind direction and stay downwind of predators.

Poison Pin Pokémon	
POKÉDEX NO.	**029**
TYPE	Poison
ABILITY	Poison Point, Rivalry
HEIGHT	1'04"
WEIGHT	15.4 lbs

Description

It uses its hard incisor teeth to crush and eat berries. The tip of a female Nidoran's horn is a bit more rounded than the tip of a male's horn.

Special Moves

Bite, Poison Sting, Fury Swipes

Evolution

NIDORAN♀   NIDORINA   NIDOQUEEN

NIDORINA

If the group is threatened, these Pokémon will band together to assault enemies with a chorus of ultrasonic waves.

Poison Pin Pokémon	
POKÉDEX NO.	**030**
TYPE	Poison
ABILITY	Poison Point, Rivalry
HEIGHT	2'07"
WEIGHT	44.1 lbs

Description

The horn on its head has atrophied. It's thought that this happens so Nidorina's children won't get poked while their mother is feeding them.

Special Moves

Double Kick, Earth Power, Fury Swipes

Evolution

NIDORAN♀　　　NIDORINA　　　NIDOQUEEN

001-100

101-200

201-300

401-442

443-500

501-600

701-800

801-898

NIDOQUEEN

It pacifies offspring by placing them in the gaps between the spines on its back. The spines will never secrete poison while young are present.

Drill Pokémon

POKÉDEX NO.	031
TYPE	Poison, Ground
ABILITY	Poison Point, Rivalry
HEIGHT	4'03"
WEIGHT	132.3 lbs

Description

Nidoqueen is better at defense than offense. With scales like armor, this Pokémon will shield its children from any kind of attack.

Special Moves

Superpower, Toxic Spikes, Earth Power

Evolution

NIDORAN♀ → NIDORINA → NIDOQUEEN

NIDORAN♂

Small but brave, this Pokémon will hold its ground and even risk its life in battle to protect the female it's friendly with.

Poison Pin Pokémon

POKÉDEX NO.	**032**
TYPE	Poison
ABILITY	Poison Point, Rivalry
HEIGHT	1'08"
WEIGHT	19.8 lbs

Description

The horn on a male Nidoran's forehead contains a powerful poison. This is a very cautious Pokémon, always straining its large ears.

Special Moves

Leer, Poison Sting, Focus Energy

Evolution

NIDORAN♂ → NIDORINO → NIDOKING

NIDORINO

001-100

101-200

201-300

401-442

443-500

501-600

701-800

801-898

It's nervous and quick to ask aggressively. The potency of its poison increases along with the level of adrenaline present in its body.

Poison Pin Pokémon

POKÉDEX NO.	**033**
TYPE	Poison
ABILITY	Poison Point, Rivalry
HEIGHT	2'11"
WEIGHT	43.0 lbs

Description

With a horn that's harder than diamond, this Pokémon goes around shattering boulders as it searches for a Moon Stone.

Special Moves

Toxic, Earth Power, Horn Attack

Evolution

NIDORAN♂   NIDORINO   NIDOKING

NIDOKING

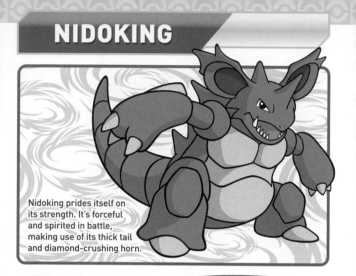

Nidoking prides itself on its strength. It's forceful and spirited in battle, making use of its thick tail and diamond-crushing horn.

Drill Pokémon	
POKÉDEX NO.	**034**
TYPE	Poison, Ground
ABILITY	Poison Point, Rivalry
HEIGHT	4'07"
WEIGHT	136.7 lbs

Description

When it goes on a rampage, it's impossible to control. But in the presence of a Nidoqueen it's lived with for a long time, Nidoking calms down.

Special Moves

Megahorn, Earth Power, Fury Attack

Evolution

NIDORAN♂ ➡ NIDORINO ➡ NIDOKING

CLEFAIRY

001-100
101-200
201-300
401-442
443-500
501-600
701-800
801-898

Its adorable behavior and cry make it highly popular. However, this cute Pokémon is rarely found.

Fairy Pokémon

POKÉDEX NO.	035
TYPE	Fairy
ABILITY	Cute Charm, Magic Guard
HEIGHT	2'00"
WEIGHT	16.5 lbs

Description

It is said that happiness will come to those who see a gathering of Clefairy dancing under a full moon.

Special Moves

Sing, Metronome, Disarming Voice

Evolution

CLEFFA → CLEFAIRY → CLEFABLE

61

CLEFABLE

Their ears are sensitive enough to hear a pin drop from over a mile away, so they're usually found in quiet places.

Fairy Pokémon	
POKÉDEX NO.	**036**
TYPE	Fairy
ABILITY	Cute Charm, Magic Guard
HEIGHT	4'03"
WEIGHT	88.2 lbs

Description

A timid fairy Pokémon that is rarely seen, it will run and hide the moment it senses people.

Special Moves

Charm, Moonlight, Moonblast

Evolution

CLEFFA ➡ CLEFAIRY ➡ CLEFABLE

VULPIX

001-
100

101-
200

201-
300

401-
442

443-
500

501-
600

701-
800

801-
898

Fox Pokémon

POKÉDEX NO.	**037**
TYPE	Fire
ABILITY	Flash Fire
HEIGHT	2'00"
WEIGHT	21.8 lbs

Description

As each tail grows, its fur becomes more lustrous. When held, it feels slightly warm.

While young, it has six gorgeous tails. When it grows, several new tails are sprouted.

Special Moves

Ember, Tail Whip, Extrasensory

Evolution

VULPIX

NINETALES

VULPIX

ALOLAN FORM

Fox Pokémon	
POKÉDEX NO.	**037**
TYPE	Ice
ABILITY	Snow Cloak
HEIGHT	2'00"
WEIGHT	21.8 lbs

Description

If you observe its curly hairs through a microscope, you'll see small ice particles springing up.

After long years in the ever-snowcapped mountains of Alola, this Vulpix has gained power over ice.

Special Moves

Powder Snow, Ice Beam, Disable

Evolution

VULPIX
(ALOLAN FORM)

NINETALES
(ALOLAN FORM)

NINETALES

001–
100

101–
200

201–
300

401–
442

443–
500

501–
600

701–
800

801–
898

Fox Pokémon

POKÉDEX NO.	038

TYPE	Fire
ABILITY	Flash Fire
HEIGHT	3'07"
WEIGHT	43.9 lbs

Description

It is said to live 1,000 years, and each of its tails is loaded with supernatural powers.

Very smart and very vengeful. Grabbing one of its many tails could result in a 1,000-year curse.

Special Moves

Flamethrower, Fire Spin, Incinerate

Evolution

VULPIX　　　NINETALES

NINETALES

ALOLAN FORM

While it will guide travelers who get lost on a snowy mountain down to the mountain's base, it won't forgive anyone who harms nature.

Fox Pokémon	
POKÉDEX NO.	**038**
TYPE	Ice, Fairy
ABILITY	Snow Cloak
HEIGHT	3'07"
WEIGHT	43.9 lbs

Description

A deity resides in the snowy mountains where this Pokémon lives. In ancient times, it was worshipped as that deity's incarnation.

Special Moves

Blizzard, Dazzling Gleam, Sheer Cold

Evolution

VULPIX
(ALOLAN FORM)

NINETALES
(ALOLAN FORM)

JIGGLYPUFF

001-100
101-200
201-300
401-442
443-500
501-600
701-800
801-898

Balloon Pokémon

POKÉDEX NO.	**039**
TYPE	Normal, Fairy
ABILITY	Cute Charm, Competitive
HEIGHT	1'08"
WEIGHT	12.1 lbs

If it inflates to sing a lullaby, it can perform longer and cause sure drowsiness in its audience.

Description

When its huge eyes waver, it sings a mysteriously soothing melody that lulls its enemies to sleep.

Special Moves

Sing, Disarming Voice, Play Rough

Evolution

IGGLYBUFF → JIGGLYPUFF → WIGGLYTUFF

WIGGLYTUFF

It's proud of its fur, which is fine and delicate. In particular, the curl on its forehead has a texture that's perfectly heavenly.

Balloon Pokémon

POKÉDEX NO.	040
TYPE	Normal, Fairy
ABILITY	Cute Charm, Competitive
HEIGHT	3'03"
WEIGHT	26.5 lbs

Description

The more air it takes in, the more it inflates. If opponents catch it in a bad mood, it will inflate itself to an enormous size to intimidate them.

Special Moves

Sweet Kiss, Hyper Voice, Charm

Evolution

IGGLYBUFF → JIGGLYPUFF → WIGGLYTUFF

ZUBAT

Bat Pokémon	
POKÉDEX NO.	**041**
TYPE	Poison, Flying
ABILITY	Inner Focus
HEIGHT	2'07"
WEIGHT	16.5 lbs

101-200
201-300
401-442
443-500
501-600
701-800
801-898

Description

Zubat live in caves, down where the sun's light won't reach. In the morning, they gather together to keep each other warm as they sleep.

It emits ultrasonic waves from its mouth to check its surroundings. Even in tight caves, Zubat flies around with skill.

Special Moves

Supersonic, Absorb, Confuse Ray

Evolution

ZUBAT → GOLBAT → CROBAT

GOLBAT

Bat Pokémon

POKÉDEX NO.	**042**
TYPE	Poison, Flying
ABILITY	Inner Focus
HEIGHT	5'03"
WEIGHT	121.3 lbs

Description

It loves to drink other creatures' blood. It's said that if it finds others of its kind going hungry, it sometimes shares the blood it's gathered.

Its feet are tiny, but this Pokémon walks skillfully. It sneaks up on sleeping prey before sinking its fangs in and slurping up blood.

Special Moves

Leech Life, Air Cutter, Poison Fang

Evolution

ZUBAT → GOLBAT → CROBAT

ODDISH

Weed Pokémon	
POKÉDEX NO.	**043**
TYPE	Grass, Poison
ABILITY	Chlorophyll
HEIGHT	1'08"
WEIGHT	11.9 lbs

Description

If exposed to moonlight, it starts to move. It roams far and wide at night to scatter its seeds.

During the day, it stays in the cold underground to avoid the sun. It grows by bathing in moonlight.

Special Moves

Poison Powder, Growth, Mega Drain

Evolution

ODDISH   GLOOM   VILEPLUME   BELLOSSOM

GLOOM

Weed Pokémon

POKÉDEX NO.	**044**
TYPE	Grass, Poison
ABILITY	Chlorophyll
HEIGHT	2'07"
WEIGHT	19.0 lbs

Its pistils exude an incredibly foul odor. The horrid stench can cause fainting at a distance of 1.25 miles.

Description

What appears to be drool is actually sweet honey. It is very sticky and clings stubbornly if touched.

Special Moves

Acid, Sweet Scent, Giga Drain

Evolution

ODDISH → GLOOM → VILEPLUME BELLOSSOM

VILEPLUME

001-100
101-200
201-300
401-442
443-500
501-600
701-800
801-898

Flower Pokémon

POKÉDEX NO.	**045**
TYPE	Grass, Poison
ABILITY	Chlorophyll
HEIGHT	3'11"
WEIGHT	41.0 lbs

Description

It has the world's largest petals. With every step, the petals shake out heavy clouds of toxic pollen.

The larger its petals, the more toxic pollen it contains. Its big head is heavy and hard to hold up.

Special Moves

Petal Blizzard, Petal Dance, Sleep Powder

Evolution

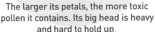
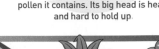

ODDISH ➡ GLOOM ➡ VILEPLUME

PARAS

Mushrooms named *tochukaso* grow on its back. They grow along with the host Paras.

Mushroom Pokémon	
POKÉDEX NO.	**046**
TYPE	Bug, Grass
ABILITY	Effect Spore, Dry Skin
HEIGHT	1'00"
WEIGHT	11.9 lbs

Description

It burrows under the ground to gnaw on tree roots. The mushrooms on its back absorb most of the nutrition.

Special Moves

Poison Powder, Aromatherapy, Fury Cutter

Evolution

PARAS

PARASECT

001-100
101-200
201-300
401-442
443-500
501-600
701-800
801-898

PARASECT

It scatters toxic spores from its mushroom cap. Once harvested, these spores can be steeped and boiled down to prepare herbal medicines.

Mushroom Pokémon

POKÉDEX NO.	**047**
TYPE	Bug, Grass
ABILITY	Effect Spore, Dry Skin
HEIGHT	3'03"
WEIGHT	65.0 lbs

Description

The bug host is drained of energy by the mushroom on its back. The mushroom appears to do all the thinking.

Special Moves

Stun Spore, Giga Drain, Spore

Evolution

PARAS

PARASECT

VENONAT

Its large eyes act as radars. In a bright place, you can see that they are clusters of many tiny eyes.

Insect Pokémon

POKÉDEX NO.	048
TYPE	Bug, Poison
ABILITY	Compound Eyes, Tinted Lens
HEIGHT	3'03"
WEIGHT	66.1 lbs

Description

Venonat is said to have evolved with a coat of thin, stiff hair that covers its entire body for protection. It possesses large eyes that never fail to spot even miniscule prey.

Special Moves

Tackle, Poison Powder, Leech Life

Evolution

VENONAT → VENOMOTH

VENOMOTH

001-100
101-200
201-300
401-442
443-500
501-600
701-800
801-898

The powdery scales on its wings are hard to remove from skin. They also contain poison that leaks out on contact.

Poison Moth Pokémon	
POKÉDEX NO.	**049**
TYPE	Bug, Poison
ABILITY	Shield Dust, Tinted Lens
HEIGHT	4'11"
WEIGHT	27.6 lbs

Description

Venomoth is nocturnal—it is a Pokémon that only becomes active at night. Its favorite prey are small insects that gather around streetlights, attracted by the light in the darkness.

Special Moves

Bug Buzz, Confusion, Psybeam

Evolution

VENONAT

VENOMOTH

DIGLETT

Mole Pokémon	
POKÉDEX NO.	**050**
TYPE	Ground
ABILITY	Sand Veil, Arena Trap
HEIGHT	0'08"
WEIGHT	1.8 lbs

If a Diglett digs through a field, it leaves the soil perfectly tilled and ideal for planting crops.

Description

It burrows through the ground at a shallow depth. It leaves raised earth in its wake, making it easy to spot.

Special Moves

Dig, Astonish, Sandstorm

Evolution

DIGLETT → DUGTRIO

DIGLETT

ALOLAN FORM

001-
100

101-
200

201-
300

401-
442

443-
500

501-
600

701-
800

801-
898

The metal-rich geology of this Pokémon's habitat caused it to develop steel whiskers on its head.

Mole Pokémon

POKÉDEX NO.	050
TYPE	Ground, Steel
ABILITY	Sand Veil, Tangling Hair
HEIGHT	0'08"
WEIGHT	2.2 lbs

Description

Its three hairs change shape depending on Diglett's mood. They're a useful communication tool among these Pokémon.

Special Moves

Metal Claw, Dig, Bulldoze

Evolution

DIGLETT
(ALOLAN FORM)

DUGTRIO
(ALOLAN FORM)

DUGTRIO

Mole Pokémon

POKÉDEX NO.	**051**
TYPE	Ground
ABILITY	Sand Veil, Arena Trap
HEIGHT	2'04"
WEIGHT	73.4 lbs

While the three of them normally get along splendidly, on rare occasions a huge fight will break out over which head gets to eat first.

Description

A team of Diglett triplets. It triggers huge earthquakes by burrowing 60 miles underground.

Special Moves

Tri Attack, Earthquake, Earth Power

Evolution

DIGLETT → DUGTRIO

DUGTRIO

ALOLAN FORM

001-100
101-200
201-300
401-442
443-900
501-600
701-800
801-898

The three of them get along very well. Through their formidable teamwork, they defeat powerful opponents.

Mole Pokémon	
POKÉDEX NO.	**051**
TYPE	Ground, Steel
ABILITY	Sand Veil, Tangling Hair
HEIGHT	2'04"
WEIGHT	146.8 lbs

Description

Their beautiful, metallic whiskers create a sort of protective helmet on their heads, and they also function as highly precise sensors.

Special Moves

Iron Head, Night Slash, Tri Attack

Evolution

DIGLETT
(ALOLAN FORM)

➡

DUGTRIO
(ALOLAN FORM)

MEOWTH

Scratch Cat Pokémon

POKÉDEX NO.	**052**

TYPE	Normal
ABILITY	Pickup, Technician
HEIGHT	1'04"
WEIGHT	9.3 lbs

It washes its face regularly to keep the coin on its forehead spotless. It doesn't get along with Galarian Meowth.

Description

It loves things that sparkle. When it sees a shiny object, the gold coin on its head shines, too.

Special Moves

Slash, Fake Out, Pay Day

Evolution

MEOWTH ➡ PERSIAN

MEOWTH

GIGANTAMAX FORM

Its body has grown incredibly long and the coin on its forehead has grown incredibly large—all thanks to Gigantamax power.

MEOWTH

001-100

101-200

201-300

401-442

443-500

501-600

701-800

801-898

Scratch Cat Pokémon	
POKÉDEX NO.	**052**
TYPE	Normal
ABILITY	Pickup, Technician
HEIGHT	108'03"+
WEIGHT	??? lbs

Description

The pattern that has appeared on its giant coin is thought to be the key to unlocking the secrets of the Dynamax* phenomenon.

Special Moves

G-Max Gold Rush

*Dynamax: A phenomenon where a Pokémon turns into a giant size. This occurs in certain areas of the Galar region.

83

MEOWTH

ALOLAN FORM

Deeply proud and keenly smart, this Pokémon moves with cunning during battle and relentlessly attacks enemies' weak points.

Scratch Cat Pokémon	
POKÉDEX NO.	**052**
TYPE	Dark
ABILITY	Pickup, Technician
HEIGHT	1'04"
WEIGHT	9.3 lbs

Description

It's accustomed to luxury because it used to live with Alolan royalty. As a result, it's very picky about food.

Special Moves

Bite, Nasty Plot, Fury Swipes

Evolution

MEOWTH
(ALOLAN FORM)

PERSIAN
(ALOLAN FORM)

MEOWTH

GALARIAN FORM

Scratch Cat Pokémon

POKÉDEX NO.	**052**

TYPE	Steel
ABILITY	Pickup, Tough Claws
HEIGHT	1'04"
WEIGHT	16.5 lbs

001-100

101-200

201-300

401-442

443-500

501-600

701-800

801-898

Living with savage, seafaring people has toughened this Pokémon's body so much that parts of it have turned to iron.

Description

These daring Pokémon have coins on their foreheads. Darker coins are harder, and harder coins garner more respect among Meowth.

Special Moves

Metal Claw, Screech, Metal Sound

Evolution

MEOWTH
(GALARIAN FORM)

➡

PERRSERKER

PERSIAN

Classy Cat Pokémon

POKÉDEX NO.	**053**

TYPE	Normal
ABILITY	Technician, Limber
HEIGHT	3'03"
WEIGHT	70.5 lbs

Its elegant and refined behavior clashes with that of the barbaric Perrserker. The relationship between the two is one of mutual disdain.

Description

Getting this prideful Pokémon to warm up to you takes a lot of effort, and it will claw at you the moment it gets annoyed.

Special Moves

Fake Out, Power Gem, Fury Swipes

Evolution

MEOWTH ➡ PERSIAN

001-100
101-200
201-300
401-442
443-500
501-600
701-800
801-898

PERSIAN

ALOLAN FORM

This Pokémon is one tough opponent. Not only does it have formidable physical abilities, but it's also not above fighting dirty.

Classy Cat Pokémon	
POKÉDEX NO.	**053**
TYPE	Dark
ABILITY	Technician, Fur Coat
HEIGHT	3'07"
WEIGHT	72.8 lbs

Description

The round face of Alolan Persian is considered to be a symbol of prosperity in the Alola region, so these Pokémon are very well cared for.

Special Moves

Nasty Plot, Night Slash, Power Gem

Evolution

MEOWTH
(ALOLAN FORM)

PERSIAN
(ALOLAN FORM)

PSYDUCK

Duck Pokémon

POKÉDEX NO.	054

TYPE	Water
ABILITY	Damp, Cloud Nine
HEIGHT	2'07"
WEIGHT	43.2 lbs

Description

It is constantly wracked by a headache. When the headache turns intense, it begins using mysterious powers.

As Psyduck gets stressed out, its headache gets progressively worse. It uses intense psychic energy to overwhelm those around it.

Special Moves

Confusion, Amnesia, Zen Headbutt

Evolution

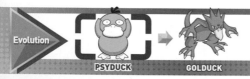

PSYDUCK → GOLDUCK

GOLDUCK

Old tales tell of Golduck punishing those that defiled its river. The guilty were dragged into the water and taken away.

Duck Pokémon

POKÉDEX NO.	055
TYPE	Water
ABILITY	Damp, Cloud Nine
HEIGHT	5'07"
WEIGHT	168.9 lbs

Description

This Pokémon lives in gently flowing rivers. It paddles through the water with its long limbs, putting its graceful swimming skills on display.

Special Moves

Hydro Pump, Aqua Tail, Soak

Evolution

PSYDUCK → GOLDUCK

MANKEY

An agile Pokémon that lives in trees. It angers easily and will not hesitate to attack anything.

Pig Monkey Pokémon	
POKÉDEX NO.	**056**
TYPE	Fighting
ABILITY	Vital Spirit, Anger Point
HEIGHT	1'08"
WEIGHT	61.7 lbs

Description

If one gets angry, all the others around it will get angry, so silence is a rare visitor in a troop of Mankey.

Special Moves

Low Kick, Focus Energy, Cross Chop

Evolution

MANKEY

PRIMEAPE

PRIMEAPE

001-100
101-200
201-300
401-442
443-500
501-600
701-800
801-898

It will never forgive opponents who have angered it. Even after it has beaten them down until they can't move, it never ever forgives.

Pig Monkey Pokémon	
POKÉDEX NO.	**057**
TYPE	Fighting
ABILITY	Vital Spirit, Anger Point
HEIGHT	3'03"
WEIGHT	70.5 lbs

Description

It stops being angry only when nobody else is around. To view this moment is very difficult.

Special Moves

Thrash, Seismic Toss, Karate Chop

Evolution

MANKEY → PRIMEAPE

GROWLITHE

Puppy Pokémon

POKÉDEX NO.	**058**
TYPE	Fire
ABILITY	Intimidate, Flash Fire
HEIGHT	2'04"
WEIGHT	41.9 lbs

Description

It has a brave and trustworthy nature. It fearlessly stands up to bigger and stronger foes.

Extremely loyal, it will fearlessly bark at any opponent to protect its own Trainer from harm.

Special Moves

Ember, Fire Fang, Agility

Evolution

 →

GROWLITHE　　　ARCANINE

ARCANINE

Legendary Pokémon	
POKÉDEX NO.	**059**
TYPE	Fire
ABILITY	Intimidate, Flash Fire
HEIGHT	6'03"
WEIGHT	341.7 lbs

A Pokémon that has long been admired for its beauty. It runs agilely as if on wings.

Description

The sight of it running over 6,200 miles in a single day and night has captivated many people.

Special Moves

Flamethrower, Flare Blitz, Extreme Speed

Evolution

GROWLITHE → ARCANINE

POLIWAG

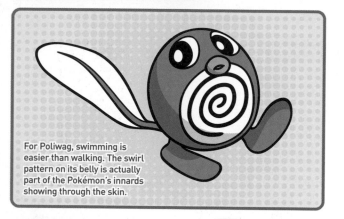

For Poliwag, swimming is easier than walking. The swirl pattern on its belly is actually part of the Pokémon's innards showing through the skin.

Tadpole Pokémon

POKÉDEX NO.	060
TYPE	Water
ABILITY	Damp, Water Absorb
HEIGHT	2'00"
WEIGHT	27.3 lbs

Description

In rivers with fast-flowing water, this Pokémon will cling to a rock by using its thick lips, which act like a suction cup.

Special Moves

Water Gun, Body Slam, Rain Dance

Evolution

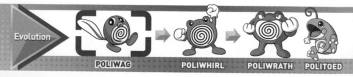

POLIWAG → POLIWHIRL → POLIWRATH   POLITOED

POLIWHIRL

Tadpole Pokémon

POKÉDEX NO.	061
TYPE	Water
ABILITY	Damp, Water Absorb
HEIGHT	3'03"
WEIGHT	44.1 lbs

This Pokémon's sweat is a slimy mucus. When captured, Poliwhirl can slither from its enemies' grasp and escape.

Description

Staring at the swirl on its belly causes drowsiness. This trait of Poliwhirl's has been used in place of lullabies to get children to go to sleep.

Special Moves

Rain Dance, Earth Power, Bubble Beam

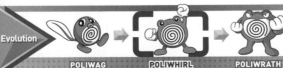

Evolution

POLIWAG → POLIWHIRL → POLIWRATH   POLITOED

POLIWRATH

Tadpole Pokémon

POKÉDEX NO.	062
TYPE	Water, Fighting
ABILITY	Damp, Water Absorb
HEIGHT	4'03"
WEIGHT	119.0 lbs

Description

Poliwrath is skilled at both swimming and martial arts. It uses its well-trained arms to dish out powerful punches.

Its body is solid muscle. When swimming through cold seas, Poliwrath uses its impressive arms to smash through drift ice and plow forward.

Special Moves

Hydro Pump, Submission, Circle Throw

Evolution

POLIWAG ➡ POLIWHIRL ➡ POLIWRATH

ABRA

This Pokémon uses its psychic powers while it sleeps. The contents of Abra's dreams affect the powers that the Pokémon wields.

Psi Pokémon	
POKÉDEX NO.	**063**
TYPE	Psychic
ABILITY	Inner Focus, Synchronize
HEIGHT	2'11"
WEIGHT	43.0 lbs

Description

Abra can teleport in its sleep. Apparently the more deeply Abra sleeps, the farther its teleportations go.

Special Moves

Teleport

Evolution

ABRA

KADABRA

ALAKAZAM

KADABRA

This Pokémon's telekinesis is immensely powerful. To prepare for evolution, Kadabra stores up psychic energy in the star on its forehead.

Psi Pokémon	
POKÉDEX NO.	**064**
TYPE	Psychic
ABILITY	Inner Focus, Synchronize
HEIGHT	4'03"
WEIGHT	124.6 lbs

Description

Using its psychic power, Kadabra levitates as it sleeps. It uses its springy tail as a pillow.

Special Moves

Confusion, Teleport, Psybeam

Evolution

ABRA → KADABRA → ALAKAZAM

ALAKAZAM

Psi Pokémon	
POKÉDEX NO.	**065**
TYPE	Psychic
ABILITY	Inner Focus, Synchronize
HEIGHT	4'11"
WEIGHT	105.8 lbs

Alakazam wields potent psychic powers. It's said that this Pokémon uses these powers to create the spoons it holds.

Description

It has an incredibly high level of intelligence. Some say that Alakazam remembers everything that ever happens to it, from birth till death.

Special Moves

Psychic, Kinesis, Future Sight

Evolution

 ABRA → KADABRA → ALAKAZAM

001-100
101-200
201-300
401-442
443-500
501-600
701-800
801-898

MEGA ALAKAZAM

It sends out psychic power from the red organ on its forehead to foresee its opponents' every move.

ALAKAZAM

Psi Pokémon	
POKÉDEX NO.	**065**
TYPE	Psychic
ABILITY	Trace
HEIGHT	3'11"
WEIGHT	105.8 lbs

Description

It's adept at precognition. When attacks completely miss Alakazam, that's because it's seeing the future.

Special Moves

Kinesis, Psycho Cut, Recover

001-100
101-200
201-300
401-442
443-500
501-600
701-800
801-898

MACHOP

Its whole body is composed of muscles. Even though it's the size of a human child, it can hurl 100 grown-ups.

Superpower Pokémon	
POKÉDEX NO.	**066**
TYPE	Fighting
ABILITY	Guts, No Guard
HEIGHT	2'07"
WEIGHT	43.0 lbs

Description

Always brimming with power, it passes time by lifting boulders. Doing so makes it even stronger.

Special Moves

Low Kick, Low Sweep, Dual Chop

Evolution

MACHOP → MACHOKE → MACHAMP

MACHOKE

Its formidable body never gets tired. It helps people by doing work such as the moving of heavy goods.

Superpower Pokémon

POKÉDEX NO.	**067**
TYPE	Fighting
ABILITY	Guts, No Guard
HEIGHT	4'11"
WEIGHT	155.4 lbs

Description

Its muscular body is so powerful, it must wear a power-save belt to be able to regulate its motions.

Special Moves

Knock Off, Low Kick, Seismic Toss

Evolution

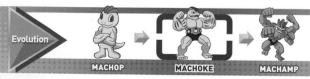

MACHOP ➡ MACHOKE ➡ MACHAMP

MACHAMP

Superpower Pokémon

POKÉDEX NO.	068
TYPE	Fighting
ABILITY	Guts, No Guard
HEIGHT	5'03"
WEIGHT	286.6 lbs

001-100

201-300

401-442

501-600

801-898

With four arms that react more quickly than it can think, it can execute many punches at once.

Description

It quickly swings its four arms to rock its opponents with ceaseless punches and chops from all angles.

Special Moves

Strength, Dynamic Punch, Cross Chop

Evolution

MACHOP

MACHOKE

MACHAMP

MACHAMP

GIGANTAMAX FORM

MACHAMP

One of these Pokémon once used its immeasurable strength to lift a large ship that was in trouble. It then carried the ship to port.

Superpower Pokémon	
POKÉDEX NO.	**068**
TYPE	Fighting
ABILITY	Guts, No Guard
HEIGHT	82'00"+
WEIGHT	??? lbs

Description

The Gigantamax energy coursing through its arms makes its punches hit as hard as bomb blasts.

Special Moves

G-Max Chi Strike

BELLSPROUT

001-100

101-200

201-300

401-442

443-500

501-600

701-800

801-898

Prefers hot and humid places. It ensnares tiny bugs with its vines and devours them.

Flower Pokémon	
POKÉDEX NO.	**069**
TYPE	Grass, Poison
ABILITY	Chlorophyll
HEIGHT	2'04"
WEIGHT	8.8 lbs

Description

Bellsprout's thin and flexible body lets it bend and sway to avoid any attack, however strong it may be. From its mouth, this Pokémon spits a corrosive fluid that melts even iron.

Special Moves

Vine Whip, Poison Powder, Slam

Evolution

BELLSPROUT → WEEPINBELL → VICTREEBEL

WEEPINBELL

When hungry, it swallows anything that moves. Its hapless prey is dissolved by strong acids.

Flycatcher Pokémon

POKÉDEX NO.	**070**
TYPE	Grass, Poison
ABILITY	Chlorophyll
HEIGHT	3'03"
WEIGHT	14.1 lbs

Description

Weepinbell has a large hook on its rear end. At night, the Pokémon hooks onto a tree branch and goes to sleep. If it moves around in its sleep, it may find itself on the ground when it wakes up.

Special Moves

Stun Spore, Acid, Razor Leaf

Evolution

BELLSPROUT → WEEPINBELL → VICTREEBEL

001-100
101-200
201-300
401-442
443-500
501-600
701-800
801-898

VICTREEBEL

Lures prey with the sweet aroma of honey. Swallowed whole, the prey is dissolved in a day, bones and all.

Flycatcher Pokémon	
POKÉDEX NO.	**071**
TYPE	Grass, Poison
ABILITY	Chlorophyll
HEIGHT	5'07"
WEIGHT	34.2 lbs

Description

Victreebel has a long vine that extends from its head. This vine is waved and flicked about as if it were an animal to attract prey. When an unsuspecting prey draws near, this Pokémon swallows it whole.

Special Moves

Leaf Tornado, Leaf Blade, Swallow

Evolution

BELLSPROUT

WEEPINBELL

VICTREEBEL

TENTACOOL

Tentacool is not a particularly strong swimmer. It drifts across the surface of shallow seas as it searches for prey.

Jellyfish Pokémon	
POKÉDEX NO.	**072**
TYPE	Water, Poison
ABILITY	Clear Body, Liquid Ooze
HEIGHT	2'11"
WEIGHT	100.3 lbs

Description

This Pokémon is mostly made of water. A Tentacool out in the ocean is very hard to spot, because its body blends in with the sea.

Special Moves

Water Gun, Poison Sting, Acid

Evolution

 →

TENTACOOL   TENTACRUEL

TENTACRUEL

001-100

101-200

201-300

401-442

443-500

501-600

701-800

801-898

When the red orbs on Tentacruel's head glow brightly, watch out. The Pokémon is about to fire off a burst of ultrasonic waves.

Jellyfish Pokémon

POKÉDEX NO.	073
TYPE	Water, Poison
ABILITY	Clear Body, Liquid Ooze
HEIGHT	5'03"
WEIGHT	121.3 lbs

Description

Its 80 tentacles can stretch and shrink freely. Tentacruel ensnares prey in a net of spread-out tentacles, delivering venomous stings to its catch.

Special Moves

Sludge Wave, Poison Jab, Hydro Pump

Evolution

TENTACOOL

TENTACRUEL

GEODUDE

Rock Pokémon	
POKÉDEX NO.	**074**
TYPE	Rock, Ground
ABILITY	Rock Head, Sturdy
HEIGHT	1'04"
WEIGHT	44.1 lbs

Description

Geodude that have lived a long life have had all their edges smoothed out until they're totally round. They also have a calm, quiet disposition.

Commonly found near mountain trails and the like. If you step on one by accident, it gets angry.

Special Moves

Defense Curl, Bulldoze, Stealth Rock

Evolution

GEODUDE → GRAVELER → GOLEM

GEODUDE

ALOLAN FORM

Geodude compete against each other with headbutts. The iron sand on their heads will stick to whichever one has stronger magnetism.

Rock Pokémon	
POKÉDEX NO.	**074**
TYPE	Rock, Electric
ABILITY	Sturdy, Magnet Pull
HEIGHT	1'04"
WEIGHT	44.8 lbs

Description

Its stone head is imbued with electricity and magnetism. If you carelessly step on one, you'll be in for a painful shock.

Special Moves

Thunder Punch, Spark, Rock Throw

Evolution

GEODUDE
(ALOLAN FORM)

GRAVELER
(ALOLAN FORM)

GOLEM
(ALOLAN FORM)

GRAVELER

Rock Pokémon

POKÉDEX NO.	**075**

TYPE	Rock, Ground
ABILITY	Rock Head, Sturdy
HEIGHT	3'03"
WEIGHT	231.5 lbs

Description

It climbs up cliffs as it heads toward the peak of a mountain. As soon as it reaches the summit, it rolls back down the way it came.

Often seen rolling down mountain trails. Obstacles are just things to roll straight over, not avoid.

Special Moves

Rock Polish, Double-Edge, Rock Throw

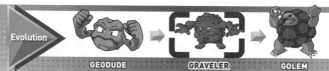

Evolution

GEODUDE → GRAVELER → GOLEM

GRAVELER

ALOLAN FORM

001-
100

101-
200

201-
300

401-
442

443-
500

501-
600

701-
800

801-
898

When two Graveler fight each other, it fills the surroundings with flashes of light and sound. People call it the "fireworks of the earth."

Rock Pokémon	
POKÉDEX NO.	**075**
TYPE	Rock, Electric
ABILITY	Sturdy, Magnet Pull
HEIGHT	3'03"
WEIGHT	242.5 lbs

Description

When it comes rolling down a mountain path, anything in its way gets zapped by electricity and is sent flying.

Special Moves

Charge, Thunder Punch, Rock Throw

Evolution

GEODUDE (ALOLAN FORM) → GRAVELER (ALOLAN FORM) → GOLEM (ALOLAN FORM)

GOLEM

Megaton Pokémon

POKÉDEX NO.	▶	**076**

TYPE	Rock, Ground
ABILITY	Rock Head, Sturdy
HEIGHT	4'07"
WEIGHT	661.4 lbs

Once it sheds its skin, its body turns tender and whitish. Its hide hardens when it's exposed to air.

Description

When Golem grow old, they stop shedding their shells. Those that have lived a long, long time have shells green with moss.

Special Moves

Heavy Slam, Rock Throw, Explosion

Evolution

GEODUDE ➡ GRAVELER ➡ GOLEM

GOLEM

ALOLAN FORM

001-100

101-200

201-300

401-442

443-500

501-600

701-800

801-898

It uses magnetism to accelerate and fire off rocks tinged with electricity. Even if it doesn't score a direct hit, the jolt of electricity will do the job.

Megaton Pokémon	
POKÉDEX NO.	**076**
TYPE	Rock, Electric
ABILITY	Sturdy, Magnet Pull
HEIGHT	5'07"
WEIGHT	696.7 lbs

Description

It's grumpy and stubborn. If you upset it, it discharges electricity from the surface of its body and growls with a voice like thunder.

Special Moves

Spark, Rock Blast, Steamroller

Evolution

GEODUDE
(ALOLAN FORM)

GRAVELER
(ALOLAN FORM)

GOLEM
(ALOLAN FORM)

PONYTA

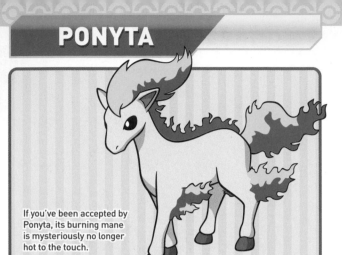

If you've been accepted by Ponyta, its burning mane is mysteriously no longer hot to the touch.

Fire Horse Pokémon	
POKÉDEX NO.	**077**
TYPE	Fire
ABILITY	Run Away, Flash Fire
HEIGHT	3'03"
WEIGHT	66.1 lbs

Description

It can't run properly when it's newly born. As it races around with others of its kind, its legs grow stronger.

Special Moves

Ember, Agility, Flame Charge

Evolution

PONYTA

RAPIDASH

PONYTA

GALARIAN FORM

001-100

101-200

201-300

401-442

443-500

501-600

701-800

801-898

Unique Horn Pokémon

POKÉDEX NO.	**077**
TYPE	Psychic
ABILITY	Run Away, Pastel Veil
HEIGHT	2'07"
WEIGHT	52.9 lbs

This Pokémon will look into your eyes and read the contents of your heart. If it finds evil there, it promptly hides away.

Description

Its small horn hides a healing power. With a few rubs from this Pokémon's horn, any slight wound you have will be healed.

Special Moves

Confusion, Psybeam, Healing Wish

Evolution

PONYTA
(GALARIAN FORM)

RAPIDASH
(GALARIAN FORM)

RAPIDASH

Fire Horse Pokémon

POKÉDEX NO.	078
TYPE	Fire
ABILITY	Run Away, Flash Fire
HEIGHT	5'07"
WEIGHT	209.4 lbs

The fastest runner becomes the leader, and it decides the herd's pace and direction of travel.

Description

This Pokémon can be seen galloping through fields at speeds of up to 150 mph, its fiery mane fluttering in the wind.

Special Moves

Inferno, Fire Blast, Smart Strike

Evolution

PONYTA → RAPIDASH

RAPIDASH

GALARIAN FORM

001–100
101–200
201–300
401–442
443–500
501–600
701–800
801–898

Unique Horn Pokémon	
POKÉDEX NO.	**078**
TYPE	Psychic, Fairy
ABILITY	Run Away, Pastel Veil
HEIGHT	5'07"
WEIGHT	176.4 lbs

Brave and prideful, this Pokémon dashes airily through the forest, its steps aided by the psychic power stored in the fur on its fetlocks.

Description

Little can stand up to its Psycho Cut. Unleashed from this Pokémon's horn, the move will punch a hole right through a thick metal sheet.

Special Moves

Psycho Cut, Fairy Wind, Take Down

Evolution

PONYTA
(GALARIAN FORM)

RAPIDASH
(GALARIAN FORM)

SLOWPOKE

Dopey Pokémon	
POKÉDEX NO.	**079**
TYPE	Water, Psychic
ABILITY	Oblivious, Own Tempo
HEIGHT	3'11"
WEIGHT	79.4 lbs

When this Pokémon's tail is soaked in water, sweetness seeps from it. Slowpoke uses this trait to lure in and fish up other Pokémon.

Description

Slow-witted and oblivious, this Pokémon won't feel any pain if its tail gets eaten. It won't notice when its tail grows back, either.

Special Moves

Tackle, Amnesia, Water Gun

Evolution

SLOWPOKE → SLOWBRO   SLOWKING

SLOWPOKE

GALARIAN FORM

Dopey Pokémon

POKÉDEX NO.	**079**
TYPE	Psychic
ABILITY	Gluttony, Own Tempo
HEIGHT	3'11"
WEIGHT	79.4 lbs

Because Galarian Slowpoke eat the seeds of a plant that grows only in Galar, their tails have developed a spicy flavor.

Description

Although this Pokémon is normally zoned out, its expression abruptly sharpens on occasion. The cause for this seems to lie in Slowpoke's diet.

Special Moves

Confusion, Zen Headbutt, Disable

Evolution

SLOWPOKE
(GALARIAN FORM)

SLOWBRO
(GALARIAN FORM)

SLOWKING
(GALARIAN FORM)

SLOWBRO

Hermit Crab Pokémon	
POKÉDEX NO.	**080**
TYPE	Water, Psychic
ABILITY	Oblivious, Own Tempo
HEIGHT	5'03"
WEIGHT	173.1 lbs

If the tail-biting Shellder is thrown off in a harsh battle, this Pokémon reverts to being an ordinary Slowpoke.

Description

When a Slowpoke went hunting in the sea, its tail was bitten by a Shellder. That made it evolve into Slowbro.

Special Moves

Psychic, Amnesia, Water Pulse

Evolution

SLOWPOKE → SLOWBRO

MEGA SLOWBRO

001–
100

101–
200

201–
300

401–
442

443–
500

501–
600

701–
800

801–
898

SLOWBRO

Having been swallowed whole by Shellder, Slowbro now has an iron defense. It's pretty comfortable in there, too.

Hermit Crab Pokémon	
POKÉDEX NO.	**080**
TYPE	Water, Psychic
ABILITY	Shell Armor
HEIGHT	6'07"
WEIGHT	264.6 lbs

Description

Under the influence of Shellder's* digestive fluids, Slowpoke has awakened, gaining a great deal of power and a little motivation to boot.

Special Moves

Withdraw, Psychic, Heal Pulse

*Shellder: A Pokémon you'll find on page 137.

SLOWBRO

GALARIAN FORM

Hermit Crab Pokémon

POKÉDEX NO.	**080**
TYPE	Poison, Psychic
ABILITY	Own Tempo, Quick Draw
HEIGHT	5'03"
WEIGHT	155.4 lbs

If this Pokémon squeezes the tongue of the Shellder biting it, the Shellder will launch a toxic liquid from the tip of its shell.

Description

A Shellder bite set off a chemical reaction with the spices inside Slowbro's body, causing Slowbro to become a Poison-type Pokémon.

Special Moves

Shell Side Arm, Psychic, Rain Dance

Evolution

SLOWPOKE
(GALARIAN FORM)

SLOWBRO
(GALARIAN FORM)

MAGNEMITE

Magnet Pokémon

POKÉDEX NO.	081

TYPE	Electric, Steel
ABILITY	Sturdy, Magnet Pull
HEIGHT	1'00"
WEIGHT	13.2 lbs

101-200

201-300

401-442

443-500

501-600

701-800

801-898

Description

At times, Magnemite runs out of electricity and ends up on the ground. If you give batteries to a grounded Magnemite, it'll start moving again.

It subsists on electricity. As Magnemite flies, it emits electromagnetic waves from the units on each side of its body.

Special Moves

Thunder Shock, Supersonic, Thunder Wave

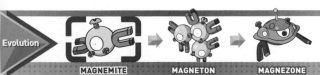

Evolution

MAGNEMITE → MAGNETON → MAGNEZONE

MAGNETON

Magnet Pokémon

POKÉDEX NO.	082

TYPE	Electric, Steel
ABILITY	Sturdy, Magnet Pull
HEIGHT	3'03"
WEIGHT	132.3 lbs

This Pokémon is three Magnemite that have linked together. Magneton sends out powerful radio waves to study its surroundings.

Description

This Pokémon is constantly putting out a powerful magnetic force. Most computers go haywire when a Magneton approaches.

Special Moves

Tri Attack, Spark, Flash Cannon

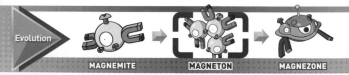

Evolution

MAGNEMITE → MAGNETON → MAGNEZONE

FARFETCH'D

001-100

101-200

201-300

401-442

443-500

501-600

701-800

801-898

They use a plant stalk as a weapon, but not all of them use it in the same way. Several distinct styles of stalk fighting have been observed.

Wild Duck Pokémon	
POKÉDEX NO.	083
TYPE	Normal, Flying
ABILITY	Keen Eye, Inner Focus
HEIGHT	2'07"
WEIGHT	33.1 lbs

Description

The stalk this Pokémon carries in its wings serves as a sword to cut down opponents. In a dire situation, the stalk can also serve as food.

Special Moves

Slash, Swords Dance, Air Slash

Evolution

FARFETCH'D

Does not evolve

127

FARFETCH'D

GALARIAN FORM

Wild Duck Pokémon

POKÉDEX NO.	**083**
TYPE	Fighting
ABILITY	Steadfast
HEIGHT	2'07"
WEIGHT	92.6 lbs

The stalks of leeks are thicker and longer in the Galar region. Farfetch'd that adapted to these stalks took on a unique form.

Description

The Farfetch'd of the Galar region are brave warriors, and they wield thick, tough leeks in battle.

Special Moves

Brutal Swing, Leaf Blade, Fury Cutter

Evolution

FARFETCH'D
[GALARIAN FORM]

SIRFETCH'D

128

DODUO

Its short wings make flying difficult. Instead, this Pokémon runs at high speed on developed legs.

Twin Bird Pokémon	
POKÉDEX NO.	**084**
TYPE	Normal, Flying
ABILITY	Run Away, Early Bird
HEIGHT	4'07"
WEIGHT	86.4 lbs

Description

Doduo's two heads never sleep at the same time. Its two heads take turns sleeping, so one head can always keep watch for enemies while the other one sleeps.

Special Moves

Quick Attack, Double Hit, Jump Kick

Evolution

DODUO → DODRIO

DODRIO

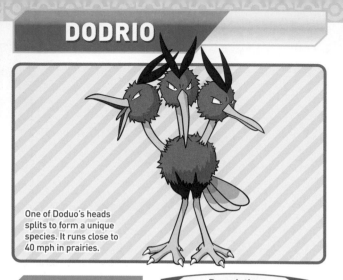

One of Doduo's heads splits to form a unique species. It runs close to 40 mph in prairies.

Triple Bird Pokémon

POKÉDEX NO.	**085**
TYPE	Normal, Flying
ABILITY	Run Away, Early Bird
HEIGHT	5'11"
WEIGHT	187.8 lbs

Description

Watch out if Dodrio's three heads are looking in three separate directions. It's a sure sign that it is on its guard. Don't go near this Pokémon if it's being wary—it may decide to peck you.

Special Moves

Tri Attack, Drill Peck, Thrash

Evolution

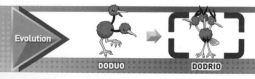

DODUO → DODRIO

SEEL

001-100

101-200

201-300

401-442

443-500

501-600

701-800

801-898

Loves freezing-cold conditions. Relishes swimming in a frigid climate of around 14 degrees Fahrenheit.

Sea Lion Pokémon	
POKÉDEX NO.	**086**
TYPE	Water
ABILITY	Thick Fat, Hydration
HEIGHT	3'07"
WEIGHT	198.4 lbs

Description

Thanks to its thick fat, cold seas don't bother it at all, but it gets tired pretty easily in warm waters.

Special Moves

Quick Attack, Wing Attack, Rock Slide

Evolution

SEEL → DEWGONG

DEWGONG

Its entire body is a snowy white. Unharmed by even intense cold, it swims powerfully in icy waters.

Sea Lion Pokémon

POKÉDEX NO.	087
TYPE	Water, Ice
ABILITY	Thick Fat, Hydration
HEIGHT	5'07"
WEIGHT	264.6 lbs

Description

It sunbathes on the beach after meals. The rise in its body temperature helps its digestion.

Special Moves

Sheer Cold, Ice Beam, Brine

Evolution

SEEL → DEWGONG

GRIMER

001-
100

101-
200

201-
300

401-
442

443-
500

501-
600

701-
800

801-
898

The wastewater coming from factories is clean these days, so Grimer have nothing to eat. They're said to be on the verge of extinction.

Sludge Pokémon	
POKÉDEX NO.	**088**
TYPE	Poison
ABILITY	Stench, Sticky Hold
HEIGHT	2'11"
WEIGHT	66.1 lbs

Description

Made of congealed sludge. It smells too putrid to touch. Even weeds won't grow in its path.

Special Moves

Poison Gas, Sludge Bomb, Gunk Shot

Evolution

GRIMER → MUK

GRIMER

ALOLAN FORM

It has a passion for trash above all else, speedily digesting it and creating brilliant crystals of sparkling poison.

Sludge Pokémon	
POKÉDEX NO.	**088**
TYPE	Poison, Dark
ABILITY	Gluttony, Poison Touch
HEIGHT	2'04"
WEIGHT	92.6 lbs

Description

There are a hundred or so of them living in Alola's waste-disposal site. They're all hard workers who eat a lot of trash.

Special Moves

Crunch, Gunk Shot, Knock Off

Evolution

GRIMER
(ALOLAN FORM)

MUK
(ALOLAN FORM)

MUK

001-
100

101-
200

201-
300

401-
442

443-
500

501-
600

701-
800

801-
898

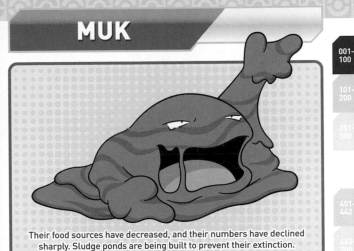

Their food sources have decreased, and their numbers have declined sharply. Sludge ponds are being built to prevent their extinction.

Sludge Pokémon	
POKÉDEX NO.	**089**
TYPE	Poison
ABILITY	Stench, Sticky Hold
HEIGHT	3'11"
WEIGHT	66.1 lbs

Description

Smells so awful it can cause fainting. Through degeneration of its nose, it lost its sense of smell.

Special Moves

Venom Drench, Sludge Wave, Acid Armor

Evolution

GRIMER → MUK

MUK

ALOLAN FORM

There are over a hundred kinds of poison inside its body. Chemical reactions between different poisons are the source of its vitality.

Sludge Pokémon	
POKÉDEX NO.	**089**
TYPE	Poison, Dark
ABILITY	Gluttony, Poison Touch
HEIGHT	3'03"
WEIGHT	114.6 lbs

Description

Muk's coloration becomes increasingly vivid the more it feasts on its favorite dish—trash.

Special Moves

Venom Drench, Poison Fang, Belch

Evolution

GRIMER
(ALOLAN FORM)

MUK
(ALOLAN FORM)

SHELLDER

001-100
101-200
201-300
401-442
443-500
501-600
701-800
801-898

Bivalve Pokémon

POKÉDEX NO.	090
TYPE	Water
ABILITY	Shell Armor, Skill Link
HEIGHT	1'00"
WEIGHT	8.8 lbs

Its hard shell repels any kind of attack. It is vulnerable only when its shell is open.

Description

It swims facing backward by opening and closing its two-piece shell. It is surprisingly fast.

Special Moves

Water Gun, Iron Defense, Withdraw

Evolution

SHELLDER   CLOYSTER

CLOYSTER

Once it slams its shell shut, it is impossible to open it, even by those with superior strength.

Bivalve Pokémon

POKÉDEX NO.	091
TYPE	Water, Ice
ABILITY	Shell Armor, Skill Link
HEIGHT	4'11"
WEIGHT	292.1 lbs

Description

For protection, it uses its harder-than-diamond shell. It also shoots spikes from the shell.

Special Moves

Icicle Spear, Shell Smash, Razor Shell

Evolution

SHELLDER

CLOYSTER

GASTLY

001-100
101-200
201-300
401-442
443-500
501-600
701-800
801-898

With its gas-like body, it can sneak into any place it desires. However, it can be blown away by the wind.

Gas Pokémon	
POKÉDEX NO.	**092**
TYPE	Ghost, Poison
ABILITY	Levitate
HEIGHT	4'03"
WEIGHT	0.2 lbs

Description

Born from gases, anyone would would faint if engulfed by its gaseous body, which contains poison.

Special Moves

Confuse Ray, Lick, Spite

Evolution

GASTLY

HAUNTER

GENGAR

HAUNTER

Gas Pokémon

POKÉDEX NO.	**093**
TYPE	Ghost, Poison
ABILITY	Levitate
HEIGHT	5'03"
WEIGHT	0.2 lbs

Description

Its tongue is made of gas. If licked, its victim starts shaking constantly until death eventually comes.

If you get the feeling of being watched in darkness when nobody is around, Haunter is there.

Special Moves

Hypnosis, Night Shade, Curse

Evolution

 GASTLY → **HAUNTER** → **GENGAR**

GENGAR

Shadow Pokémon

POKÉDEX NO.	**094**
TYPE	Ghost, Poison
ABILITY	Cursed Body
HEIGHT	4'11"
WEIGHT	89.3 lbs

001-100
101-200
201-300
401-442
663-500
501-600
701-800
801-898

It is said to emerge from darkness to steal the lives of those who become lost in the mountains.

Description

On the night of a full moon, if shadows move on their own and laugh, it must be Gengar's doing.

Special Moves

Shadow Ball, Mean Look, Dream Eater

Evolution

GASTLY → HAUNTER → GENGAR

GENGAR

It lays traps, hoping to steal the lives of those it catches. If you stand in front of its mouth, you'll hear your loved ones' voices calling out to you.

GENGAR

Shadow Pokémon	
POKÉDEX NO.	**094**
TYPE	Ghost, Poison
ABILITY	Cursed Body
HEIGHT	65'07"+
WEIGHT	??? lbs

Description

Rumor has it that its gigantic mouth leads not into its body, filled with cursed energy, but instead directly to the afterlife.

Special Moves

G-Max Terror

MEGA GENGAR

001-100
101-200
201-300
401-442
443-500
501-600
701-800
801-898

GENGAR

It can pass through other dimensions and can appear anywhere. It caused a stir when it stuck just one leg out of a wall.

Shadow Pokémon	
POKÉDEX NO.	**094**
TYPE	Ghost, Poison
ABILITY	Shadow Tag
HEIGHT	4'07"
WEIGHT	89.3 lbs

Description

It tries to take the lives of anyone and everyone. It will even try to curse the Trainer who is its master!

Special Moves

Shadow Punch, Shadow Ball, Dark Pulse

ONIX

It rapidly bores through the ground at 50 mph by squirming and twisting its massive, rugged body.

Rock Snake Pokémon	
POKÉDEX NO.	**095**
TYPE	Rock, Ground
ABILITY	Rock Head, Sturdy
HEIGHT	28'10"
WEIGHT	463.0 lbs

Description

As it digs through the ground, it absorbs many hard objects. This is what makes its body so solid.

Special Moves

Bind, Rock Slide, Iron Tail

Evolution

ONIX

STEELIX

DROWZEE

001-100

101-200

201-300

401-442

443-500

501-600

701-800

801-898

If you sleep by it all the time, it will sometimes show you dreams it ate in the past.

Hypnosis Pokémon	
POKÉDEX NO.	**096**
TYPE	Psychic
ABILITY	Insomnia, Forewarn
HEIGHT	3'03"
WEIGHT	71.4 lbs

Description

It can be spotted near recreational facilities, intending to eat the pleasant dreams of children who enjoyed themselves there that day.

Special Moves

Hypnosis, Confusion, Psybeam

Evolution

DROWZEE → HYPNO

HYPNO

There are some Hypno that assist doctors with patients who can't sleep at night in hospitals.

Hypnosis Pokémon

POKÉDEX NO.	097
TYPE	Psychic
ABILITY	Insomnia, Forewarn
HEIGHT	5'03"
WEIGHT	166.7 lbs

Description

Avoid eye contact if you come across one. It will try to put you to sleep using its pendulum.

Special Moves

Hypnosis, Psychic, Nightmare

Evolution

DROWZEE

HYPNO

KRABBY

001-100
101-200
201-300
401-442
443-500
501-600
701-800
801-898

If it senses danger approaching, it cloaks itself with bubbles from its mouth so it will look bigger.

River Crab Pokémon	
POKÉDEX NO.	**098**
TYPE	Water
ABILITY	Shell Armor, Hyper Cutter
HEIGHT	1'04"
WEIGHT	14.3 lbs

Description

It can be found near the sea. The large pincers grow back if they are torn out of their sockets.

Special Moves

Water Gun, Harden, Bubble Beam

Evolution

KRABBY

➡

KINGLER

KINGLER

Its oversized claw is very powerful, but when it's not in battle, the claw just gets in the way.

Pincer Pokémon	
POKÉDEX NO.	**099**
TYPE	Water
ABILITY	Shell Armor, Hyper Cutter
HEIGHT	4'03"
WEIGHT	132.3 lbs

Description

The larger pincer has 10,000-horsepower strength. However, it is so heavy, it is difficult to aim.

Special Moves

Metal Claw, Crabhammer, Stomp

Evolution

KRABBY

KINGLER

001-100
101-200
201-300
401-442
443-500
501-600

KINGLER

GIGANTAMAX FORM

KINGLER

The bubbles it spews out are strongly alkaline. Any opponents hit by them will have their bodies quickly melted away.

Pincer Pokémon	
POKÉDEX NO.	**099**
TYPE	Water
ABILITY	Shell Armor, Hyper Cutter
HEIGHT	62'04"+
WEIGHT	??? lbs

Description

The flow of Gigantamax energy has spurred this Pokémon's left pincer to grow to an enormous size. That claw can pulverize anything.

Special Moves

G-Max Foam Burst

VOLTORB

It's usually found in power plants. Easily mistaken for a Poké Ball, it has zapped many people.

Ball Pokémon	
POKÉDEX NO.	100
TYPE	Electric
ABILITY	Static, Soundproof
HEIGHT	1'08"
WEIGHT	22.9 lbs

Description

Voltorb was first sighted at a company that manufactures Poké Balls. The link between that sighting and the fact that this Pokémon looks very similar to a Poké Ball remains a mystery.

Special Moves

Charge, Swift, Electro Ball

Evolution

 ➡

VOLTORB   ELECTRODE

ELECTRODE

Ball Pokémon	
POKÉDEX NO.	**101**
TYPE	Electric
ABILITY	Static, Soundproof
HEIGHT	3'11"
WEIGHT	146.8 lbs

It stores an overflowing amount of electric energy inside its body. Even a small shock makes it explode.

Description

Electrode eats electricity in the atmosphere. On days when lightning strikes, you can see this Pokémon exploding all over the place from eating too much electricity.

Special Moves

Sonic Boom, Explosion, Eerie Impulse

Evolution

VOLTORB → ELECTRODE

001-100
101-200
201-300
401-442
443-500
501-600
701-800
801-898

EXEGGCUTE

Egg Pokémon

POKÉDEX NO.	**102**
TYPE	Grass, Psychic
ABILITY	Chlorophyll
HEIGHT	1'04"
WEIGHT	5.5 lbs

These Pokémon get nervous when they're not in a group of six. The minute even one member of the group goes missing, Exeggcute become cowardly.

Description

Though it may look like it's just a bunch of eggs, it's a proper Pokémon. Exeggcute communicates with others of its kind via telepathy, apparently.

Special Moves

Hypnosis, Absorb, Giga Drain

Evolution

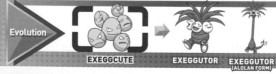

EXEGGCUTE → EXEGGUTOR   EXEGGUTOR (ALOLAN FORM)

EXEGGUTOR

Coconut Pokémon

POKÉDEX NO.	**103**
TYPE	Grass, Psychic
ABILITY	Chlorophyll
HEIGHT	6'07"
WEIGHT	264.6 lbs

001-100
101-200
201-300
401-442
443-509
501-600
701-800
801-898

Description

Each of Exeggutor's three heads is thinking different thoughts. The three don't seem to be very interested in one another.

When they work together, Exeggutor's three heads can put out powerful psychic energy. Cloudy days make this Pokémon sluggish.

Special Moves

Bullet Seed, Stomp, Leaf Storm

Evolution

EXEGGCUTE

EXEGGUTOR

EXEGGUTOR

ALOLAN FORM

Coconut Pokémon

POKÉDEX NO.	**103**
TYPE	Grass, Dragon
ABILITY	Frisk
HEIGHT	35'09"
WEIGHT	916.2 lbs

Description

Blazing sunlight has brought out the true form and powers of this Pokémon.

This Pokémon's psychic powers aren't as strong as they once were. The head on this Exeggutor's tail scans surrounding areas with weak telepathy.

Special Moves

Dragon Hammer, Seed Bomb, Absorb

Evolution

EXEGGCUTE

EXEGGUTOR
[ALOLAN FORM]

154

CUBONE

Lonely Pokémon	
POKÉDEX NO.	104

TYPE	Ground
ABILITY	Rock Head, Lightening Rod
HEIGHT	1'04"
WEIGHT	14.3 lbs

Description

Cubone pines for the mother it will never see again. Seeing a likeness of its mother in the full moon, it cries. The stains on the skull the Pokémon wears are made by the tears it sheds.

Special Moves

Mud-Slap, Thrash, Bone Rush

If it is sad or lonely, the skull it wears shakes, and emits a plaintive and mournful sound.

Evolution

CUBONE   MAROWAK   MAROWAK (ALOLAN FORM)

001-100
101-200
201-300
401-442
443-500
501-600
701-800
801-898

MAROWAK

Bone Keeper Pokémon

POKÉDEX NO.	**105**
TYPE	Ground
ABILITY	Rock Head, Lightning Rod
HEIGHT	3'03"
WEIGHT	99.2 lbs

Description

When this Pokémon evolved, the skull of its mother fused to it. Marowak's temperament also turned vicious at the same time.

Special Moves

Bonemerang, Bone Rush, Stomping Tantrum

The bone it holds is its key weapon. It throws the bone skillfully like a boomerang to KO targets.

Evolution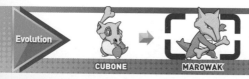

CUBONE → MAROWAK

MAROWAK

001-100

101-200

201-300

401-442

443-500

501-600

701-800

801-898

ALOLAN FORM

This Pokémon sets the bone it holds on fire and dances through the night as a way to mourn its fallen allies.

Bone Keeper Pokémon

POKÉDEX NO.	105
TYPE	Fire, Ghost
ABILITY	Lightning Rod, Cursed Body
HEIGHT	3'03"
WEIGHT	75.0 lbs

Description

The cursed flames that light up the bone carried by this Pokémon are said to cause both mental and physical pain that will never fade.

Special Moves

Shadow Bone, Flare Blitz, Will-O-Wisp

Evolution

CUBONE

MAROWAK
[ALOLAN FORM]

HITMONLEE

Kicking Pokémon

POKÉDEX NO.	106

TYPE	Fighting
ABILITY	Limber, Reckless
HEIGHT	4'11"
WEIGHT	109.8 lbs

This amazing Pokémon has an awesome sense of balance. It can kick in succession from any position.

Description

The legs freely contract and stretch. The stretchy legs allow it to hit a distant foe with a rising kick.

Special Moves

Low Sweep, Mega Kick, High Jump Kick

Evolution

TYROGUE

HITMONLEE

HITMONCHAN

001-100

101-200

201-300

401-442

443-500

501-600

701-800

801-898

The arm-twisting punches it throws pulverize even concrete. It rests after three minutes of fighting.

Punching Pokémon	
POKÉDEX NO.	**107**
TYPE	Fighting
ABILITY	Keen Eye, Iron Fist
HEIGHT	4'07"
WEIGHT	110.7 lbs

Description

Its punches slice the air. They are launched at such high speed, even a slight graze could cause a burn.

Special Moves

Bullet Punch, Close Combat, Counter

Evolution

TYROGUE ➡ **HITMONCHAN**

LICKITUNG

Bug Pokémon are Lickitung's main food source. This Pokémon paralyzes its prey with a lick from its long tongue, then swallows the prey whole.

Licking Pokémon	
POKÉDEX NO.	**108**
TYPE	Normal
ABILITY	Oblivious, Own Tempo
HEIGHT	3'11"
WEIGHT	144.4 lbs

Description

If this Pokémon's sticky saliva gets on you and you don't clean it off, an intense itch will set in. The itch won't go away, either.

Special Moves

Lick, Slam, Wrap

Evolution

LICKITUNG → LICKILICKY

KOFFING

Its body is full of poisonous gas. It floats into garbage dumps, seeking out the fumes of raw, rotting trash.

Poison Gas Pokémon	
POKÉDEX NO.	**109**
TYPE	Poison
ABILITY	Levitate, Neutralizing Gas
HEIGHT	2'00"
WEIGHT	2.2 lbs

Description

It adores polluted air. Some claim that Koffing used to be more plentiful in the Galar region than they are now.

Special Moves

Poison Gas, Sludge Bomh, Haze

Evolution

KOFFING

WEEZING

WEEZING
(GALARIAN FORM)

001-100
101-200
201-300
401-442
443-500
501-600
701-800
801-898

WEEZING

It can't suck in air quite as well as a Galarian Weezing, but the toxins it creates are more potent than those of its counterpart.

Poison Gas Pokémon	
POKÉDEX NO.	**110**
TYPE	Poison
ABILITY	Levitate, Neutralizing Gas
HEIGHT	3'11"
WEIGHT	20.9 lbs

Description

It mixes gases between its two bodies. It's said that these Pokémon were seen all over the Galar region back in the day.

Special Moves

Double Hit, Sludge, Self-Destruct

Evolution

KOFFING → WEEZING

WEEZING

GALARIAN FORM

Poison Gas Pokémon

POKÉDEX NO.	110
TYPE	Poison, Fairy
ABILITY	Levitate, Neutralizing Gas
HEIGHT	9'10"
WEIGHT	35.3 lbs

001-100
101-200
201-300
401-442
443-500
501-600
701-800
801-898

Long ago, during a time when droves of factories fouled the air with pollution, Weezing changed into this form for some reason.

Description

This Pokémon consumes particles that contaminate the air. Instead of leaving droppings, it expels clean air.

Special Moves

Strange Steam, Aromatic Mist, Destiny Bond

Evolution

KOFFING

WEEZING
(GALARIAN FORM)

RHYHORN

Spikes Pokémon

POKÉDEX NO.	**111**
TYPE	Ground, Rock
ABILITY	Rock Head, Lightning Rod
HEIGHT	3'03"
WEIGHT	253.5 lbs

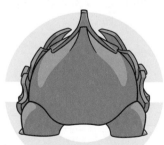

Strong, but not too bright, this Pokémon can shatter even a skyscraper with its charging tackles.

Description

It can remember only one thing at a time. Once it starts rushing, it forgets why it started.

Special Moves

Take Down, Stone Edge, Horn Drill

Evolution

RHYHORN → RHYDON → RHYPERIOR

RHYDON

Protected by an armor-like hide, it is capable of living in molten lava of 3,600 degrees Fahrenheit.

001-100
101-200
201-300
401-442
443-500
501-600
701-800
801-898

Drill Pokémon	
POKÉDEX NO.	**112**
TYPE	Ground, Rock
ABILITY	Rock Head, Lightning Rod
HEIGHT	6'03"
WEIGHT	264.6 lbs

Description

It begins walking on its hind legs after evolution. It can punch holes through boulders with its horn.

Special Moves

Drill Run, Hammer Arm, Earthquake

Evolution

RHYHORN → RHYDON → RHYPERIOR

165

CHANSEY

Egg Pokémon

POKÉDEX NO.	**113**
TYPE	Normal
ABILITY	Natural Cure, Serene Grace
HEIGHT	3'07"
WEIGHT	76.3 lbs

The egg Chansey carries is not only delicious but also packed with nutrition. It's used as a high-class cooking ingredient.

Description

This species was once very slow. To protect their eggs from other creatures, these Pokémon became able to flee quickly.

Special Moves

Soft-Boiled, Heal Pulse, Echoed Voice

Evolution

HAPPINY → CHANSEY → BLISSEY

TANGELA

Vine Pokémon	
POKÉDEX NO.	**114**
TYPE	Grass
ABILITY	Chlorophyll, Leaf Guard
HEIGHT	3'03"
WEIGHT	77.2 lbs

Hidden beneath a tangle of vines that grows nonstop even if they are torn off, this Pokémon's true appearance remains a mystery.

Description

The vines of a Tangela have a distinct scent. In some parts of Galar, Tangela vines are used as herbs.

Special Moves

Bind, Giga Drain, Power Whip

Evolution

TANGELA → TANGROWTH

001-100

101-200

201-300

401-442

443-500

501-600

701-800

801-898

KANGASKHAN

There are records of a lost human child being raised by a childless Kangaskhan.

Parent Pokémon

POKÉDEX NO.	115
TYPE	Normal
ABILITY	Early Bird, Scrappy
HEIGHT	7'03"
WEIGHT	176.4 lbs

Description

Although it's carrying its baby in a pouch on its belly, Kangaskhan is swift on its feet. It intimidates its opponents with quick jabs.

Special Moves

Double Hit, Outrage, Focus Energy

Evolution

KANGASKHAN

Does not evolve

MEGA KANGASKHAN

When the mother sees the back of her Mega-Evolved child, it makes her think of the day when her child will inevitably leave her.

KANGASKHAN

001-100

101-200

201-300

401-442

443-500

501-600

701-800

801-898

Parent Pokémon

POKÉDEX NO.	115
TYPE	Normal
ABILITY	Parental Bond
HEIGHT	7'03"
WEIGHT	220.5 lbs

Description

Its child has grown rapidly, thanks to the energy of Mega Evolution. Mother and child show off their harmonious teamwork in battle.

Special Moves

Comet Punch, Mega Punch, Double Hit

HORSEA

Dragon Pokémon

POKÉDEX NO.	**116**
TYPE	Water
ABILITY	Swift Swim, Sniper
HEIGHT	1'04"
WEIGHT	17.6 lbs

They swim with dance-like motions and cause whirlpools to form. Horsea compete to see which of them can generate the biggest whirlpool.

Description

Horsea makes its home in oceans with gentle currents. If this Pokémon is under attack, it spits out pitch-black ink and escapes.

Special Moves

Water Gun, Dragon Breath, Rain Dance

Evolution

HORSEA → SEADRA → KINGDRA

SEADRA

Seadra's mouth is slender, but its suction power is strong. In an instant, Seadra can suck in food that's larger than the opening of its mouth.

001-100
101-200
201-300
401-442
443-500
501-600
701-800
801-898

Dragon Pokémon	
POKÉDEX NO.	**117**
TYPE	Water
ABILITY	Poison Point, Sniper
HEIGHT	3'11"
WEIGHT	55.1 lbs

Description

It's the males that raise the offspring. While Seadra are raising young, the spines on their backs secrete thicker and stronger poison.

Special Moves

Dragon Pulse, Hydro Pump, Twister

Evolution

HORSEA → SEADRA → KINGDRA

GOLDEEN

Its dorsal and pectoral fins are strongly developed like muscles. It can swim at a speed of five knots.*

Goldfish Pokémon	
POKÉDEX NO.	**118**
TYPE	Water
ABILITY	Swift Swim, Water Veil
HEIGHT	2'00"
WEIGHT	33.1 lbs

Description

Its dorsal, pectoral, and tail fins wave elegantly in water. That is why it is known as the Water Dancer.

Special Moves

Supersonic, Horn Drill, Aqua Ring

Evolution

GOLDEEN

SEAKING

*Knot: A measurement of a ship's speed. Five knots is roughly 5.6 miles per hour.

SEAKING

In autumn, its body becomes more fatty in preparing to propose to a mate. It takes on beautiful colors.

Goldfish Pokémon

POKÉDEX NO.	119
TYPE	Water
ABILITY	Swift Swim, Water Veil
HEIGHT	4'03"
WEIGHT	86.0 lbs

Description

Using its horn, it bores holes in riverbed boulders, making nests to prevent its eggs from washing away.

Special Moves

Megahorn, Water Pulse, Waterfall

Evolution

GOLDEEN → SEAKING

001-100
101-200
201-300
401-442
443-500
501-600
701-800
801-898

STARYU

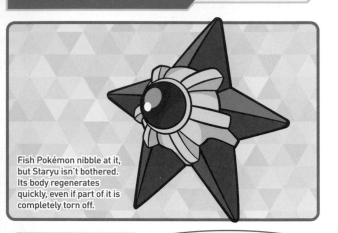

Fish Pokémon nibble at it, but Staryu isn't bothered. Its body regenerates quickly, even if part of it is completely torn off.

Star Shape Pokémon	
POKÉDEX NO.	**120**
TYPE	Water
ABILITY	Natural Cure, Illuminate
HEIGHT	2'07"
WEIGHT	76.1 lbs

Description

If you visit a beach at the end of summer, you'll be able to see groups of Staryu lighting up in a steady rhythm.

Special Moves

Water Gun, Psybeam, Harden

Evolution

STARYU

STARMIE

STARMIE

This Pokémon has an organ known as its core. The organ glows in seven colors when Starmie is unleashing its potent psychic powers.

Mysterious Pokémon

POKÉDEX NO.	121
TYPE	Water, Psychic
ABILITY	Natural Cure, Illuminate
HEIGHT	3'07"
WEIGHT	176.4 lbs

Description

Starmie swims by spinning its body at high speed. As this Pokémon cruises through the ocean, it absorbs tiny plankton.

Special Moves

Psychic, Brine, Recover

Evolution

 ➡

STARYU → STARMIE

D01-100
101-200
201-300
401-442
443-500
501-600
701-800
801-898

MR. MIME

Barrier Pokémon

POKÉDEX NO.	122
TYPE	Psychic, Fairy
ABILITY	Soundproof, Filter
HEIGHT	4'03"
WEIGHT	120.2 lbs

The broadness of its hands may be no coincidence—many scientists believe its palms become enlarged specifically for pantomiming.

Description

It's known for its top-notch pantomime skills. It protects itself from all sorts of attacks by emitting auras from its fingers to create walls.

Special Moves

Mimic, Light Screen, Dazzling Gleam

Evolution

MIME JR.

MR. MIME

MR. MIME

GALARIAN FORM

001-100
101-200
201-300
401-442
443-500
501-600
701-800
801-898

Dancing Pokémon

POKÉDEX NO.	122
TYPE	Ice, Psychic
ABILITY	Vital Spirit, Screen Cleaner
HEIGHT	4'07"
WEIGHT	125.2 lbs

It can radiate chilliness from the bottoms of its feet. It'll spend the whole day tap-dancing on a frozen floor.

Description

Its talent is tap-dancing. It can also manipulate temperatures to create a floor of ice, which this Pokémon can kick up to use as a barrier.

Special Moves

Freeze-Dry, Icy Shard, Mimic

Evolution

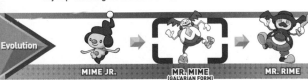

MIME JR. ➡ MR. MIME (GALARIAN FORM) ➡ MR. RIME

177

SCYTHER

Mantis Pokémon

POKÉDEX NO.	123
TYPE	Bug, Flying
ABILITY	Swarm, Technician
HEIGHT	4'11"
WEIGHT	123.5 lbs

As Scyther fights more and more battles, its scythes become sharper and sharper. With a single slice, Scyther can fell a massive tree.

Description

If you come across an area in a forest where a lot of trees have been cut down, what you've found is a Scyther's territory.

Special Moves

Slash, Swords Dance, X-Scissor

Evolution

SCYTHER → SCIZOR

JYNX

In certain parts of Galar, Jynx was once feared and worshipped as the Queen of Ice.

001-100

101-200

201-300

401-442

443-500

501-600

701-800

801-898

Human Shape Pokémon

POKÉDEX NO.	**124**
TYPE	Ice, Psychic
ABILITY	Oblivious, Forewarn
HEIGHT	4'07"
WEIGHT	89.5 lbs

Description

The Jynx of Galar often have beautiful and delicate voices. Some of these Pokémon have even gathered a fan base.

Special Moves

Sweet Kiss, Psychic, Blizzard

Evolution

SMOOCHUM

JYNX

ELECTABUZZ

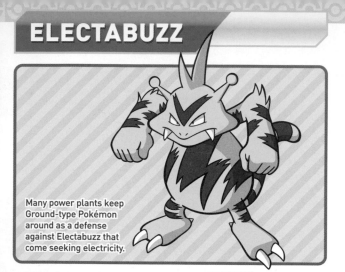

Many power plants keep Ground-type Pokémon around as a defense against Electabuzz that come seeking electricity.

Electric Pokémon

POKÉDEX NO.	125
TYPE	Electric
ABILITY	Static
HEIGHT	3'07"
WEIGHT	66.1 lbs

Description

With the coming of a storm, many of these Pokémon will gather under tall trees and sit there waiting for lightning to strike.

Special Moves

Thunder Shock, Thunder Punch, Discharge

Evolution

ELEKID → ELECTABUZZ → ELECTIVIRE

MAGMAR

001-100

101-200

201-300

401-442

443-500

501-600

701-800

801-898

These Pokémon's bodies are constantly burning. Magmar are feared as one of the causes behind fires.

Spitfire Pokémon	
POKÉDEX NO.	**126**
TYPE	Fire
ABILITY	Flame Body
HEIGHT	4'03"
WEIGHT	98.1 lbs

Description

Magmar dispatches its prey with fire. But it regrets this habit once it realizes that it has burned its intended prey to a charred crisp.

Special Moves

Flamethrower, Fire Blast, Low Kick

Evolution

MAGBY → MAGMAR → MAGMORTAR

PINSIR

These Pokémon judge one another based on pincers. Thicker, more impressive pincers make for more popularity with the opposite gender.

Stag Beetle Pokémon	
POKÉDEX NO.	**127**
TYPE	Bug
ABILITY	Hyper Cutter, Mold Breaker
HEIGHT	4'11"
WEIGHT	121.3 lbs

Description

This Pokémon clamps its pincers down on its prey and then either splits the prey in half or flings it away.

Special Moves

Guillotine, Strength, X-Scissor

Evolution

PINSIR

Does not evolve

MEGA PINSIR

With its vaunted horns, it can lift an opponent 10 times heavier than itself and fly about with ease.

PINSIR

001-100

101-200

201-300

401-442

443-500

501-600

701-800

801-898

Stag Beetle Pokémon

POKÉDEX NO.	**127**
TYPE	Bug, Flying
ABILITY	Aerilate
HEIGHT	5'07"
WEIGHT	130.1 lbs

Description

After Mega Evolution, it becomes able to fly. Perhaps because it's so happy, it rarely touches the ground.

Special Moves

Guillotine, Submission, Double Hit

TAUROS

The Tauros of Galar are volatile in nature, and they won't allow people to ride on their backs.

Wild Bull Pokémon

POKÉDEX NO.	128
TYPE	Normal
ABILITY	Intimidate, Anger Point
HEIGHT	4'07"
WEIGHT	194.9 lbs

Description

When Tauros begins whipping itself with its tails, it's a warning that the Pokémon is about to charge with astounding speed.

Special Moves

Take Down, Horn Attack, Giga Impact

Evolution

TAUROS

Does not evolve

MAGIKARP

Fish Pokémon

POKÉDEX NO.	129
TYPE	Water
ABILITY	Swift Swim
HEIGHT	2'11"
WEIGHT	22.0 lbs

Description

This weak and pathetic Pokémon gets easily pushed along rivers when there are strong currents.

It is virtually worthless in terms of both power and speed. It is the most weak and pathetic Pokémon in the world.

Special Moves

Splash, Tackle, Flail

001-100
101-200
201-300
401-442
463-500
501-600
701-800
801-898

Evolution

MAGIKARP → GYARADOS

GYARADOS

Atrocious Pokémon

POKÉDEX NO.	**130**
TYPE	Water, Flying
ABILITY	Intimidate
HEIGHT	21'04"
WEIGHT	518.1 lbs

It has an extremely aggressive nature. The Hyper Beam it shoots from its mouth totally incinerates all targets.

Description

Once it begins to rampage, a Gyarados will burn everything down, even in a harsh storm.

Special Moves

Hyper Beam, Hydro Cannon, Thrash

Evolution

MAGIKARP → GYARADOS

MEGA GYARADOS

001-
100

101-
200

201-
300

401-
442

443-
500

501-
600

701-
800

801-
898

Mega Evolution places a burden on its body. The stress causes it to become all the more ferocious.

GYARADOS

Atrocious Pokémon	
POKÉDEX NO.	**130**
TYPE	Water, Dark
ABILITY	Mold Breaker
HEIGHT	21'04"
WEIGHT	672.4 lbs

Description

Although it obeys its instinctive drive to destroy everything within its reach, it will respond to orders from a Trainer it truly trusts.

Special Moves

Hyper Beam, Hydro Pump, Dragon Rage

LAPRAS

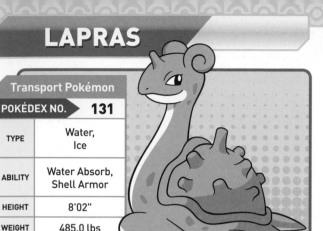

Transport Pokémon

POKÉDEX NO.	**131**
TYPE	Water, Ice
ABILITY	Water Absorb, Shell Armor
HEIGHT	8'02"
WEIGHT	485.0 lbs

Crossing icy seas is no issue for this cold-resistant Pokémon. Its smooth skin is a little cool to the touch.

Description

A smart and kindhearted Pokémon, it glides across the surface of the sea while its beautiful song echoes around it.

Special Moves

Ice Beam, Icy Shard, Brine

Evolution

LAPRAS

Does not evolve

LAPRAS

GIGANTAMAX FORM

It surrounds itself with a huge ring of gathered ice particles. It uses the ring to smash any icebergs that might impede its graceful swimming.

LAPRAS

001-100

101-200

201-300

401-442

443-500

501-600

701-800

801-898

Transport Pokémon	
POKÉDEX NO.	**131**
TYPE	Water, Ice
ABILITY	Water Absorb, Shell Armor
HEIGHT	78'09"+
WEIGHT	??? lbs

Description

Over 5,000 people can ride on its shell at once. And it's a very comfortable ride, without the slightest shaking or swaying.

Special Moves

G-Max Resonance

DITTO

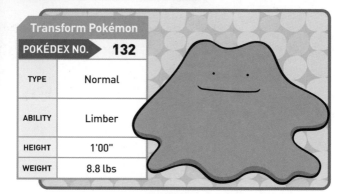

Transform Pokémon

POKÉDEX NO.	132
TYPE	Normal
ABILITY	Limber
HEIGHT	1'00"
WEIGHT	8.8 lbs

Description

It can reconstitute its entire cellular structure to change into what it sees, but it returns to normal when it relaxes.

Special Moves

Transform

When it encounters another Ditto, it will move faster than normal to duplicate that opponent exactly.

Evolution | DITTO | Does not evolve

190

EEVEE

Evolution Pokémon

POKÉDEX NO.	133

TYPE	Normal
ABILITY	Run Away, Adaptability
HEIGHT	1'00"
WEIGHT	14.3 lbs

It has the ability to alter the composition of its body to suit its surrounding environment.

Description

Thanks to its unstable genetic makeup, this special Pokémon conceals many different possible evolutions.

Special Moves

Swift, Charm, Baby-Doll Eyes

001-100
101-200
201-300
401-442
443-500
501-600
701-800
801-898

Evolution

EEVEE

→ VAPOREON FLAREON UMBREON GLACEON

JOLTEON ESPEON LEAFEON SYLVEON

EEVEE

Having gotten even friendlier and more innocent, Eevee tries to play with anyone around, only to end up crushing them with its immense body.

EEVEE

Evolution Pokémon	
POKÉDEX NO.	**133**
TYPE	Normal
ABILITY	Run Away, Adaptability
HEIGHT	59'01"+
WEIGHT	??? lbs

Description

Gigantamax energy upped the fluffiness of the fur around Eevee's neck. The fur will envelop a foe, capturing its body and captivating its mind.

Special Moves

G-Max Cuddle

VAPOREON

001-100
101-200
201-300
401-442
443-500
501-600
701-800
801-898

Bubble Jet Pokémon

POKÉDEX NO.	**134**
TYPE	Water
ABILITY	Water Absorb
HEIGHT	3'03"
WEIGHT	63.9 lbs

Description

When Vaporeon's fins begin to vibrate, it is a sign that rain will come within a few hours.

Its cell composition is similar to water molecules. As a result, it can't be seen when it melts away into water.

Special Moves

Water Gun,
Hydro Pump, Haze

Evolution

EEVEE   VAPOREON

JOLTEON

Lightning Pokémon

POKÉDEX NO.	135
TYPE	Electric
ABILITY	Volt Absorb
HEIGHT	2'07"
WEIGHT	54.0 lbs

Description

It accumulates negative ions in the atmosphere to blast out 10,000-volt lightning bolts.

If agitated, it uses electricity to straighten out its fur and launch it in small bunches.

Special Moves

Thunder Shock, Thunder Fang, Double Kick

Evolution

EEVEE   JOLTEON

FLAREON

001-100
101-200
201-300
401-442
443-500
501-600
701-800
801-898

Flame Pokémon

POKÉDEX NO.	**136**
TYPE	Fire
ABILITY	Flash Fire
HEIGHT	2'11"
WEIGHT	55.1 lbs

Description

It stores some of the air it inhales in its internal flame pouch, which heats it to 3,000 degrees Fahrenheit.

Once it has stored up enough heat, this Pokémon's body temperature can reach up to 1,700 degrees Fahrenheit.

Special Moves

Ember, Fire Fang, Flare Blitz

Evolution

EEVEE → FLAREON

195

PORYGON

In recent years, this species has been very helpful in cyberspace. These Pokémon will go around checking to make sure no suspicious data exists.

Virtual Pokémon

POKÉDEX NO.	137
TYPE	Normal
ABILITY	Trace, Download
HEIGHT	2'07"
WEIGHT	80.5 lbs

Description

State-of-the-art technology was used to create Porygon. It was the first artificial Pokémon to be created via computer programming.

Special Moves

Tri Attack, Recover, Zap Cannon

Evolution

PORYGON

PORYGON2

PORYGON-Z

OMANYTE

This Pokémon is a member of an ancient, extinct species. Omanyte paddles through water with its 10 tentacles, looking like it's just drifting along.

Spiral Pokémon

POKÉDEX NO.	138
TYPE	Rock, Water
ABILITY	Shell Armor, Swift Swim
HEIGHT	1'04"
WEIGHT	16.5 lbs

Description

Because some Omanyte manage to escape after being restored or are released into the wild by people, this species is becoming a problem.

Special Moves

Withdraw, Ancient Power, Surf

Evolution

OMANYTE

OMASTAR

OMASTAR

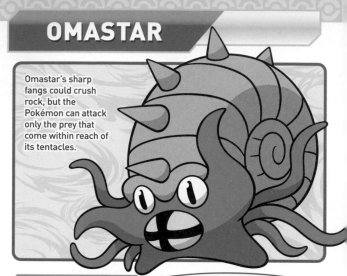

Omastar's sharp fangs could crush rock, but the Pokémon can attack only the prey that come within reach of its tentacles.

Spiral Pokémon

POKÉDEX NO.	139
TYPE	Rock, Water
ABILITY	Shell Armor, Swift Swim
HEIGHT	3'03"
WEIGHT	77.2 lbs

Description

Weighed down by a large and heavy shell, Omastar couldn't move very fast. Some say it went extinct because it was unable to catch food.

Special Moves

Crunch, Hydro Pump, Shell Smash

Evolution

OMANYTE → OMASTAR

KABUTO

001-100
101-200
201-300
401-442
443-500
501-600
701-800
801-898

While some say this species has gone extinct, Kabuto sightings are apparently fairly common in some places.

Shellfish Pokémon	
POKÉDEX NO.	140
TYPE	Rock, Water
ABILITY	Swift Swim, Battle Armor
HEIGHT	1'08"
WEIGHT	25.4 lbs

Description

This species is almost entirely extinct. Kabuto molt every three days, making their shells harder and harder.

Special Moves

Absorb, Ancient Power, Mud Shot

Evolution

KABUTO

KABUTOPS

KABUTOPS

Kabutops slices its prey apart and sucks out the fluids. The discarded body parts become food for other Pokémon.

Shellfish Pokémon	
POKÉDEX NO.	141
TYPE	Rock, Water
ABILITY	Swift Swim, Battle Armor
HEIGHT	4'03"
WEIGHT	89.3 lbs

Description

The cause behind the extinction of this species is unknown. Kabutops were aggressive Pokémon that inhabited warm seas.

Special Moves

Slash, Stone Edge, Liquidation

Evolution

KABUTO

KABUTOPS

AERODACTYL

This is a ferocious Pokémon from ancient times. Apparently, even modern technology is incapable of producing a perfectly restored specimen.

001-100

101-200

201-300

401-442

443-500

501-600

701-800

801-898

Fossil Pokémon	
POKÉDEX NO.	142
TYPE	Rock, Flying
ABILITY	Rock Head, Pressure
HEIGHT	5'11"
WEIGHT	130.1 lbs

Description

Aerodactyl's sawlike fangs can shred skin to tatters—even the skin of Steel-type Pokémon.

Special Moves

Ancient Power, Wing Attack, Rock Slide

Evolution

Does not evolve

AERODACTYL

MEGA AERODACTYL

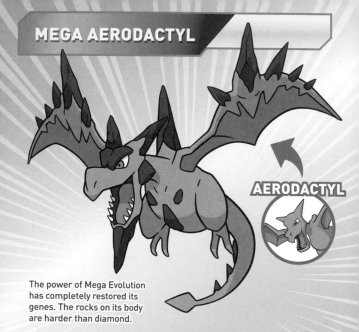

AERODACTYL

The power of Mega Evolution has completely restored its genes. The rocks on its body are harder than diamond.

Fossil Pokémon

POKÉDEX NO.	**142**
TYPE	Rock, Flying
ABILITY	Tough Claws
HEIGHT	6'11"
WEIGHT	174.2 lbs

Description

It will attack anything that moves. Mega Evolution is a burden on its body, so it's incredibly irritated.

Special Moves

Hyper Beam, Giga Impact, Iron Head

SNORLAX

001-100
101-200
201-300
401-442
443-500
501-600
701-800
801-898

Sleeping Pokémon

POKÉDEX NO.	143

TYPE	Normal
ABILITY	Thick Fat, Immunity
HEIGHT	6'11"
WEIGHT	1014.1 lbs

Description

It is not satisfied unless it eats over 880 pounds of food every day. When it is done eating, it goes promptly to sleep.

This Pokémon's stomach is so strong, even eating moldy or rotten food will not affect it.

Special Moves

Rest, High Horsepower, Heavy Slam

Evolution

MUNCHLAX → SNORLAX

203

SNORLAX

GIGANTAMAX FORM

Terrifyingly strong, this Pokémon is the size of a mountain—and moves about as much as one as well.

SNORLAX

Sleeping Pokémon	
POKÉDEX NO.	**143**
TYPE	Normal
ABILITY	Thick Fat, Immunity
HEIGHT	114'10"+
WEIGHT	??? lbs

Description

Gigantamax energy has affected stray seeds and even pebbles that got stuck to Snorlax, making them grow to a huge size.

Special Moves

G-Max Replenish

ARTICUNO

Freeze Pokémon	
POKÉDEX NO.	**144**
TYPE	Ice, Flying
ABILITY	Pressure
HEIGHT	5'07"
WEIGHT	122.1 lbs

001-100

101-200

201-300

401-442

443-500

501-600

701-800

801-898

Description

It's said that this Pokémon's beautiful blue wings are made of ice. Articuno flies over snowy mountains, its long tail fluttering along behind it.

This Pokémon can control ice at will. Articuno is said to live in snowy mountains riddled with permafrost.

Special Moves

Ice Beam, Blizzard, Sheer Cold

Evolution

ARTICUNO

Does not evolve

ARTICUNO

GALARIAN FORM

Cruel Pokémon		
POKÉDEX NO.		**144**
TYPE	Psychic, Flying	
ABILITY	Competitive	
HEIGHT	5'07"	
WEIGHT	112.2 lbs	

Its feather-like blades are composed of psychic energy and can shear through thick iron sheets as if they were paper.

Description

Known as Articuno, this Pokémon fires beams that can immobilize opponents as if they had been frozen solid.

Special Moves

Freezing Glare, Psycho Cut, Hurricane

Evolution Does not evolve

ARTICUNO
(GALARIAN FORM)

ZAPDOS

Electric Pokémon

POKÉDEX NO.	**145**
TYPE	Electric, Flying
ABILITY	Pressure
HEIGHT	5'03"
WEIGHT	116.0 lbs

This Pokémon has complete control over electricity. There are tales of Zapdos nesting in the dark depths of pitch-black thunderclouds.

Description

Zapdos is a Legendary Bird Pokémon. It's said that when Zapdos rubs its feathers together, lightning will fall immediately after.

Special Moves

Thunder, Drill Peck, Zap Cannon

Evolution Does not evolve

ZAPDOS

001-100
101-200
201-300
401-442
443-500
501-600
701-800
801-898

ZAPDOS

GALARIAN FORM

Strong Legs Pokémon

POKÉDEX NO.	145
TYPE	Fighting, Flying
ABILITY	Defiant
HEIGHT	5'03"
WEIGHT	128.3 lbs

When its feathers rub together, they produce a crackling sound like the zapping of electricity. That's why this Pokémon is called Zapdos.

Description

One kick from its powerful legs will pulverize a dump truck. Supposedly, this Pokémon runs through the mountains at over 180 mph.

Special Moves

Thunderous Kick, Close Combat, Rock Smash

Evolution

ZAPDOS
[GALARIAN FORM]

Does not evolve

MOLTRES

Flame Pokémon

POKÉDEX NO.	**146**
TYPE	Fire, Flying
ABILITY	Pressure
HEIGHT	6'07"
WEIGHT	132.3 lbs

It's one of the Legendary Bird Pokémon. When Moltres flaps its flaming wings, they glimmer with a dazzling red glow.

Description

There are stories of this Pokémon using its radiant, flame-cloaked wings to light up paths for those lost in the mountains.

Special Moves

Incinerate, Burn Up, Sky Attack

Evolution

MOLTRES

Does not evolve

101-200
201-300
401-442
443-500
501-600
701-800
801-898

MOLTRES

GALARIAN FORM

Malevolent Pokémon

POKÉDEX NO.	**146**

TYPE	Dark, Flying
ABILITY	Berserk
HEIGHT	6'07"
WEIGHT	145.5 lbs

The sinister aura that blazes like molten fire around this Pokémon is what inspired the name Moltres.

Description

This Pokémon's sinister, flame-like aura will consume the spirit of any creature it hits. Victims become burned-out shadows of themselves.

Special Moves

Fiery Wrath, Nasty Plot, Hurricane

Evolution Does not evolve

MOLTRES
(GALARIAN FORM)

DRATINI

This Pokémon was long considered to be no more than a myth. The small lump on a Dratini's forehead is actually a horn that's still coming in.

001-100
101-200
201-300
401-442
443-500
501-600
701-800
801-898

Dragon Pokémon

POKÉDEX NO.	147
TYPE	Dragon
ABILITY	Shed Skin
HEIGHT	5'11"
WEIGHT	7.3 lbs

Description

Dratini dwells near bodies of rapidly flowing water, such as the plunge pools of waterfalls. As it grows, Dratini will shed its skin many times.

Special Moves

Wrap, Aqua Tail, Slam

Evolution

DRATINI → DRAGONAIR → DRAGONITE

DRAGONAIR

This Pokémon lives in pristine oceans and lakes. It can control the weather, and it uses this power to fly into the sky, riding on the wind.

Dragon Pokémon

POKÉDEX NO.	**148**
TYPE	Dragon
ABILITY	Shed Skin
HEIGHT	13'01"
WEIGHT	36.4 lbs

Description

This Pokémon gathers power in the orbs on its tail and controls the weather. When enshrouded by an aura, Dragonair has a mystical appearance.

Special Moves

Aqua Tail, Agility,
Rain Dance

Evolution

DRATINI → DRAGONAIR → DRAGONAIR

DRAGONITE

Dragon Pokémon	
POKÉDEX NO.	**149**
TYPE	Dragon, Flying
ABILITY	Inner Focus
HEIGHT	7'03"
WEIGHT	463.0 lbs

This Pokémon is known as the Sea Incarnate. Figureheads that resemble Dragonite decorate the bows of many ships.

001-100

101-200

201-300

401-442

443-500

501-600

701-800

801-898

Description

It's a kindhearted Pokémon. If it spots a drowning person or Pokémon, Dragonite simply must help them.

Special Moves

Hyper Beam, Dragon Rush, Hurricane

Evolution

DRATINI ➡ DRAGONAIR ➡ DRAGONITE

MEWTWO

Genetic Pokémon

POKÉDEX NO.	150
TYPE	Psychic
ABILITY	Pressure
HEIGHT	6'07"
WEIGHT	269.0 lbs

The research efforts of a certain scientist ultimately resulted in this Pokémon. Its powers are dedicated to battling.

Description

Created from the DNA of Mew, this Pokémon is a dangerous combination of overwhelming power and a savage heart.

Special Moves

Psychic, Amnesia, Psystrike

Evolution

MEWTWO

Does not evolve

MEW

001-100

101-200

201-300

401-442

443-500

501-600

701-800

801-898

New Species Pokémon	
POKÉDEX NO.	**151**
TYPE	Psychic
ABILITY	Synchronize
HEIGHT	1'04"
WEIGHT	8.8 lbs

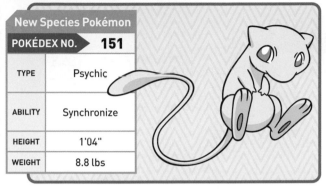

Description

This mythical Pokémon is said to be extinct, but sightings of it are still being reported to this day.

It's very intelligent and can use an incredible variety of moves. Many believe that all other Pokémon are descendants of this one.

Special Moves

Psychic, Metronome, Transform

Evolution  Does not evolve

MEW

CHIKORITA

Leaf Pokémon

POKÉDEX NO.	152

TYPE	Grass
ABILITY	Overgrow
HEIGHT	2'11"
WEIGHT	14.1 lbs

Description

In battle, Chikorita waves its leaf around to keep the foe at bay. However, a sweet fragrance also wafts from the leaf, becalming the battling Pokémon and creating a cozy, friendly atmosphere all around.

It uses the leaf on its head to determine the air's temperature and humidity. It loves to sunbathe.

Special Moves

Body Slam, Razor Leaf, Synthesis

Evolution

CHIKORITA → BAYLEEF → MEGANIUM

BAYLEEF

001-100
101-200
201-300
401-442
443-500
501-600
701-800
801-898

Leaf Pokémon	
POKÉDEX NO.	**153**
TYPE	Grass
ABILITY	Overgrow
HEIGHT	3'11"
WEIGHT	34.8 lbs

Description

Bayleef's neck is ringed by curled-up leaves. Inside each tubular leaf is a small shoot of a tree. The fragrance of this shoot makes people peppy.

Special Moves

Magical Leaf, Poison Powder, Synthesis

The buds that ring its neck give off a spicy aroma that perks people up.

Evolution

CHIKORITA

BAYLEEF

MEGANIUM

MEGANIUM

Herb Pokémon

POKÉDEX NO.	**154**
TYPE	Grass
ABILITY	Overgrow
HEIGHT	5'11"
WEIGHT	221.6 lbs

Meganium's breath has the power to revive dead grass and plants. It can make them healthy again.

Description

The fragrance of Meganium's flower soothes and calms emotions. In battle, this Pokémon gives off more of its becalming scent to blunt the foe's fighting spirit.

Special Moves

Petal Dance,
Petal Blizzard, Reflect

Evolution

CHIKORITA

BAYLEEF

MEGANIUM

CYNDAQUIL

Fire Mouse Pokémon

POKÉDEX NO.	155
TYPE	Fire
ABILITY	Blaze
HEIGHT	1'08"
WEIGHT	17.4 lbs

It has a timid nature. If it is startled, the flames on its back burn more vigorously.

Description

Cyndaquil protects itself by flaring up the flames on its back. The flames are vigorous if the Pokémon is angry. However, if it is tired, the flames sputter fitfully with incomplete combustion.

Special Moves

Tackle, Ember, Flame Charge

Evolution

CYNDAQUIL → QUILAVA → TYPHLOSION

001-100
101-200
201-300
401-442
443-500
501-600
701-800
801-898

QUILAVA

Volcano Pokémon

POKÉDEX NO.	**156**
TYPE	Fire
ABILITY	Blaze
HEIGHT	2'11"
WEIGHT	41.9 lbs

Description

Quilava keeps its foes at bay with the intensity of its flames and gusts of superheated air. This Pokémon applies its outstanding nimbleness to dodge attacks even while scorching the foes with flames.

Special Moves

Swift, Flame Charge, Lava Plume

Before battle, it turns its back on its opponent to demonstrate how ferociously its fire blazes.

Evolution

CYNDAQUIL → QUILAVA → TYPHLOSION

TYPHLOSION

Volcano Pokémon

POKÉDEX NO.	**157**
TYPE	Fire
ABILITY	Blaze
HEIGHT	5'07"
WEIGHT	175.3 lbs

If its rage peaks, it becomes so hot that anything that touches it will instantly go up in flames.

Description

Typhlosion obscures itself behind a shimmering heat haze that it creates using its intensely hot flames. This Pokémon creates blazing explosive blasts that burn everything to cinders.

Special Moves

Eruption, Flamethrower, Flame Wheel

Evolution

CYNDAQUIL ➡ QUILAVA ➡ TYPHLOSION

001-100
101-200
201-300
401-442
443-500
501-600
701-800
801-898

TOTODILE

Big Jaw Pokémon

POKÉDEX NO.	158
TYPE	Water
ABILITY	Torrent
HEIGHT	2'00"
WEIGHT	20.9 lbs

Description

Despite the smallness of its body, Totodile's jaws are very powerful. While the Pokémon may think it is just playfully nipping, its bite has enough power to cause serious injury.

Special Moves

Scratch, Water Gun, Leer

It is small but rough and tough. It won't hesitate to take a bite out of anything that moves.

Evolution

TOTODILE → CROCONAW → FERALIGATR

CROCONAW

Big Jaw Pokémon

POKÉDEX NO.	159
TYPE	Water
ABILITY	Torrent
HEIGHT	3'07"
WEIGHT	55.1 lbs

001-100

101-200

201-300

401-442

443-500

501-600

701-800

801-898

If it loses a fang, a new one grows back in its place. There are always 48 fangs lining Its mouth.

Description

Once Croconaw has clamped its jaws on its foe, it will absolutely not let go. Because the tips of its fangs are forked back like barbed fishhooks, they become impossible to remove when they have sunk in.

Special Moves

Slash, Aqua Tail, Ice Fang

Evolution

TOTODILE
→

CROCONAW
→

FERALIGATR

FERALIGATR

Big Jaw Pokémon	
POKÉDEX NO.	**160**
TYPE	Water
ABILITY	Torrent
HEIGHT	7'07"
WEIGHT	195.8 lbs

Description

Feraligatr intimidates its foes by opening its huge mouth. In battle, it will kick the ground hard with its thick and powerful hind legs to charge at the foe at an incredible speed.

Special Moves

Hydro Pump, Thrash, Superpower

It usually moves slowly, but it goes at blinding speed when it attacks and bites prey.

Evolution

TOTODILE → CROCONAW → FERALIGATR

SENTRET

Scout Pokémon	
POKÉDEX NO.	**161**
TYPE	Normal
ABILITY	Keen Eye, Run Away
HEIGHT	2'07"
WEIGHT	13.2 lbs

001-100
101-200
201-300
401-442
443-500
501-600
701-800
801-898

When acting as a lookout,
it warns others of danger by screeching
and hitting the ground with its tail.

Description

When Sentret sleeps, it does so while another stands guard. The sentry wakes the others at the first sign of danger. When this Pokémon becomes separated from its pack, it becomes incapable of sleep due to fear.

Special Moves

Foresight, Baton Pass, Quick Attack

Evolution

SENTRET → FURRET

FURRET

The mother puts its offspring to sleep by curling up around them. It corners foes with speed.

Long Body Pokémon	
POKÉDEX NO.	**162**
TYPE	Normal
ABILITY	Keen Eye, Run Away
HEIGHT	5'11"
WEIGHT	71.7 lbs

Description

Furret has a very slim build. When under attack, it can slickly squirm through narrow spaces and get away. In spite of its short limbs, this Pokémon is very nimble and fleet.

Special Moves

Agility, Hyper Voice, Me First

Evolution

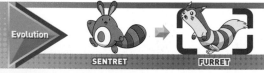

SENTRET → FURRET

HOOTHOOT

Owl Pokémon	
POKÉDEX NO.	**163**
TYPE	Normal, Flying
ABILITY	Keen Eye, Insomnia
HEIGHT	2'04"
WEIGHT	46.7 lbs

It begins to hoot at the same time every day. Some Trainers use them in place of clocks.

Description

It always stands on one foot. It changes feet so fast, the movement can rarely be seen.

Special Moves

Peck, Extrasensory, Hypnosis

Evolution

HOOTHOOT → NOCTOWL

001-100
101-200
201-300
401-442
443-500
501-600
701-800
801-898

NOCTOWL

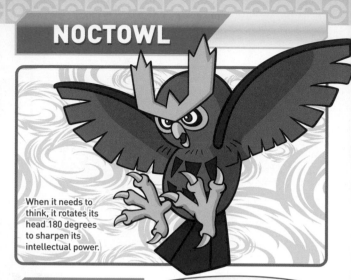

When it needs to think, it rotates its head 180 degrees to sharpen its intellectual power.

Owl Pokémon	
POKÉDEX NO.	164
TYPE	Normal, Flying
ABILITY	Keen Eye, Insomnia
HEIGHT	5'03"
WEIGHT	89.9 lbs

Description

Its eyes are specially developed to enable it to see clearly even in murky darkness and minimal light.

Special Moves

Echoed Voice, Air Slash, Roost

Evolution

HOOTHOOT

NOCTOWL

LEDYBA

Five Star Pokémon

POKÉDEX NO.	**165**
TYPE	Bug, Flying
ABILITY	Swarm, Early Bird
HEIGHT	3'03"
WEIGHT	23.8 lbs

These very cowardly Pokémon join together and use Reflect to protect their nest.

Description

This Pokémon is very sensitive to cold. In the warmth of Alola, it appears quite lively.

Special Moves

Tackle, Air Slash, Supersonic

Evolution

LEDYBA → LEDIAN

001-100
101-200
201-300
401-442
443-500
501-600
701-800
801-898

LEDIAN

It flies through the night sky, sprinkling sparkly dust. According to some, if that dust sticks to you, good things will happen to you.

Five Star Pokémon

POKÉDEX NO.	166
TYPE	Bug, Flying
ABILITY	Swarm, Early Bird
HEIGHT	4'07"
WEIGHT	78.5 lbs

Description

It's said that the patterns on its back are related to the stars in the night sky, but the details of that relationship remain unclear.

Special Moves

Tackle, Bug Buzz, Mach Punch

Evolution

LEDYBA → LEDIAN

SPINARAK

001-100

101-200

201-300

401-442

443-500

501-600

701-800

801-898

String Spit Pokémon

POKÉDEX NO.	**167**
TYPE	Bug, Poison
ABILITY	Swarm, Insomnia
HEIGHT	1'08"
WEIGHT	18.7 lbs

Description

Although the poison from its fangs isn't that strong, it's potent enough to weaken prey that get caught in its web.

With threads from its mouth, it fashions sturdy webs that won't break even if you set a rock on them.

Special Moves

String Shot, Poison Sting, Cross Poison

Evolution

SPINARAK

ARIADOS

ARIADOS

There are some areas where people use the string Ariados spins for their own weaving. The resulting cloth is popular for its strength.

Long Leg Pokémon

POKÉDEX NO.	168
TYPE	Bug, Poison
ABILITY	Swarm, Insomnia
HEIGHT	3'07"
WEIGHT	73.9 lbs

Description

Every night, it wanders around in search of prey, whose movements it restrains by spewing threads before it bites into them with its fangs.

Special Moves

Sticky Web, Pin Missile, Spider Web

Evolution

SPINARAK → ARIADOS

CROBAT

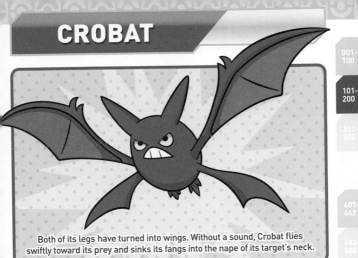

Both of its legs have turned into wings. Without a sound, Crobat flies swiftly toward its prey and sinks its fangs into the nape of its target's neck.

Bat Pokémon	
POKÉDEX NO.	**169**
TYPE	Poison, Flying
ABILITY	Inner Focus
HEIGHT	5'11"
WEIGHT	165.3 lbs

Description

This Pokémon flaps its four wings skillfully. Crobat can fly through cramped caves without needing to slow down.

Special Moves

Mean Look, Toxic, Air Cutter

Evolution

ZUBAT

GOLBAT

CROBAT

001-100
101-200
201-300
401-442
443-500
501-600
701-800
801-898

CHINCHOU

Angler Pokémon

POKÉDEX NO.	170
TYPE	Water, Electric
ABILITY	Illuminate, Volt Absorb
HEIGHT	1'08"
WEIGHT	26.5 lbs

On the dark ocean floor, its only means of communication is its constantly flashing lights.

Description

Its antennae, which evolved from a fin, have both positive and negative charges flowing through them.

Special Moves

Supersonic, Water Gun, Thunder Wave

Evolution

CHINCHOU ➡ LANTURN

LANTURN

This Pokémon flashes a bright light that blinds its prey. This creates an opening for it to deliver an electrical attack.

Light Pokémon	
POKÉDEX NO.	**171**
TYPE	Water, Electric
ABILITY	Illuminate, Volt Absorb
HEIGHT	3'11"
WEIGHT	49.6 lbs

Description

The light it emits is so bright that it can illuminate the sea's surface from a depth of over three miles.

Special Moves

Electro Ball, Eerie Impulse, Confuse Ray

Evolution

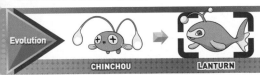

CHINCHOU → LANTURN

001-100
101-200
201-300
401-442
443-500
501-600
701-800
801-898

PICHU

Tiny Mouse Pokémon	
POKÉDEX NO.	**172**
TYPE	Electric
ABILITY	Static
HEIGHT	1'00"
WEIGHT	4.4 lbs

The electric sacs in its cheeks are small. If even a little electricity leaks, it becomes shocked.

Description

Despite its small size, it can zap even adult humans. However, if it does so, it also surprises itself.

Special Moves

Thunder Shock, Charm, Nuzzle

Evolution

PICHU → PIKACHU → RAICHU → RAICHU (ALOLAN FORM)

CLEFFA

001-100
101-200
201-300
401-442
443-500
501-600
701-800
801-898

Star Shape Pokémon

POKÉDEX NO.	173
TYPE	Fairy
ABILITY	Cute Charm, Magic Guard
HEIGHT	1'00"
WEIGHT	6.6 lbs

According to local rumors, Cleffa are often seen in places where shooting stars have fallen.

Description

Because of its unusual, starlike silhouette, people believe that it came here on a meteor.

Special Moves

Copy Cat, Sweet Kiss, Disarming Voice

Evolution

CLEFFA → CLEFAIRY → CLEFABLE

IGGLYBUFF

Balloon Pokémon

POKÉDEX NO.	174
TYPE	Normal, Fairy
ABILITY	Cute Charm, Competitive
HEIGHT	1'00"
WEIGHT	2.2 lbs

Taking advantage of the softness of its body, Igglybuff moves as if bouncing. Its body turns a deep pink when its temperature rises.

Description

Igglybuff loves to sing. Its marshmallow-like body gives off a faint sweet smell.

Special Moves

Sing, Sweet Kiss, Disarming Voice

Evolution

IGGLYBUFF → JIGGLYPUFF → WIGGLYTUFF

TOGEPI

001-100
101-200
201-300
401-442
443-500
501-600
701-800
801-898

Spike Ball Pokémon

POKÉDEX NO.	175

TYPE	Fairy
ABILITY	Serene Grace, Hustle
HEIGHT	1'00"
WEIGHT	3.3 lbs

Description

The shell seems to be filled with joy. It is said that it will share good luck when treated kindly.

A proverb claims that happiness will come to anyone who can make a sleeping Togepi stand up.

Special Moves

Growl, Life Dew, Metronome

Evolution

TOGEPI → TOGETIC → TOGEKISS

TOGETIC

Happiness Pokémon

POKÉDEX NO. **176**

TYPE	Fairy, Flying
ABILITY	Serene Grace, Hustle
HEIGHT	2'00"
WEIGHT	7.1 lbs

Description

It grows dispirited if it is not with kind people. It can float in midair without moving its wings.

They say that it will appear before kindhearted, caring people and shower them with happiness.

Special Moves

Sweet Kiss, Fairy Wind, Charm

Evolution

TOGEPI → TOGETIC → TOGEKISS

NATU

Tiny Bird Pokémon

POKÉDEX NO.	**177**
TYPE	Psychic, Flying
ABILITY	Synchronize, Early Bird
HEIGHT	0'08"
WEIGHT	4.4 lbs

It is extremely good at climbing tree trunks and likes to eat the new sprouts on the trees.

Description

Because its wings aren't yet fully grown, it has to hop to get around. It is always staring at something.

Special Moves

Leer, Night Shade, Future Sight

Evolution

NATU → XATU

XATU

This odd Pokémon can see both the past and the future. It eyes the sun's movement all day.

Mystic Pokémon	
POKÉDEX NO.	**178**
TYPE	Psychic, Flying
ABILITY	Synchronize, Early Bird
HEIGHT	4'11"
WEIGHT	33.1 lbs

Description

They say that it stays still and quiet because it is seeing both the past and future at the same time.

Special Moves

Psychic, Psycho Shift, Future Sight

Evolution

NATU → XATU

MAREEP

Clothing made from Mareep's fleece is easily charged with static electricity, so a special process is used on it.

001-100
101-200
201-300
401-442
443-500
501-600
701-800
801-898

Wool Pokémon	
POKÉDEX NO.	**179**
TYPE	Electric
ABILITY	Static
HEIGHT	2'00"
WEIGHT	17.2 lbs

Description

Rubbing its fleece generates electricity. You'll want to pet it because it's cute, but if you use your bare hand, you'll get a painful shock.

Special Moves

Discharge, Light Screen, Cotton Guard

Evolution

MAREEP → FLAAFFY → AMPHAROS

245

FLAAFFY

Wool Pokémon

POKÉDEX NO.	180
TYPE	Electric
ABILITY	Static
HEIGHT	2'07"
WEIGHT	29.3 lbs

In the places on its body where fleece doesn't grow, its skin is rubbery and doesn't conduct electricity. Those spots are safe to touch.

Description

It stores electricity in its fluffy fleece. If it stores up too much, it will start to go bald in those patches.

Special Moves

Thunder Shock, Electro Ball, Charge

Evolution

MAREEP → FLAAFFY → AMPHAROS

AMPHAROS

Light Pokémon

POKÉDEX NO.	**181**
TYPE	Electric
ABILITY	Static
HEIGHT	4'07"
WEIGHT	135.6 lbs

Its tail shines bright and strong.
It has been prized since long ago
as a beacon for sailors.

Description

The light from its tail
can be seen from
space. This is why you
can always tell exactly
where it is, which is
why it usually keeps
the light off.

Special Moves

Thunder Punch, Thunder
Wave, Dragon Pulse

Evolution

MAREEP → FLAAFFY → AMPHAROS

001-
100

101-
200

201-
300

401-
442

443-
500

501-
600

701-
800

801-
898

MEGA AMPHAROS

Massive amounts of energy intensely stimulated Ampharos's cells, apparently awakening its long-sleeping dragon's blood.

AMPHAROS

Light Pokémon	
POKÉDEX NO.	**181**
TYPE	Electric, Dragon
ABILITY	Mold Breaker
HEIGHT	4'07"
WEIGHT	135.6 lbs

Description

Excess energy from Mega Evolution stimulates its genes, and the wool it had lost grows in again.

Special Moves

Dragon Pulse, Signal Beam, Ion Deluge

BELLOSSOM

Flower Pokémon

POKÉDEX NO.	182
TYPE	Grass
ABILITY	Chlorophyll
HEIGHT	1'04"
WEIGHT	12.8 lbs

Description

Bellossom gather at times and appear to dance. They say that the dance is a ritual to summon the sun.

Plentiful in the tropics. When it dances, its petals rub together and make a pleasant ringing sound.

Special Moves

Petal Blizzard, Grassy Terrain, Toxic

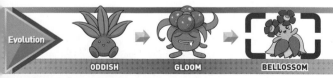

Evolution

ODDISH → GLOOM → BELLOSSOM

001-100
101-200
201-300
401-442
443-500
501-600
701-800
801-898

MARILL

Aqua Mouse Pokémon

POKÉDEX NO.	183
TYPE	Water, Fairy
ABILITY	Thick Fat, Huge Power
HEIGHT	1'04"
WEIGHT	18.7 lbs

Even after Marill swims in a cold sea, its water-repellent fur dries almost as soon as Marill leaves the water. That's why this Pokémon is never cold.

Description

This Pokémon uses its round tail as a float. The ball of Marill's tail is filled with nutrients that have been turned into an oil.

Special Moves

Defense Curl, Rollout, Bubble Beam

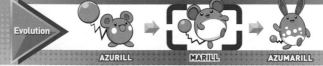

Evolution

AZURILL ➡ MARILL ➡ AZUMARILL

AZUMARILL

These Pokémon create air-filled bubbles. When Azurill play in rivers, Azumarill will cover them with these bubbles.

001-100

101-200

201-300

401-442

443-500

501-600

701-800

801-898

Aqua Rabbit Pokémon

POKÉDEX NO.	184
TYPE	Water, Fairy
ABILITY	Thick Fat, Huge Power
HEIGHT	2'07"
WEIGHT	62.8 lbs

Description

It spends most of its time in the water. On sunny days, Azumarill floats on the surface of the water and sunbathes.

Special Moves

Hydro Pump, Slam, Rain Dance

Evolution

AZURILL ➡ MARILL ➡ AZUMARILL

SUDOWOODO

Imitation Pokémon

POKÉDEX NO.	185

TYPE	Rock
ABILITY	Rock Head, Sturdy
HEIGHT	3'11"
WEIGHT	83.8 lbs

It's so popular with the elderly that there's a magazine devoted to this Pokémon. Fans obsess over the particular length and angle of its arms.

Description

It disguises itself as a tree to avoid attack. It hates water, so it will disappear if it starts raining.

Special Moves

Copycat, Wood Hammer, Block

Evolution

BONSLY → SUDOWOODO

POLITOED

The cry of a male is louder than that of a female. Male Politoed with deep, menacing voices find more popularity with the opposite gender.

Frog Pokémon	
POKÉDEX NO.	**186**
TYPE	Water
ABILITY	Damp, Water Absorb
HEIGHT	3'07"
WEIGHT	74.7 lbs

Description

At nightfall, these Pokémon appear on the shores of lakes. They announce their territorial claims by letting out cries that sound like shouting.

Special Moves

Perish Song, Mud Shot, Belly Drum

Evolution

POLIWAG → POLIWHIRL → POLITOED

001-100
101-200
201-300
401-442
443-500
501-600
701-800
801-898

HOPPIP

Its body is so light, it must grip the ground firmly with its feet to keep from being blown away.

Cottonweed Pokémon	
POKÉDEX NO.	**187**
TYPE	Grass, Flying
ABILITY	Chlorophyll, Leaf Guard
HEIGHT	1'04"
WEIGHT	1.1 lbs

Description

This Pokémon drifts and floats with the wind. If it senses the approach of strong winds, Hoppip links its leaves with other Hoppip to avoid being blown away.

Special Moves

Absorb, Acrobatics, Rage Powder

Evolution

HOPPIP → SKIPLOOM → JUMPLUFF

SKIPLOOM

It spreads its petals to absorb sunlight. It also floats in the air to get closer to the sun.

Cottonweed Pokémon	
POKÉDEX NO.	**188**
TYPE	Grass, Flying
ABILITY	Chlorophyll, Leaf Guard
HEIGHT	2'00"
WEIGHT	2.2 lbs

Description

Skiploom's flower blossoms when the temperature rises above 64 degrees Fahrenheit. How much the flower opens depends on the temperature. For that reason, this Pokémon is sometimes used as a thermometer.

Special Moves

Poison Powder, U-turn, Mega Drain

Evolution

HOPPIP → SKIPLOOM → JUMPLUFF

001-100
101-200
201-300
401-442
443-500
501-600
701-800
801-898

JUMPLUFF

Even in the fiercest wind, it can control its fluff to make its way to any place in the world it wants.

Cottonweed Pokémon	
POKÉDEX NO.	**189**
TYPE	Grass, Flying
ABILITY	Chlorophyll, Leaf Guard
HEIGHT	2'07"
WEIGHT	6.6 lbs

Description

Jumpluff rides warm southernwinds to cross the sea and fly to foreign lands. The Pokémon descends to the ground when it encounters cold air while it is floating.

Special Moves

Bullet Seed, Synthesis, Cotton Spore

Evolution

HOPPIP ➡ SKIPLOOM ➡ JUMPLUFF

AIPOM

Long Tail Pokémon

POKÉDEX NO.	**190**

TYPE	Normal
ABILITY	Run Away, Pickup
HEIGHT	2'07"
WEIGHT	25.4 lbs

Its tail is so powerful that it can use it to grab a tree branch and hold itself up in the air.

Description

As it did more and more with its tail, its hands became clumsy. It makes its nest high in the treetops.

Special Moves

Tail Whip, Fling, Nasty Plot

001-100

101-200

201-300

401-442

443-500

501-600

701-800

801-898

Evolution

 ➡

AIPOM → AMBIPOM

SUNKERN

It may plummet from the sky. If attacked by a Spearow,* it will violently shake its leaves.

Seed Pokémon	
POKÉDEX NO.	**191**
TYPE	Grass
ABILITY	Chlorophyll, Solar Power
HEIGHT	1'00"
WEIGHT	4.0 lbs

Description

Sunkern tries to move as little as it possibly can. It does so because it tries to conserve all the nutrients it has stored in its body for its evolution. It will not eat a thing, subsisting only on morning dew.

Special Moves

Growth, Sunny Day, Leech Seed

Evolution

SUNKERN ➡ SUNFLORA

 *Spearow: A Pokémon you'll find on page 42.

SUNFLORA

As the hot season approaches, the petals on this Pokémon's face become more vivid and lively.

001-100
101-200
201-300
401-442
443-500
501-600
701-800
801-898

Sun Pokémon

POKÉDEX NO.	**192**
TYPE	Grass
ABILITY	Chlorophyll, Solar Power
HEIGHT	2'07"
WEIGHT	18.7 lbs

Description

Sunflora converts solar energy into nutrition. It moves around actively in the daytime when it is warm. It stops moving as soon as the sun goes down for the night.

Special Moves

Flower Shield, Leaf Storm, Grass Whistle

Evolution

 ➡

SUNKERN   SUNFLORA

259

YANMA

If it flaps its wings really fast, it can generate shock waves that will shatter windows in the area.

Clear Wing Pokémon

POKÉDEX NO.	193
TYPE	Bug, Flying
ABILITY	Compound Eyes, Speed Boost
HEIGHT	3'11"
WEIGHT	83.8 lbs

Description

Its eyes can see 360 degrees without moving its head. It won't miss prey—even those behind it.

Special Moves

Wing Attack, U-turn, Double Team

Evolution

YANMA

YANMEGA

WOOPER

001-100
101-200
201-300
401-442
463-500
501-600
701-800
801-898

Water Fish Pokémon

POKÉDEX NO.	**194**
TYPE	Water, Ground
ABILITY	Damp, Water Absorb
HEIGHT	1'04"
WEIGHT	18.7 lbs

Description

This Pokémon lives in cold water. It will leave the water to search for food when it gets cold outside.

When it walks around on the ground, it coats its body with a slimy, poisonous film.

Special Moves

Water Gun, Mud Shot, Muddy Water

Evolution

WOOPER → QUAGSIRE

QUAGSIRE

It has a sluggish nature. It lies at the river's bottom, waiting for prey to stray into its mouth.

Water Fish Pokémon

POKÉDEX NO.	**195**
TYPE	Water, Ground
ABILITY	Damp, Water Absorb
HEIGHT	4'07"
WEIGHT	165.3 lbs

Description

A dim-witted Pokémon. It doesn't care if it bumps its head into boats or rocks while swimming.

Special Moves

Slam, Aqua Tail, Earthquake

Evolution

WOOPER → QUAGSIRE

ESPEON

001-100
101-200
201-300
401-442
443-500
501-600
701-800
801-898

Sun Pokémon

POKÉDEX NO.	196
TYPE	Psychic
ABILITY	Synchronize
HEIGHT	2'11"
WEIGHT	58.4 lbs

It unleashes psychic power from the orb on its forehead. When its power is exhausted, the orb grows dull and dark.

Description

By reading air currents, it can predict things such as the weather or its foe's next move.

Special Moves

Confusion, Psybeam, Psychic

Evolution

EEVEE → ESPEON

UMBREON

UMBREON

Moonlight Pokémon

POKÉDEX NO.	197
TYPE	Dark
ABILITY	Synchronize
HEIGHT	3'03"
WEIGHT	59.5 lbs

On the night of a full moon, or when it gets excited, the ring patterns on its body glow yellow.

Description

When this Pokémon becomes angry, its pores secrete a poisonous sweat, which it sprays at its opponent's eyes.

Special Moves

Snarl, Dark Pulse, Moonlight

Evolution

EEVEE

UMBREON

MURKROW

001-100
101-200
201-300
401-442
443-500
501-600
701-800
801-898

Darkness Pokémon

POKÉDEX NO.	198
TYPE	Dark, Flying
ABILITY	Insomnia, Super Luck
HEIGHT	1'08"
WEIGHT	4.6 lbs

Description

It searches for shiny things for its boss. Murkrow's presence is said to be unlucky, so many people detest it.

It has a weakness for shiny things. It's been known to sneak into the nests of Gabite*—noted collectors of jewels—in search of treasure.

Special Moves

Wing Attack, Taunt, Feint Attack

Evolution

MURKROW → HONCHKROW

---

*Gabite: A Pokémon you'll find in volume 2.

SLOWKING

Slowking can solve any problem presented to it, but no one can understand a thing Slowking says.

Royal Pokémon	
POKÉDEX NO.	**199**
TYPE	Water, Psychic
ABILITY	Oblivious, Own Tempo
HEIGHT	6'07"
WEIGHT	175.3 lbs

Description

When its head was bitten, toxins entered Slowpoke's head and unlocked an extraordinary power.

Special Moves

Psychic, Zen Headbutt, Surf

Evolution

SLOWPOKE

SLOWKING

SLOWKING

001-100
101-200
201-300
401-442
443-500
501-600
701-800
801-898

GALARIAN FORM

Hexpert Pokémon

POKÉDEX NO.	**199**
TYPE	Poison, Psychic
ABILITY	Own Tempo, Curious Medicine
HEIGHT	5'11"
WEIGHT	175.3 lbs

Description

A combination of toxins and the shock of evolving has increased Shellder's* intelligence to the point that Shellder now controls Slowking.

While chanting strange spells, this Pokémon combines its internal toxins with what it's eaten, creating strange potions.

Special Moves

Eerie Spell, Acid, Curse

Evolution

 →

SLOWPOKE
(GALARIAN FORM)

SLOWKING
(GALARIAN FORM)

*Shellder: A Pokémon you'll find on page 137.

267

MISDREAVUS

Screech Pokémon

POKÉDEX NO.	200
TYPE	Ghost
ABILITY	Levitate
HEIGHT	2'04"
WEIGHT	2.2 lbs

Description

What gives meaning to its life is surprising others. If you set your ear against the red orbs around its neck, you can hear shrieking.

What makes it happy is imitating the voices of weeping people and scaring everyone. It doesn't deal well with folks who aren't easily frightened.

Special Moves

Psywave, Grudge, Pain Split

Evolution

MISDREAVUS → MISMAGIUS

UNOWN

001-100
101-200
201-300
401-442
443-500
501-600
701-800
801-898

Symbol Pokémon

POKÉDEX NO.	201
TYPE	Psychic
ABILITY	Levitate
HEIGHT	1'08"
WEIGHT	11.0 lbs

Its flat, thin body is always stuck on walls. Its shape appears to have some meaning.

Description

This Pokémon is shaped like ancient writing. It is a mystery as to which came first, the ancient writings or the various Unown. Research into this topic is ongoing but nothing is known.

Special Moves

Hidden Power

Evolution  Does not evolve

UNOWN

WOBBUFFET

Patient Pokémon

POKÉDEX NO.	**202**
TYPE	Psychic
ABILITY	Shadow Tag
HEIGHT	4'03"
WEIGHT	62.8 lbs

Description

To keep its pitch-black tail hidden, it lives quietly in the darkness. It is never first to attack.

It hates light and shock. If attacked, it inflates its body to pump up its counterstrike.

Special Moves

Counter, Safeguard, Mirror Coat

Evolution

WYNAUT → WOBBUFFET

GIRAFARIG

Girafarig's rear head contains a tiny brain that is too small for thinking. However, the rear head doesn't need to sleep, so it can keep watch over its surroundings 24 hours a day.

001-100

101-200

201-300

401-442

443-500

501-600

701-800

801-898

Long Neck Pokémon

POKÉDEX NO.	203
TYPE	Normal, Psychic
ABILITY	Inner Focus, Early Bird
HEIGHT	4'11"
WEIGHT	91.5 lbs

Description

Girafarig's rear head also has a brain, but it is small. The rear head attacks in response to smells and sounds. Approaching this Pokémon from behind can cause the rear head to suddenly lash out and bite.

Special Moves

Double Hit, Power Swap, Stomp

Evolution Does not evolve

GIRAFARIG

PINECO

It sticks tree bark to itself with its saliva, making itself thicker and larger. Elderly Pineco are ridiculously huge.

Bagworm Pokémon	
POKÉDEX NO.	**204**
TYPE	Bug
ABILITY	Sturdy
HEIGHT	2'00"
WEIGHT	15.9 lbs

Description

Pineco hangs from a tree branch and patiently waits for prey to come along. If the Pokémon is disturbed while eating by someone shaking its tree, it drops down to the ground and explodes with no warning.

Special Moves

Gyro Ball, Self-Destruct, Rapid Spin

Evolution

PINECO → FORRETRESS

FORRETRESS

001-100
101-200
201-300
301-400
401-442
443-500
501-600
701-800
801-898

In the moment that it gulps down its prey, the inside of its shell is exposed, but to this day, no one has ever seen that sight.

Bagworm Pokémon	
POKÉDEX NO.	**205**
TYPE	Bug, Steel
ABILITY	Sturdy
HEIGHT	3'11"
WEIGHT	277.3 lbs

Description

When something approaches it, it fires off fragments of its steel shell in attack. This is not a conscious action but a conditioned reflex.

Special Moves

Mirror Shot, Heavy Slam, Iron Defense

Evolution

PINECO

FORRETRESS

DUNSPARCE

The nests Dunsparce live in are mazes of tunnels. They never get lost in their own nests—they can tell where they are by the scent of the dirt.

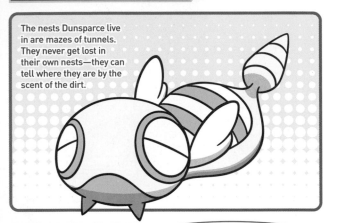

Land Snake Pokémon	
POKÉDEX NO.	**206**
TYPE	Normal
ABILITY	Run Away, Serene Grace
HEIGHT	4'11"
WEIGHT	30.9 lbs

Description

This Pokémon's tiny wings have some scientists saying that Dunsparce used to fly through the sky in ancient times.

Special Moves

Body Slam, Ancient Power, Glare

Evolution

DUNSPARCE

Does not evolve

GLIGAR

Fly Scorpion Pokémon

POKÉDEX NO.	207
TYPE	Ground, Flying
ABILITY	Sand Veil, Hyper Cutter
HEIGHT	3'07"
WEIGHT	142.9 lbs

001-100
101-200
201-300
401-442
443-500
501-600
701-800
801-898

It usually clings to cliffs. When it spots its prey, it spreads its wings and glides down to attack.

Description

Gligar glides through the air without a sound as if it were sliding. This Pokémon hangs on to the face of its foe using its clawed hind legs and the large pincers on its forelegs, then injects the prey with its poison barb.

Special Moves

Poison Sting, Acrobatics, Sky Uppercut

Evolution

  →

GLIGAR   GLISCOR

STEELIX

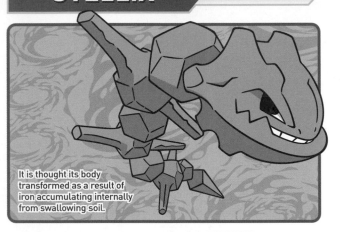

It is thought its body transformed as a result of iron accumulating internally from swallowing soil.

Iron Snake Pokémon

POKÉDEX NO.	**208**
TYPE	Steel, Ground
ABILITY	Rock Head, Sturdy
HEIGHT	30'02"
WEIGHT	881.8 lbs

Description

It is said that if an Onix lives for over 100 years, its composition changes to become diamond-like.

Special Moves

Dig, Iron Tail, Slam

Evolution

ONIX ➡ STEELIX

MEGA STEELIX

001-100
101-200
201-300
401-442
443-500
501-600
701-800
801-898

STEELIX

It chews its way through boulders with its sturdy jaws. Its eyes can see in the darkness underground.

Iron Snake Pokémon	
POKÉDEX NO.	**208**
TYPE	Steel, Ground
ABILITY	Sand Force
HEIGHT	34'05"
WEIGHT	1631.4 lbs

Description

The iron it ingested with the soil it swallowed transformed its body and made it harder than diamonds.

Special Moves

Iron Tail, Stone Edge, Rock Tomb

SNUBBULL

It grows close to others easily and is also easily spoiled. The disparity between its face and its actions makes many young people wild about it.

Fairy Pokémon	
POKÉDEX NO.	**209**
TYPE	Fairy
ABILITY	Run Away, Intimidate
HEIGHT	2'00"
WEIGHT	17.2 lbs

Description

In contrast to its appearance, it's quite timid. When playing with other puppy Pokémon, it sometimes gets bullied.

Special Moves

Scary Face, Crunch, Lick

Evolution

SNUBBULL → GRANBULL

GRANBULL

Although it's popular with young people, Granbull is timid and sensitive, so it's totally incompetent as a watchdog.

Fairy Pokémon

POKÉDEX NO. 210

TYPE	Fairy
ABILITY	Intimidate, Quick Feet
HEIGHT	4'07"
WEIGHT	107.4 lbs

Description

While it has powerful jaws, it doesn't care for disputes, so it rarely has a chance to display its might.

Special Moves

Thunder Fang, Ice Fang, Outrage

001-100
101-200
201-300
401-442
443-500
501-600
701-800
801-898

Evolution

SNUBBULL   GRANBULL

QWILFISH

The small spikes covering its body developed from scales. They inject a toxin that causes fainting.

Balloon Pokémon	
POKÉDEX NO.	**211**
TYPE	Water, Poison
ABILITY	Poison Point, Swift Swim
HEIGHT	1'08"
WEIGHT	8.6 lbs

Description

When faced with a larger opponent, it swallows as much water as it can to match the opponent's size.

Special Moves

Poison Sting, Pin Missile, Fell Stinger

Evolution

QWILFISH

Does not evolve

SCIZOR

Pincer Pokémon

POKÉDEX NO.	**212**
TYPE	Bug, Steel
ABILITY	Swarm, Technician
HEIGHT	5'11"
WEIGHT	260.1 lbs

Description

Bulky pincers account for one-third of Scizor's body weight. A single swing of one of these pincers will crush a boulder completely.

Special Moves

Bullet Punch, Slash, X-Scissor

Though its body is slim, Scizor has tremendous attacking power. Even Scizor's muscles are made of metal.

Evolution

SCYTHER

SCIZOR

001-100
101-200
201-300
401-442
443-500
501-600
701-800
801-898

MEGA SCIZOR

SCIZOR

It's better at beating things than grasping them. When it battles for a long time, the weight of its pincers becomes too much to bear.

Pincer Pokémon

POKÉDEX NO.	212
TYPE	Bug, Steel
ABILITY	Technician
HEIGHT	6'07"
WEIGHT	275.6 lbs

Description

It stores the excess energy from Mega Evolution, so after a long time passes, its body starts to melt.

Special Moves

Bullet Punch, Iron Head, Double Hit

SHUCKLE

The berries stored in its vaselike shell eventually become a thick, pulpy juice.

Mold Pokémon	
POKÉDEX NO.	**213**
TYPE	Bug, Rock
ABILITY	Sturdy, Gluttony
HEIGHT	2'00"
WEIGHT	45.2 lbs

Description

It stores berries inside its shell. To avoid attacks, it hides beneath rocks and remains completely still.

Special Moves

Withdraw, Rock Throw, Sticky Web

Evolution

SHUCKLE

Does not evolve

001-100
101-200
201-300
401-442
443-500
501-600
701-800
801-898

HERACROSS

Heracross loves sweet sap and will go looking through forests for it. The Pokémon uses its two antennae to pick up scents as it searches.

Single Horn Pokémon

POKÉDEX NO.	**214**
TYPE	Bug, Fighting
ABILITY	Swarm, Guts
HEIGHT	4'11"
WEIGHT	119.0 lbs

Description

This Pokémon takes pride in its strength, which allows it to lift things 100 times heavier than itself with no trouble at all.

Special Moves

Throat Chop, Megahorn, Horn Attack

Evolution

HERACROSS

Does not evolve

MEGA HERACROSS

001-100
101-200
201-300
401-442
443-500
501-600
701-800
801-898

HERACROSS

A tremendous influx of energy builds it up, but when Mega Evolution ends, Heracross is bothered by terrible soreness in its muscles.

Single Horn Pokémon

POKÉDEX NO.	214
TYPE	Bug, Fighting
ABILITY	Skill Link
HEIGHT	5'07"
WEIGHT	137.8 lbs

Description

It can grip things with its two horns and lift 500 times its own body weight.

Special Moves

Bullet Seed, Close Combat, Aerial Ace

285

SNEASEL

POKÉDEX NO.	**215**

TYPE	Dark, Ice
ABILITY	Keen Eye, Inner Focus
HEIGHT	2'11"
WEIGHT	61.7 lbs

Description

Its paws conceal sharp claws. If attacked, it suddenly extends the claws and startles its enemy.

It has a cunning yet savage disposition. It waits for parents to leave their nests, and then it sneaks in to steal their eggs.

Special Moves

Fury Swipes, Metal Claw, Hone Claws

Evolution

SNEASEL   →   WEAVILE

TEDDIURSA

001-100

101-200

201-300

401-442

443-500

501-600

701-800

801-898

Little Bear Pokémon

POKÉDEX NO.	**216**
TYPE	Normal
ABILITY	Pickup, Quick Feet
HEIGHT	2'00"
WEIGHT	19.4 lbs

Before food becomes scarce in wintertime, its habit is to hoard food in many hidden locations.

Description

This Pokémon likes to lick its palms that are sweetened by being soaked in honey. Teddiursa concocts its own honey by blending fruits and pollen collected by Beedrill.*

Special Moves

Fling, Baby-Doll Eyes, Play Nice

Evolution

TEDDIURSA   URSARING

*Beedrill: A Pokémon you'll find on page 32.

287

URSARING

With its ability to distinguish any aroma, it unfailingly finds all food buried deep underground.

Hibernator Pokémon	
POKÉDEX NO.	**217**
TYPE	Normal
ABILITY	Guts, Quick Feet
HEIGHT	5'11"
WEIGHT	277.3 lbs

Description

In the forests inhabited by Ursaring, it is said that there are many streams and towering trees where they gather food. This Pokémon walks through its forest gathering food every day.

Special Moves

Hammer Arm, Thrash, Scary Face

Evolution ➡

TEDDIURSA   URSARING

SLUGMA

Slugma does not have any blood in its body. Instead, intensely hot magma circulates throughout this Pokémon's body, carrying essential nutrients and oxygen to its organs.

001-100

101-200

201-300

401-442

443-500

501-600

701-800

801-898

Lava Pokémon	
POKÉDEX NO.	**218**
TYPE	Fire
ABILITY	Flame Body, Magma Armor
HEIGHT	2'04"
WEIGHT	77.2 lbs

Description

Molten magma courses throughout Slugma's circulatory system. If this Pokémon is chilled, the magma cools and hardens. Its body turns brittle and chunks fall off, reducing its size.

Special Moves

Ember, Incinerate, Ancient Power

Evolution

SLUGMA   MAGCARGO

289

MAGCARGO

Magcargo's body temperature is approximately 18,000 degrees Fahrenheit. Water is vaporized on contact. If this Pokémon is caught in the rain, the raindrops instantly turn into steam, cloaking the area in a thick fog.

Description

Magcargo's shell is actually its skin that hardened as a result of cooling. Its shell is very brittle and fragile—just touching it causes it to crumble apart. This Pokémon returns to its original size by dipping itself in magma.

Lava Pokémon	
POKÉDEX NO.	**219**
TYPE	Fire, Rock
ABILITY	Flame Body, Magma Armor
HEIGHT	2'07"
WEIGHT	121.3 lbs

Special Moves

Flamethrower, Rock Throw, Recover

Evolution

SLUGMA → MAGCARGO

SWINUB

001-100
101-200
201-300
401-442
443-500
501-600
701-800
801-898

Pig Pokémon

POKÉDEX NO.	**220**
TYPE	Ice, Ground
ABILITY	Oblivious, Snow Cloak
HEIGHT	1'04"
WEIGHT	14.3 lbs

Description

It rubs its snout on the ground to find and dig up food. It sometimes discovers hot springs.

If it smells something enticing, it dashes off headlong to find the source of the aroma.

Special Moves

Mud-Slap, Icy Wind, Ice Shard

Evolution

SWINUB → PILOSWINE → MAMOSWINE

PILOSWINE

Although its legs are short, its rugged hooves prevent it from slipping, even on icy ground.

Swine Pokémon

POKÉDEX NO.	**221**
TYPE	Ice, Ground
ABILITY	Oblivious, Snow Cloak
HEIGHT	3'07"
WEIGHT	123.0 lbs

Description

If it charges at an enemy, the hairs on its back stand up straight. It is very sensitive to sound.

Special Moves

Ice Fang, Blizzard, Icy Wind

Evolution

SWINUB → PILOSWINE → MAMOSWINE

CORSOLA

Coral Pokémon	
POKÉDEX NO.	**222**
TYPE	Water, Rock
ABILITY	Natural Cure, Hustle
HEIGHT	2'00"
WEIGHT	11.0 lbs

These Pokémon live in warm seas. In prehistoric times, many lived in the oceans around the Galar region as well.

Description

It will regrow any branches that break off its head. People keep particularly beautiful Corsola branches as charms to promote safe childbirth.

Special Moves

Water Gun, Tackle, Power Gem

Evolution · CORSOLA · Does not evolve

001-100
101-200
201-300
401-442
443-500
501-600
701-800
801-898

CORSOLA

GALARIAN FORM

Coral Pokémon

POKÉDEX NO.	222
TYPE	Ghost
ABILITY	Weak Armor
HEIGHT	2'00"
WEIGHT	1.1 lbs

Sudden climate change wiped out this ancient kind of Corsola. This Pokémon absorbs others' life force through its branches.

Description

Watch your step when wandering areas oceans once covered. What looks like a stone could be this Pokémon, and it will curse you if you kick it.

Special Moves

Night Shade, Strength Sap, Curse

Evolution

CORSOLA
(GALARIAN FORM)

CURSOLA

REMORAID

001-100
101-200
201-300
401-442
443-500
501-600
701-800
801-898

Jet Pokémon

POKÉDEX NO.	**223**
TYPE	Water
ABILITY	Sniper, Hustle
HEIGHT	2'00"
WEIGHT	26.5 lbs

The water they shoot from their mouths can hit moving prey from more than 300 feet away.

Description

Using its dorsal fin as a suction pad, it clings to Mantine's* underside to scavenge for leftovers.

Special Moves

Lock-On, Ice Beam, Water Pulse

Evolution

REMORAID → OCTILLERY

---

*Mantine: A Pokémon you'll find on page 298.

295

OCTILLERY

It traps enemies with its suction-cupped tentacles, then smashes them with its rock-hard head.

Jet Pokémon	
POKÉDEX NO.	**224**
TYPE	Water
ABILITY	Sniper, Suction Cups
HEIGHT	2'11"
WEIGHT	62.8 lbs

Description

It has a tendency to want to be in holes. It prefers rock crags or pots and sprays ink from them before attacking.

Special Moves

Octazooka, Hydro Pump, Soak

Evolution

REMORAID → OCTILLERY

DELIBIRD

Delivery Pokémon

POKÉDEX NO.	225
TYPE	Ice, Flying
ABILITY	Vital Spirit, Hustle
HEIGHT	2'11"
WEIGHT	35.3 lbs

It has a generous habit of sharing its food with people and Pokémon, so it's always scrounging around for more food.

Description

It carries food all day long. There are tales about lost people who were saved by the food it had.

Special Moves

Present, Drill Peck

Evolution

DELIBIRD

Does not evolve

001-100
101-200
201-300
401-442
443-500
501-600
701-800
801-898

MANTINE

As it majestically swims, it doesn't care if Remoraid* attach to it to scavenge for its leftovers.

Kite Pokémon

POKÉDEX NO.	226
TYPE	Water, Flying
ABILITY	Water Absorb, Swift Swim
HEIGHT	6'11"
WEIGHT	485.0 lbs

Description

If it builds up enough speed swimming, it can jump out above the waves and glide for over 300 feet.

Special Moves

Bounce, Hydro Pump, Aqua Ring

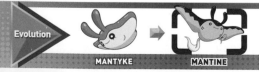

Evolution

MANTYKE → MANTINE

*Remoraid: A Pokémon you'll find on page 295.

001-100
101-200
201-300
401-442
443-500
501-600
701-800
801-898

SKARMORY

People fashion swords from Skarmory's shed feathers, so this Pokémon is a popular element in heraldic designs.

Armor Bird Pokémon

POKÉDEX NO.	227
TYPE	Steel, Flying
ABILITY	Keen Eye, Sturdy
HEIGHT	5'07"
WEIGHT	111.3 lbs

Description

The pointed feathers of these Pokémon are sharper than swords. Skarmory and Corviknight fight viciously over territory.

Special Moves

Metal Claw, Brave Bird, Fury Attack

Evolution

Does not evolve

SKARMORY

HOUNDOUR

They make repeated eerie howls before dawn to call attention to their pack.

Dark Pokémon	
POKÉDEX NO.	**228**
TYPE	Dark, Fire
ABILITY	Flash Fire, Early Bird
HEIGHT	2'00"
WEIGHT	23.8 lbs

Description

It cooperates with others skillfully. When it becomes your partner, it's very loyal to you as its Trainer and will obey your orders.

Special Moves

Fire Fang, Beat Up, Odor Sleuth

Evolution

HOUNDOUR → HOUNDOOM

HOUNDOOM

Identifiable by its eerie howls, people a long time ago thought it was the grim reaper and feared it.

Dark Pokémon	
POKÉDEX NO.	**229**
TYPE	Dark, Fire
ABILITY	Flash Fire, Early Bird
HEIGHT	4'07"
WEIGHT	77.2 lbs

Description

They spew flames mixed with poison to finish off their opponents. They divvy up their prey evenly among the members of their pack.

Special Moves

Flamethrower, Inferno, Fire Fang

Evolution

HOUNDOUR

HOUNDOOM

001-100
101-200
201-300
401-442
443-500
501-600
701-800
801-898

MEGA HOUNDOOM

HOUNDOOM

Houndoom's entire body generates heat when it Mega Evolves. Its fearsome fiery breath turns its opponents to ash.

Dark Pokémon

POKÉDEX NO.	**229**
TYPE	Dark, Fire
ABILITY	Solar Power
HEIGHT	6'03"
WEIGHT	109.1 lbs

Description

Its red claws and the tip of its tail are melting from high internal temperatures that are painful to Houndoom itself.

Special Moves

Flamethrower, Fire Fang, Crunch

KINGDRA

Scales shed by this Pokémon have such a splendorous gleam to them that they've been given to royalty as gifts.

Dragon Pokémon	
POKÉDEX NO.	**230**
TYPE	Water, Dragon
ABILITY	Swift Swim, Sniper
HEIGHT	5'11"
WEIGHT	335.1 lbs

Description

With the arrival of a storm at sea, this Pokémon will show itself on the surface. When a Kingdra and a Dragonite meet, a fierce battle ensues.

Special Moves

Dragon Breath, Dragon Pulse, Twister

Evolution

HORSEA → SEADRA → KINGDRA

001-100
101-200
201-300
401-442
443-500
501-600
701-800
801-898

PHANPY

Long Nose Pokémon

POKÉDEX NO.	**231**
TYPE	Ground
ABILITY	Pickup
HEIGHT	1'08"
WEIGHT	73.9 lbs

Description

For its nest, Phanpy digs a vertical pit in the ground at the edge of a river. It marks the area around its nest with its trunk to let the others know that the area has been claimed.

Phanpy uses its long nose to shower itself. When others gather around, they thoroughly douse each other with water. These Pokémon can be seen drying their soaking-wet bodies at the edge of water.

Special Moves

Flail, Tackle, Double-Edge

Evolution

PHANPY → DONPHAN

DONPHAN

001-100
101-200
201-300
401-442
443-500
501-600
701-800
801-898

Donphan's favorite attack is curling its body into a ball, then charging at its foe while rolling at high speed. Once it starts rolling, this Pokémon can't stop very easily.

Armor Pokémon	
POKÉDEX NO.	**232**
TYPE	Ground
ABILITY	Sturdy
HEIGHT	3'07"
WEIGHT	264.6 lbs

Description

If Donphan were to tackle with its hard body, even a house could be destroyed. Using its massive strength, the Pokémon helps clear rock and mud slides that block mountain trails.

Special Moves

Fury Attack, Horn Attack, Magnitude

Evolution

PHANPY → DONPHAN

PORYGON2

Virtual Pokémon	
POKÉDEX NO.	**233**
TYPE	Normal
ABILITY	Trace, Download
HEIGHT	2'00"
WEIGHT	71.7 lbs

This is a Porygon that was updated with special data. Porygon2 develops itself by learning about many different subjects all on its own.

Description

After artificial intelligence was implemented in Porygon2, the Pokémon began using a strange language that only other Porygon2 understand.

Special Moves

Hyper Beam, Discharge, Conversion 2

Evolution

PORYGON ➡ PORYGON2 ➡ PORYGON-Z

STANTLER

Staring at its antlers creates an odd sensation as if one were being drawn into their centers.

Big Horn Pokémon	
POKÉDEX NO.	**234**
TYPE	Normal
ABILITY	Intimidate, Frisk
HEIGHT	4'07"
WEIGHT	157.0 lbs

Description

Stantler's magnificent antlers were traded at high prices as works of art. As a result, this Pokémon was hunted close to extinction by those who were after the priceless antlers.

Special Moves

Take Down, Zen Headbutt, Confuse Ray

Evolution

STANTLER

Does not evolve

001-100
101-200
201-300
401-442
443-500
501-600
701-800
801-898

SMEARGLE

The fluid of Smeargle's tail secretions changes in the intensity of its hue as the Pokémon's emotions change.

Painter Pokémon

POKÉDEX NO.	235
TYPE	Normal
ABILITY	Technician, Own Tempo
HEIGHT	3'11"
WEIGHT	127.9 lbs

Description

It draws symbols with the fluid that oozes from the tip of its tail. Depending on the symbol, Smeargle fanatics will pay big money for them.

Special Moves

Sketch

Evolution

SMEARGLE

Does not evolve

TYROGUE

Scuffle Pokémon

POKÉDEX NO.	236
TYPE	Fighting
ABILITY	Guts, Steadfast
HEIGHT	2'04"
WEIGHT	46.3 lbs

Even though it is small, it can't be ignored because it will slug any handy target without warning.

Description

It is always bursting with energy. To make itself stronger, it keeps on fighting even if it loses.

Special Moves

Tackle, Fake Out, Focus Energy

Evolution

TYROGUE → HITMONLEE HITMONCHAN HITMONTOP

001-100
101-200
201-300
401-442
443-500
501-600
701-800
801-898

HITMONTOP

It launches kicks while spinning. If it spins at high speed, it may bore its way into the ground.

Handstand Pokémon	
POKÉDEX NO.	**237**
TYPE	Fighting
ABILITY	Intimidate, Technician
HEIGHT	4'07"
WEIGHT	105.8 lbs

Description

After doing a handstand to throw off the opponent's timing, it presents its fancy kick moves.

Special Moves

Rapid Spin, Triple Kick, Sucker Punch

Evolution

TYROGUE

HITMONTOP

SMOOCHUM

Kiss Pokémon	
POKÉDEX NO.	**238**
TYPE	Ice, Psychic
ABILITY	Oblivious, Forewarn
HEIGHT	1'04"
WEIGHT	13.2 lbs

001-100
101-200
201-300
401-442
501-600
701-800
801-898

This is a very curious Pokémon. Smoochum decides what it likes and dislikes by touching things with its lips.

Description

If its face gets even slightly dirty, Smoochum will bathe immediately. But if its body gets dirty, Smoochum doesn't really seem to care.

Special Moves

Lick, Sweet Kiss, Fake Tears

Evolution

SMOOCHUM → JYNX

ELEKID

When a storm approaches, this Pokémon gets restless. Once Elekid hears the sound of thunder, it gets full-on rowdy.

Electric Pokémon	
POKÉDEX NO.	**239**
TYPE	Electric
ABILITY	Static
HEIGHT	2'00"
WEIGHT	51.8 lbs

Description

It's not good at storing electricity yet. This Pokémon sneaks into people's homes, looking for electrical outlets to eat electricity from.

Special Moves

Quick Attack, Thunder Punch, Thunder Wave

Evolution

ELEKID → ELECTABUZZ → ELECTIVIRE

MAGBY

Live Coal Pokémon

POKÉDEX NO.	240
TYPE	Fire
ABILITY	Flame Body
HEIGHT	2'04"
WEIGHT	47.2 lbs

This Pokémon is small and timid. Whenever Magby gets excited or surprised, flames leak from its mouth and its nose.

Description

This Pokémon makes its home near volcanoes. At the end of the day, Magby soaks in magma, resting and recovering from the day's fatigue.

Special Moves

Smog, Fire Punch, Flame Wheel

Evolution

MAGBY → MAGMAR → MAGMORTAR

001-100
101-200
201-300
401-442
443-500
501-600
701-800
801-898

MILTANK

Milk Cow Pokémon

POKÉDEX NO.	241
TYPE	Normal
ABILITY	Thick Fat, Scrappy
HEIGHT	3'11"
WEIGHT	166.4 lbs

Description

Miltank produces highly nutritious milk, so it's been supporting the lives of people and other Pokémon since ancient times.

This Pokémon needs to be milked every day, or else it will fall ill. The flavor of Miltank milk changes with the seasons.

Special Moves

Milk Drink, High Horsepower, Body Slam

Evolution MILTANK — Does not evolve

BLISSEY

Blissey lays mysterious eggs that are filled with happiness. It's said that anyone who eats a Blissey egg will start acting kindly to all others.

Happiness Pokémon	
POKÉDEX NO.	**242**
TYPE	Normal
ABILITY	Natural Cure, Serene Grace
HEIGHT	4'11"
WEIGHT	103.2 lbs

Description

Whenever a Blissey finds a weakened Pokémon, it will share its egg and offer its care until the other Pokémon is all better.

Special Moves

Soft-Roiled, Disarming Voice, Light Screen

Evolution

HAPPINY → CHANSEY → BLISSEY

001-100
101-200
201-300
401-442
443-500
501-600
701-800
801-898

315

RAIKOU

Thunder Pokémon

POKÉDEX NO.	243

TYPE	Electric
ABILITY	Pressure
HEIGHT	6'03"
WEIGHT	392.4 lbs

The rain clouds it carries let it fire thunderbolts at will. They say that it descended with lightning.

Description

Raikou embodies the speed of lightning. The roars of this Pokémon send shock waves shuddering through the air and shake the ground as if lightning bolts have come crashing down.

Special Moves

Thunder, Thunder Fang, Zap Cannon

Evolution

Does not evolve

RAIKOU

ENTEI

Volcano Pokémon	
POKÉDEX NO.	**244**
TYPE	Fire
ABILITY	Pressure
HEIGHT	6'11"
WEIGHT	436.5 lbs

001-100

101-200

201-300

401-442

443-500

501-600

701-800

801-898

It is said that when it roars, a volcano erupts somewhere around the globe.

Description

Entei embodies the passion of magma. This Pokémon is thought to have been born in the eruption of a volcano. It sends up massive bursts of fire that utterly consume all that they touch.

Special Moves

Sacred Fire, Fire Blast, Flame Wheel

Evolution

ENTEI

Does not evolve

SUICUNE

Aurora Pokémon

POKÉDEX NO. 245

TYPE	Water
ABILITY	Pressure
HEIGHT	6'07"
WEIGHT	412.3 lbs

Description

Suicune embodies the compassion of a pure spring of water. It runs across the land with gracefulness. This Pokémon has the power to purify dirty water.

Special Moves

Sheer Cold, Ice Fang, Surf

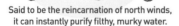

Said to be the reincarnation of north winds, it can instantly purify filthy, murky water.

Evolution   Does not evolve

SUICUNE

LARVITAR

001-100
101-200
201-300
401-442
443-500
501-600
701-800
801-898

Rock Skin Pokémon

POKÉDEX NO.	**246**
TYPE	Rock, Ground
ABILITY	Guts
HEIGHT	2'00"
WEIGHT	158.7 lbs

Description

Born deep underground, it comes aboveground and becomes a pupa once it has finished eating the surrounding soil.

It feeds on soil. After it has eaten a large mountain, it will fall asleep so it can grow.

Special Moves

Rock Slide, Sandstorm, Stone Edge

Evolution

LARVITAR → **PUPITAR** → **TYRANITAR**

PUPITAR

It will not stay still, even while it's a pupa. It already has arms and legs under its solid shell.

Hard Shell Pokémon

POKÉDEX NO.	247
TYPE	Rock, Ground
ABILITY	Shed Skin
HEIGHT	3'11"
WEIGHT	335.1 lbs

Description

Even sealed in its shell, it can move freely. Hard and fast, it has outstanding destructive power.

Special Moves

Iron Defense, Dark Pulse, Hyper Beam

Evolution

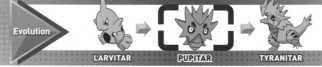

LARVITAR → PUPITAR → TYRANITAR

TYRANITAR

Armor Pokémon

POKÉDEX NO.	**248**
TYPE	Rock, Dark
ABILITY	Sand Stream
HEIGHT	6'07"
WEIGHT	445.3 lbs

Description

The quakes caused when it walks make even great mountains crumble and change the surrounding terrain.

Its body can't be harmed by any sort of attack, so it is very eager to make challenges against enemies.

Special Moves

Giga Impact, Thrash, Hyper Beam

Evolution

 ➡ ➡

LARVITAR　　**PUPITAR**　　**TYRANITAR**

001-100
101-200
201-300
401-442
443-500
501-600
701-800
801-898

MEGA TYRANITAR

Due to the colossal power poured into it, this Pokémon's back split right open. Its destructive instincts are the only thing keeping it moving.

TYRANITAR

Armor Pokémon

POKÉDEX NO.	248
TYPE	Rock, Dark
ABILITY	Sand Stream
HEIGHT	8'02"
WEIGHT	562.2 lbs

Description

The effects of Mega Evolution make it more ferocious than ever. It's unclear whether it can even hear its Trainer's orders.

Special Moves

Giga Impact, Hyper Beam, Stone Edge

LUGIA

Diving Pokémon

POKÉDEX NO.	**249**
TYPE	Psychic, Flying
ABILITY	Pressure
HEIGHT	17'01"
WEIGHT	476.2 lbs

It is said to be the guardian of the seas. It is rumored to have been seen on the night of a storm.

Description

Lugia's wings pack devastating power—a light fluttering of its wings can blow apart regular houses. As a result, this Pokémon chooses to live out of sight deep under the sea.

Special Moves

Acroblast, Sky Attack, Future Sight

Evolution

Does not evolve

LUGIA

1-100
101-200
201-300
401-442
443-500
501-600
701-800
801-898

HO-OH

Rainbow Pokémon

POKÉDEX NO.	**250**

TYPE	Fire, Flying
ABILITY	Pressure
HEIGHT	12'06"
WEIGHT	438.7 lbs

It will reveal itself before a pure-hearted Trainer by shining its bright, rainbow-colored wings.

Description

Ho-Oh's feathers glow in seven colors depending on the angle at which they are struck by light. These feathers are said to bring happiness to the bearers. This Pokémon is said to live at the foot of a rainbow.

Special Moves

Sacred Fire, Sky Attack, Burn Up

Evolution

HO-OH

Does not evolve

CELEBI

Time Travel Pokémon

POKÉDEX NO.	**251**
TYPE	Psychic, Grass
ABILITY	Natural Cure
HEIGHT	2'00"
WEIGHT	11.0 lbs

This Pokémon traveled through time to come from the future. It bolsters grass and trees with its own strength, and it can heal wounds, too.

001-
100

101-
200

201-
300

401-
442

443-
500

501-
600

701-
800

801-
898

Description

This Pokémon has the ability to move through time. Records describing it as a forest deity can be found in many different eras.

Special Moves

Leaf Storm, Future Sight, Recover

Evolution

CELEBI

Does not evolve

TREECKO

Wood Gecko Pokémon

POKÉDEX NO.	252

TYPE	Grass
ABILITY	Overgrow
HEIGHT	1'08"
WEIGHT	11.0 lbs

Description

Treecko has small hooks on the bottom of its feet that enable it to scale vertical walls. This Pokémon attacks by slamming foes with its thick tail.

Treecko is cool, calm, and collected—it never panics under any situation. If a bigger foe were to glare at this Pokémon, it would glare right back without conceding an inch of ground.

Special Moves

Energy Ball, Quick Attack, Leafage

Evolution

TREECKO → GROVYLE → SCEPTILE

GROVYLE

Wood Gecko Pokémon

POKÉDEX NO.	**253**
TYPE	Grass
ABILITY	Overgrow
HEIGHT	2'11"
WEIGHT	47.6 lbs

001-100
101-200
201-300
401-442
443-500
501-600
701-800
801-898

The leaves growing out of Grovyle's body are convenient for camouflaging it from enemies in the forest. This Pokémon is a master at climbing trees in jungles.

Description

This Pokémon adeptly flies from branch to branch in trees. In a forest, no Pokémon can ever hope to catch a fleeing Grovyle however fast they may be.

Special Moves

Fury Cutter, Giga Drain, False Swipe

Evolution

TREECKO → GROVYLE → SCEPTILE

SCEPTILE

Forest Pokémon

POKÉDEX NO.	254
TYPE	Grass
ABILITY	Overgrow
HEIGHT	5'07"
WEIGHT	115.1 lbs

Description

The leaves growing on Sceptile's body are very sharp edged. This Pokémon is very agile—it leaps all over the branches of trees and jumps on its foe from above or behind.

Sceptile has seeds growing on its back. They are said to be bursting with nutrients that revitalize trees. This Pokémon raises the trees in a forest with loving care.

Special Moves

Leaf Blade, Dual Chop, Detect

Evolution

TREECKO → GROVYLE → SCEPTILE

MEGA SCEPTILE

001-100
101-200
201-300
401-442
443-500
501-600
701-800
801-898

SCEPTILE

It agilely leaps about the jungle and uses the sharp leaves on its arms to strike its prey.

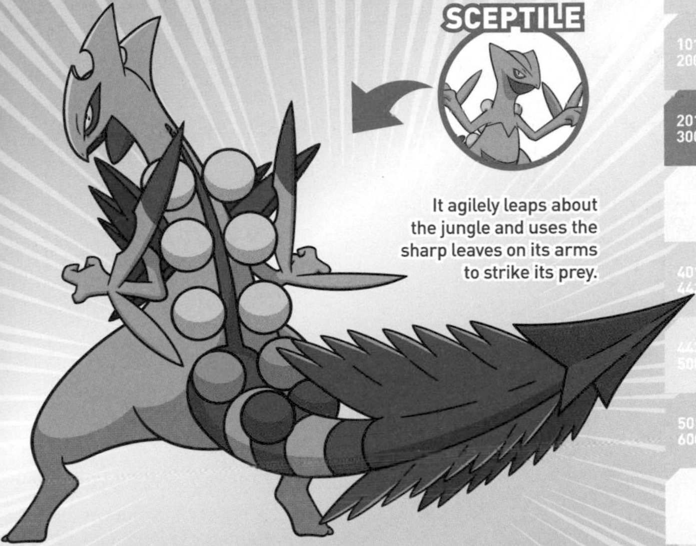

Forest Pokémon	
POKÉDEX NO.	254
TYPE	Grass, Dragon
ABILITY	Lightning Rod
HEIGHT	6'03"
WEIGHT	121.7 lbs

Description

The leaves that grow on its arms can slice down thick trees. It is without peer in jungle combat.

Special Moves

Leaf Storm, Leaf Blade, X-Scissor

TORCHIC

Chick Pokémon

POKÉDEX NO.	**255**
TYPE	Fire
ABILITY	Blaze
HEIGHT	1'04"
WEIGHT	5.5 lbs

Description

Torchic has a place inside its body where it keeps its flame. Give it a hug—it will be glowing with warmth. This Pokémon is covered all over by a fluffy coat of down.

Torchic sticks with its Trainer, following behind with unsteady steps. This Pokémon breathes fire of 1,800 degrees Fahrenheit, including fireballs that leave the foe scorched black.

Special Moves

Ember, Quick Attack, Bounce

Evolution

TORCHIC

COMBUSKEN

BLAZIKEN

COMBUSKEN

Young Fowl Pokémon

POKÉDEX NO.	**256**
TYPE	Fire, Fighting
ABILITY	Blaze
HEIGHT	2'11"
WEIGHT	43.0 lbs

Combusken battles with the intensely hot flames it spews from its beak and with outstandingly destructive kicks. This Pokémon's cry is very loud and distracting.

Description

Combusken toughens up its legs and thighs by running through fields and mountains. This Pokémon's legs possess both speed and power, enabling it to dole out 10 kicks in one second.

Special Moves

Flame Charge, Aerial Ace, Double Kick

001-100
101-200
201-300
401-442
443-500
501-600
701-800
801-898

Evolution

TORCHIC → COMBUSKEN → BLAZIKEN

BLAZIKEN

Blaze Pokémon	
POKÉDEX NO.	**257**
TYPE	Fire, Fighting
ABILITY	Blaze
HEIGHT	6'03"
WEIGHT	114.6 lbs

In battle, Blaziken blows out intense flames from its wrists and attacks foes courageously. The stronger the foe, the more intensely this Pokémon's wrists burn.

Description

It learns martial arts that use punches and kicks. Every several years, its old feathers burn off, and new, supple feathers grow back in their place.

Special Moves

Flare Blitz, Blaze Kick, Slash

Evolution

TORCHIC → COMBUSKEN → BLAZIKEN

MEGA BLAZIKEN

001-
100

101-
200

201-
300

401-
442

443-
500

501-
600

701-
800

801-
898

BLAZIKEN

Flames spout from its wrists, enveloping its knuckles. Its punches scorch its foes.

Blaze Pokémon	
POKÉDEX NO.	**257**
TYPE	Fire, Fighting
ABILITY	Speed Boost
HEIGHT	6'03"
WEIGHT	114.6 lbs

Description

Blaziken has incredibly strong legs—it can easily clear a 30-story building in one leap. This Pokémon's blazing punches leave its foes scorched and blackened.

Special Moves

Sky Uppercut, Brave Bird, Blaze Kick

MUDKIP

Mud Fish Pokémon

POKÉDEX NO.	258
TYPE	Water
ABILITY	Torrent
HEIGHT	1'04"
WEIGHT	16.8 lbs

Description

The fin on Mudkip's head acts as highly sensitive radar. Using this fin to sense movements of water and air, this Pokémon can determine what is taking place around it without using its eyes.

In water, Mudkip breathes using the gills on its cheeks. If it is faced with a tight situation in battle, this Pokémon will unleash its amazing power—it can crush rocks bigger than itself.

Special Moves

Water Gun, Rock Slide, Supersonic

Evolution

MUDKIP → MARSHTOMP → SWAMPERT

MARSHTOMP

Mud Fish Pokémon

POKÉDEX NO.	259
TYPE	Water, Ground
ABILITY	Torrent
HEIGHT	2'04"
WEIGHT	61.7 lbs

Description

The surface of Marshtomp's body is enveloped by a thin, sticky film that enables it to live on land. This Pokémon plays in mud on beaches when the ocean tide is low.

Marshtomp is much faster at traveling through mud than it is at swimming. This Pokémon's hindquarters exhibit obvious development, giving it the ability to walk on just its hind legs.

Special Moves

Water Pulse, Mud Shot, Rock Slide

Evolution

MUDKIP → MARSHTOMP → SWAMPERT

001-100
101-200
201-300
401-442
443-500
501-600
701-800
801-898

SWAMPERT

Mud Fish Pokémon	
POKÉDEX NO.	**260**
TYPE	Water, Ground
ABILITY	Torrent
HEIGHT	4'11"
WEIGHT	180.6 lbs

Swampert is very strong. It has enough power to easily drag a boulder weighing more than a ton. This Pokémon also has powerful vision that lets it see even in murky water.

Description

Swampert predicts storms by sensing subtle differences in the sounds of waves and tidal winds with its fins. If a storm is approaching, it piles up boulders to protect itself.

Special Moves

Hammer Arm, Hydro Pump, Earthquake

Evolution

MUDKIP ➡ MARSHTOMP ➡ SWAMPERT

MEGA SWAMPERT

Its arms are hard as rock. With one swing, it can break a boulder into pieces.

SWAMPERT

001-100
101-200
201-300
401-442
443-500
501-600
701-800
801-898

Mud Fish Pokémon	
POKÉDEX NO.	**260**
TYPE	Water, Ground
ABILITY	Swift Swim
HEIGHT	6'03"
WEIGHT	224.9 lbs

Description

It can swim while towing a large ship. It bashes down foes with a swing of its thick arms.

Special Moves

Hammer Arm, Sludge Bomb, Mud Shot

POOCHYENA

Poochyena is an omnivore—it will eat anything. A distinguishing feature is how large its fangs are compared to its body. This Pokémon tries to intimidate its foes by making the hair on its tail bristle out.

Bite Pokémon	
POKÉDEX NO.	**261**
TYPE	Dark
ABILITY	Run Away, Quick Feet
HEIGHT	1'08"
WEIGHT	30.0 lbs

Description

At first sight, Poochyena takes a bite at anything that moves. This Pokémon chases after prey until the victim becomes exhausted. However, it may turn tail if the prey strikes back.

Special Moves

Crunch, Tackle, Odor Sleuth

Evolution

POOCHYENA → MIGHTYENA

MIGHTYENA

Mightyena travel and act as a pack in the wild. The memory of its life in the wild compels the Pokémon to obey only those Trainers that it recognizes to possess superior skill.

Bite Pokémon	
POKÉDEX NO.	**262**
TYPE	Dark
ABILITY	Intimidate, Quick Feet
HEIGHT	3'03"
WEIGHT	81.6 lbs

Description

Mightyena gives obvious signals when it is preparing to attack. It starts to growl deeply and then flattens its body. This Pokémon will bite savagely with its sharply pointed fangs.

Special Moves

Snarl, Fire Fang, Take Down

Evolution

POOCHYENA   MIGHTYENA

001-100
101-200
201-300
401-442
443-500
501-600
701-800
801-898

ZIGZAGOON

Tiny Raccoon Pokémon

POKÉDEX NO.	263
TYPE	Normal
ABILITY	Pickup, Gluttony
HEIGHT	1'04"
WEIGHT	38.6 lbs

It marks its territory by rubbing its bristly fur on trees. This variety of Zigzagoon is friendlier and calmer than the kind native to Galar.

Description

Zigzagoon that adapted to regions outside Galar acquired this appearance. If you've lost something, this Pokémon can likely find it.

Special Moves

Tackle, Double-Edge, Tail Whip

Evolution

ZIGZAGOON → LINOONE

ZIGZAGOON

GALARIAN FORM

Tiny Raccoon Pokémon

POKÉDEX NO.	263
TYPE	Dark, Normal
ABILITY	Pickup, Gluttony
HEIGHT	1'04"
WEIGHT	38.6 lbs

001-100

101-200

201-300

301-400

401-442

443-500

501-600

601-700

701-800

801-898

Thought to be the oldest form of Zigzagoon, it moves in zigzags and wreaks havoc upon its surroundings.

Description

Its restlessness has it constantly running around. If it sees another Pokémon, it will purposely run into them in order to start a fight.

Special Moves

Snarl, Take Down, Pin Missile

Evolution

ZIGZAGOON (GALARIAN FORM) → LINOONE (GALARIAN FORM) → OBSTAGOON

LINOONE

It uses its explosive speed and razor-sharp claws to bring down prey. Running along winding paths is not its strong suit.

Rushing Pokémon	
POKÉDEX NO.	**264**
TYPE	Normal
ABILITY	Pickup, Gluttony
HEIGHT	1'08"
WEIGHT	71.7 lbs

Description

Its fur is strong and supple. Shaving brushes made with shed Linoone hairs are highly prized.

Special Moves

Double-Edge, Fury Swipes, Take Down

Evolution

ZIGZAGOON → LINOONE

LINOONE

GALARIAN FORM

Rushing Pokémon

POKÉDEX NO.	264

TYPE	Dark, Normal
ABILITY	Pickup, Gluttony
HEIGHT	1'08"
WEIGHT	71.7 lbs

001-100
101-200
201-300
401-442
443-500
501-600
701-800
801-898

Description

It uses its long tongue to taunt opponents. Once the opposition is enraged, this Pokémon hurls itself at the opponent, tackling them forcefully.

Special Moves

Night Slash, Double-Edge, Snarl

This very aggressive Pokémon will recklessly challenge opponents stronger than itself.

Evolution

ZIGZAGOON
(GALARIAN FORM)

LINOONE
(GALARIAN FORM)

OBSTAGOON

WURMPLE

Using the spikes on its rear end, Wurmple peels the bark off trees and feeds on the sap that oozes out. This Pokémon's feet are tipped with suction pads that allow it to cling to glass without slipping.

Worm Pokémon	
POKÉDEX NO.	**265**
TYPE	Bug
ABILITY	Shield Dust
HEIGHT	1'00"
WEIGHT	7.9 lbs

Description

Wurmple is targeted by Swellow as prey. This Pokémon will try to resist by pointing the spikes on its rear at the attacking predator. It will weaken the foe by leaking poison from the spikes.

Special Moves

Tackle, String Shot, Poison Sting

Evolution

  WURMPLE

 SILCOON BEAUTIFLY

 CASCOON DUSTOX

SILCOON

001-100
101-200
201-300
401-442
443-500
501-600
701-800
R01 898

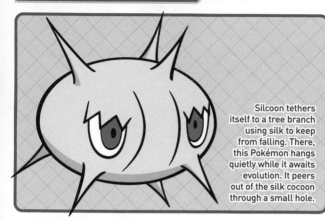

Silcoon tethers itself to a tree branch using silk to keep from falling. There, this Pokémon hangs quietly while it awaits evolution. It peers out of the silk cocoon through a small hole.

Cocoon Pokémon	
POKÉDEX NO.	**266**
TYPE	Bug
ABILITY	Shed Skin
HEIGHT	2'00"
WEIGHT	22.0 lbs

Description

Silcoon was once thought to endure hunger and not consume anything before its evolution. However, it is now thought that this Pokémon slakes its thirst by drinking rainwater that collects on its silk.

Special Moves

Harden

Evolution

WURMPLE → SILCOON → BEAUTIFLY

345

BEAUTIFLY

Beautifly's favorite food is the sweet pollen of flowers. If you want to see this Pokémon, just leave a potted flower by an open window. Beautifly is sure to come looking for pollen.

Butterfly Pokémon

POKÉDEX NO.	267
TYPE	Bug, Flying
ABILITY	Swarm
HEIGHT	3'03"
WEIGHT	62.6 lbs

Description

Beautifly has a long mouth like a coiled needle, which is very convenient for collecting pollen from flowers. This Pokémon rides the spring winds as it flits around gathering pollen.

Special Moves

Air Cutter, Silver Wind, Whirlwind

Evolution

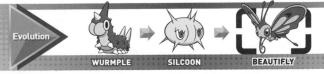

WURMPLE → SILCOON → BEAUTIFLY

CASCOON

001-100
101-200
201-300
401-442
443-500
501-600
701-800
801-898

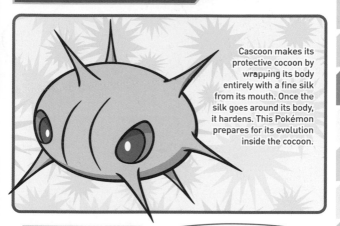

Cascoon makes its protective cocoon by wrapping its body entirely with a fine silk from its mouth. Once the silk goes around its body, it hardens. This Pokémon prepares for its evolution inside the cocoon.

Cocoon Pokémon	
POKÉDEX NO.	268
TYPE	Bug
ABILITY	Shed Skin
HEIGHT	2'04"
WEIGHT	25.4 lbs

Description

If it is attacked, Cascoon remains motionless however badly it may be hurt. It does so because if it were to move, its body would be weak upon evolution. This Pokémon will also not forget the pain it endured.

Special Moves

Harden

Evolution

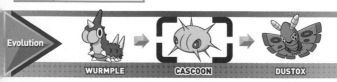

WURMPLE → CASCOON → DUSTOX

DUSTOX

When Dustox flaps its wings, a fine dust is scattered all over. This dust is actually a powerful poison that will even make a pro wrestler sick. This Pokémon searches for food using its antennae like radar.

Poison Moth Pokémon

POKÉDEX NO.	269
TYPE	Bug, Poison
ABILITY	Shield Dust
HEIGHT	3'11"
WEIGHT	69.7 lbs

Description

Dustox is instinctively drawn to light. Swarms of this Pokémon are attracted by the bright lights of cities, where they wreak havoc by stripping the leaves off roadside trees for food.

Special Moves

Quiver Dance, Bug Buzz, Toxic

Evolution

WURMPLE CASCOON DUSTOX

348

LOTAD

Water Weed Pokémon

POKÉDEX NO.	270	
TYPE	Water, Grass	
ABILITY	Swift Swim, Rain Dish	
HEIGHT	1'08"	
WEIGHT	5.7 lbs	

Its leaf grew too large for it to live on land. That is how it began to live floating in the water.

Description

It searches about for clean water. If it does not drink water for too long, the leaf on its head wilts.

Special Moves

Rain Dance, Energy Ball, Water Gun

Evolution

 → →

LOTAD   LOMBRE   LUDICOLO

001-100
101-200
201-300
401-442
443-500
501-600
701-800
801-89R

LOMBRE

It lives at the water's edge where it is sunny. It sleeps on a bed of water grass by day and becomes active at night.

Jolly Pokémon	
POKÉDEX NO.	**271**
TYPE	Water, Grass
ABILITY	Swift Swim, Rain Dish
HEIGHT	3'11"
WEIGHT	71.7 lbs

Description

Lombre's entire body is covered by a slippery, slimy film. It feels horribly unpleasant to be touched by this Pokémon's hands. Lombre is often mistaken for a human child.

Special Moves

Bubble Beam, Mega Drain, Rain Dance

Evolution

LOTAD → LOMBRE → LUDICOLO

LUDICOLO

Carefree Pokémon

POKÉDEX NO.	**272**
TYPE	Water, Grass
ABILITY	Swift Swim, Rain Dish
HEIGHT	4'11"
WEIGHT	121.3 lbs

Description

The rhythm of bright, festive music activates Ludicolo's cells, making it more powerful.

If it hears festive music, all its muscles fill with energy. It can't help breaking out into a dance.

Special Moves

Hydro Pump, Giga Drain, Mist

 Evolution

LOTAD → LOMBRE → LUDICOLO

001-100
101-200
201-300
401-442
443-500
501-600
701-800
801-898

SEEDOT

It attaches itself to a tree branch using the top of its head. Strong winds can sometimes make it fall.

Acorn Pokémon	
POKÉDEX NO.	**273**
TYPE	Grass
ABILITY	Chlorophyll, Early Bird
HEIGHT	1'08"
WEIGHT	8.8 lbs

Description

If it remains still, it looks just like a real nut. It delights in surprising foraging Pokémon.

Special Moves

Sunny Day, Mega Drain, Nature Power

Evolution

SEEDOT → NUZLEAF → SHIFTRY

NUZLEAF

It lives deep in forests. With the leaf on its head, it makes a flute whose song makes listeners uneasy.

Wily Pokémon	
POKÉDEX NO.	**274**
TYPE	Grass, Dark
ABILITY	Chlorophyll, Early Bird
HEIGHT	3'03"
WEIGHT	61.7 lbs

Description

Nuzleaf lives in densely overgrown forests. They occasionally venture out of the forest to startle people. This Pokémon dislikes having its long nose pinched.

Special Moves

Razor Leaf, Explosion, Sucker Punch

Evolution

SEEDOT → NUZLEAF → SHIFTRY

001-100
101-200
201-300
401-442
443-500
501-600
701-800
801-898

SHIFTRY

A Pokémon that was feared as a forest guardian. It can read the foe's mind and take preemptive action.

Wicked Pokémon

POKÉDEX NO.	**275**
TYPE	Grass, Dark
ABILITY	Chlorophyll, Early Bird
HEIGHT	4'03"
WEIGHT	131.4 lbs

Description

It lives quietly in the deep forest. It is said to create chilly winter winds with the fans it holds.

Special Moves

Leaf Tornado, Leaf Blade, Swagger

Evolution

SEEDOT

NUZLEAF

SHIFTRY

TAILLOW

001-100
101-200
201-300
401-442
443-500
501-600
601-700
701-800
801-898

Tiny Swallow Pokémon

POKÉDEX NO.	**276**
TYPE	Normal, Flying
ABILITY	Guts
HEIGHT	1'00"
WEIGHT	5.1 lbs

Description

Taillow courageously stands its ground against foes, however strong they may be. This gutsy Pokémon will remain defiant even after a loss. On the other hand, it cries loudly if it becomes hungry.

It dislikes cold seasons. They migrate to other lands in search of warmth, flying over 180 miles a day.

Special Moves

Peck, Wing Attack, Agility

Evolution

TAILLOW → SWELLOW

355

SWELLOW

Swallow Pokémon

POKÉDEX NO.	**277**
TYPE	Normal, Flying
ABILITY	Guts
HEIGHT	2'04"
WEIGHT	43.7 lbs

Description

Swellow is very conscientious about the upkeep of its glossy wings. Once two Swellow are gathered, they diligently take care of cleaning each other's wings.

Swellow flies high above our heads, making graceful arcs in the sky. This Pokémon dives at a steep angle as soon as it spots its prey. The hapless prey is tightly grasped by Swellow's clawed feet, preventing escape.

Special Moves

Aerial Ace, Air Slash, Focus Energy

Evolution

TAILLOW → SWELLOW

WINGULL

001-100
101-200
201-300
401-442
443-500
501-600
701-800
801-898

It soars on updrafts without flapping its wings. It makes nests on sheer cliffs at the sea's edge.

Seagull Pokémon	
POKÉDEX NO.	**278**
TYPE	Water, Flying
ABILITY	Keen Eye, Hydration
HEIGHT	2'00"
WEIGHT	20.9 lbs

Description

Fishermen keep an eye out for Wingull in the sky, because wherever they're circling, the ocean is sure to be teeming with fish Pokémon.

Special Moves

Wing Attack, Water Gun, Roost

Evolution

WINGULL

PELIPPER

357

PELIPPER

Skimming the water's surface, it dips its large bill in the sea, scoops up food and water, and carries it away.

Water Bird Pokémon

POKÉDEX NO.	**279**
TYPE	Water, Flying
ABILITY	Keen Eye, Drizzle
HEIGHT	3'11"
WEIGHT	61.7 lbs

Description

It is a messenger of the skies, carrying small Pokémon and eggs to safety in its bill.

Special Moves

Hyrdo Pump, Stockpile, Swallow

Evolution

WINGULL → PELIPPER

RALTS

001-100
101-200
201-300
401-442
443-500
501-600
601-700
701-800
801-898

Feeling Pokémon

POKÉDEX NO.	**280**
TYPE	Psychic, Fairy
ABILITY	Synchronize, Trace
HEIGHT	1'04"
WEIGHT	14.6 lbs

It is highly attuned to the emotions of people and Pokémon. It hides if it senses hostility.

Description

If its horns capture the warm feelings of people or Pokémon, its body warms up slightly.

Special Moves

Disarming Voice, Confusion, Teleport

Evolution

RALTS → KIRLIA → GARDEVOIR → GALLADE (MALE ONLY)

KIRLIA

Emotion Pokémon

POKÉDEX NO.	**281**
TYPE	Psychic, Fairy
ABILITY	Synchronize, Trace
HEIGHT	2'07"
WEIGHT	44.5 lbs

It has a psychic power that enables it to distort the space around it and see into the future.

Description

If its Trainer becomes happy, it overflows with energy, dancing joyously while spinning about.

Special Moves

Psybeam, Draining Kiss, Calm Mind

Evolution

RALTS → KIRLIA → GARDEVOIR → GALLADE (MALE ONLY)

GARDEVOIR

Embrace Pokémon

POKÉDEX NO.	**282**
TYPE	Psychic, Fairy
ABILITY	Synchronize, Trace
HEIGHT	5'03"
WEIGHT	106.7 lbs

001-100
101-200
201-300
401-442
443-500
501-600
701-800
801-898

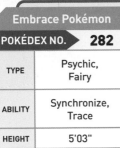

Description

To protect its Trainer, it will expend all its psychic power to create a small black hole.

It has the power to predict the future. Its power peaks when it is protecting its Trainer.

Special Moves

Dazzling Gleam, Teleport, Dream Eater

Evolution

RALTS ➡ KIRLIA ➡ GARDEVOIR

MEGA GARDEVOIR

Gardevoir has the psychokinetic power to distort the dimensions and create a small black hole. This Pokémon will try to protect its Trainer even at the risk of its own life.

GARDEVOIR

Embrace Pokémon

POKÉDEX NO.	**282**
TYPE	Psychic, Fairy
ABILITY	Pixilate
HEIGHT	5'03"
WEIGHT	106.7 lbs

Description

Gardevoir has the ability to read the future. If it senses impending danger to its Trainer, this Pokémon is said to unleash its psychokinetic energy at full power.

Special Moves

Moonblast, Misty Terrain, Psychic

SURSKIT

It lives in ponds and marshes that feature lots of plant life. It often fights with Dewpider, whose habitat and diet are similar.

001-100

101-200

201-300

301-358

401-442

443-500

501-600

601-700

701-800

801-898

Pond Skater Pokémon	
POKÉDEX NO.	**283**
TYPE	Water, Bug
ABILITY	Swift Swim
HEIGHT	1'08"
WEIGHT	3.7 lbs

Description

If it's in a pinch, it will secrete a sweet liquid from the tip of its head. Syrup made from gathering that liquid is tasty on bread.

Special Moves

Bubble, Bubble Beam, Aqua Jet

Evolution

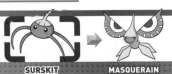

SURSKIT → MASQUERAIN

MASQUERAIN

Masquerain intimidates enemies with the eyelike patterns of its eyespots. If that doesn't work, it deftly makes its escape on its set of four wings.

Eyeball Pokémon

POKÉDEX NO.	284
TYPE	Bug, Flying
ABILITY	Intimidate
HEIGHT	2'07"
WEIGHT	7.9 lbs

Description

Its thin, winglike antennae are highly absorbent. It waits out rainy days in tree hollows.

Special Moves

Water Sport, Air Cutter, Silver Wind

Evolution

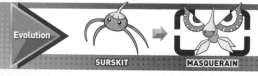

SURSKIT → MASQUERAIN

SHROOMISH

If Shroomish senses danger, it shakes its body and scatters spores from the top of its head. This Pokémon's spores are so toxic, they make trees and weeds wilt.

001-100

101-200

201-300

401-442

443-500

501-600

701-800

801-898

Mushroom Pokémon	
POKÉDEX NO.	**285**
TYPE	Grass
ABILITY	Effect Spore, Poison Heal
HEIGHT	1'04"
WEIGHT	9.9 lbs

Description

Shroomish live in damp soil in the dark depths of forests. They are often found keeping still under fallen leaves. This Pokémon feeds on compost that is made up of fallen, rotted leaves.

Special Moves

Absorb, Stun Spore, Spore

Evolution

SHROOMISH → BRELOOM

BRELOOM

The seeds ringing Breloom's tail are made of hardened toxic spores. It is horrible to eat the seeds. Just taking a bite of this Pokémon's seed will cause your stomach to rumble.

Mushroom Pokémon

POKÉDEX NO.	**286**
TYPE	Grass, Fighting
ABILITY	Effect Spore, Poison Heal
HEIGHT	3'11"
WEIGHT	86.4 lbs

Description

Breloom closes in on its foe with light and sprightly footwork, then throws punches with its stretchy arms. This Pokémon's fighting technique puts boxers to shame.

Special Moves

Mach Punch, Sky Uppercut, Feint

Evolution

SHROOMISH

→

BRELOOM

SLAKOTH

Slakoth's heart beats just once a minute. Whatever happens, it is content to loaf around motionless. It is rare to see this Pokémon in motion.

Slacker Pokémon

POKÉDEX NO.	287
TYPE	Normal
ABILITY	Truant
HEIGHT	2'07"
WEIGHT	52.9 lbs

Description

Slakoth lolls around for over 20 hours every day. Because it moves so little, it does not need much food. This Pokémon's sole daily meal consists of just three leaves.

Special Moves

Slack Off, Feint Attack, Chip Away

Evolution

SLAKOTH → VIGOROTH → SLAKING

001-100
101-200
201-300
401-442
443-500
501-600
701-800
801-898

VIGOROTH

Vigoroth is simply incapable of remaining still. Even when it tries to sleep, the blood in its veins grows agitated, compelling this Pokémon to run wild throughout the jungle before it can settle down.

Wild Monkey Pokémon	
POKÉDEX NO.	**288**
TYPE	Normal
ABILITY	Vital Spirit
HEIGHT	4'07"
WEIGHT	102.5 lbs

Description

Vigoroth is always itching and agitated to go on a wild rampage. It simply can't tolerate sitting still for even a minute. This Pokémon's stress level rises if it can't be moving constantly.

Special Moves

Focus Punch, Focus Energy, Fury Swipes

Evolution

SLAKOTH → VIGOROTH → SLAKING

SLAKING

Lazy Pokémon	
POKÉDEX NO.	**289**
TYPE	Normal
ABILITY	Truant
HEIGHT	6'07"
WEIGHT	287.7 lbs

Description

Slaking spends all day lying down and lolling about. It eats grass growing within its reach. If it eats all the grass it can reach, this Pokémon reluctantly moves to another spot.

Wherever Slaking live, rings of over a yard in diameter appear in grassy fields. They are made by the Pokémon as it eats all the grass within reach while lying prone on the ground.

Special Moves

Swagger, Hammer Arm, Fling

Evolution

SLAKOTH ➡ VIGOROTH ➡ SLAKING

001-100
101-200
201-300
301-400
443-500
501-600
701-800
801-898

NINCADA

It can sometimes live underground for more than 10 years. It absorbs nutrients from the roots of trees.

Trainee Pokémon	
POKÉDEX NO.	**290**
TYPE	Bug, Ground
ABILITY	Compound Eyes
HEIGHT	1'08"
WEIGHT	12.1 lbs

Description

Because it lives almost entirely underground, it is nearly blind. It uses its antennae instead.

Special Moves

Sand Attack, Dig, Fury Swipes

Evolution

NINCADA → NINJASK   SHEDINJA

NINJASK

Its cry leaves a lasting headache if heard for too long. It moves so quickly that it is almost invisible.

Ninja Pokémon

POKÉDEX NO.	**291**
TYPE	Bug, Flying
ABILITY	Speed Boost
HEIGHT	2'07"
WEIGHT	26.5 lbs

Description

This Pokémon is so quick, it is said to be able to avoid any attack. It loves to feed on tree sap.

Special Moves

Double Team, Fury Cutter, Bug Bite

Evolution

NINCADA

NINJASK

001-100
101-200
201-300
401-442
443-500
501-600
701-800
801-898

SHEDINJA

A strange Pokémon—it flies without moving its wings, has a hollow shell for a body, and does not breathe.

Shed Pokémon

POKÉDEX NO.	292
TYPE	Bug, Ghost
ABILITY	Wonder Guard
HEIGHT	2'07"
WEIGHT	2.6 lbs

Description

A most peculiar Pokémon that somehow appears in a Poké Ball when a Nincada evolves.

Special Moves

Shadow Sneak, Phantom Force, Shadow Ball

Evolution

NINCADA

SHEDINJA

WHISMUR

The cry of a Whismur is over 100 decibels.* If you're close to a Whismur when it lets out a cry, you'll be stuck with an all-day headache.

Whisper Pokémon	
POKÉDEX NO.	**293**
TYPE	Normal
ABILITY	Soundproof
HEIGHT	2'00"
WEIGHT	35.9 lbs

Description

When Whismur cries, the sound of its own voice startles it, making the Pokémon cry even louder. It cries until it's exhausted, then it falls asleep.

Special Moves

Supersonic, Uproar, Echoed Voice

Evolution

WHISMUR → LOUDRED → EXPLOUD

*Decibel: The measurement for the intensity of sound.

373

LOUDRED

POKÉDEX NO.	**294**
TYPE	Normal
ABILITY	Soundproof
HEIGHT	3'03"
WEIGHT	89.3 lbs

Description

Loudred's ears serve as speakers, and they can put out sound waves powerful enough to blow away a house.

The force of this Pokémon's loud voice isn't just the sound—it's also the wave of air pressure that blows opponents away and damages them.

Special Moves

Hyper Voice, Bite, Screech

Evolution

WHISMUR → LOUDRED → EXPLOUD

EXPLOUD

This Pokémon can do more than just shout. To communicate with others of its kind, it'll emit all sorts of sounds from the holes in its body.

Loud Noise Pokémon

POKÉDEX NO.	295
TYPE	Normal
ABILITY	Soundproof
HEIGHT	4'11"
WEIGHT	185.2 lbs

Description

In the past, people would use the loud voices of these Pokémon as a means of communication between distant cities.

Special Moves

Crunch, Hyper Beam, Boomburst

Evolution

WHISMUR → LOUDRED → EXPLOUD

001-100
101-200
201-300
401-442
443-500
501-600
701-800
801-898

MAKUHITA

There's a rumor of a traditional recipe for stew that Trainers can use to raise strong Makuhita.

Guts Pokémon

POKÉDEX NO.	**296**
TYPE	Fighting
ABILITY	Guts, Thick Fat
HEIGHT	3'03"
WEIGHT	190.5 lbs

Description

It practices its slaps by repeatedly slapping tree trunks. It has been known to slap an Exeggutor and get flung away.

Special Moves

Arm Thrust, Vital Throw, Wake-Up Slap

Evolution

MAKUHITA → HARIYAMA

HARIYAMA

Hariyama that are big and fat aren't necessarily strong. There are some small ones that move nimbly and use moves skillfully.

001-100
101-200
201-300
401-442
443-500
501-600
701-800
801-898

Arm Thrust Pokémon

POKÉDEX NO.	297
TYPE	Fighting
ABILITY	Guts, Thick Fat
HEIGHT	7'07"
WEIGHT	559.5 lbs

Description

Although they enjoy comparing their strength, they're also kind. They value etiquette, praising opponents they battle.

Special Moves

Seismic Toss, Force Palm, Heavy Slam

Evolution

MAKUHITA

HARIYAMA

AZURILL

Polka Dot Pokémon

POKÉDEX NO.	298

TYPE	Normal, Fairy
ABILITY	Thick Fat, Huge Power
HEIGHT	0'08"
WEIGHT	4.4 lbs

The ball on Azurill's tail bounces like a rubber ball, and it's full of the nutrients the Pokémon needs to grow.

Description

Although Azurill are normally docile, an angry one will swing around the big ball on its tail and try to smash its opponents.

Special Moves

Splash, Water Gun, Bubble Beam

Evolution

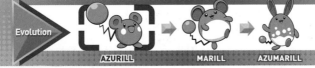

AZURILL → MARILL → AZUMARILL

NOSEPASS

It moves less than an inch a year, but when it's in a jam, it will spin and drill down into the ground in a split second.

Compass Pokémon	
POKÉDEX NO.	**299**
TYPE	Rock
ABILITY	Sturdy, Magnet Pull
HEIGHT	3'03"
WEIGHT	213.8 lbs

Description

It hunts without twitching a muscle by pulling in its prey with powerful magnetism. But sometimes it pulls natural enemies in close.

Special Moves

Thunder Wave, Rock Throw, Earth Power

Evolution

NOSEPASS → PROBOPASS

001-100
101-200
201-300
401-442
443-500
501-600
701-800
801-890

SKITTY

Kitten Pokémon

POKÉDEX NO.	**300**
TYPE	Normal
ABILITY	Cute Charm, Normalize
HEIGHT	2'00"
WEIGHT	24.3 lbs

Skitty is known to chase around playfully after its own tail. In the wild, this Pokémon lives in holes in the trees of forests. It is very popular as a pet because of its adorable looks.

Description

Skitty has the habit of becoming fascinated by moving objects and chasing them around. This Pokémon is known to chase after its own tail and become dizzy.

Special Moves

Fake Out, Disarming Voice, Assist

Evolution

SKITTY ➡ DELCATTY

DELCATTY

Delcatty sleeps anywhere it wants without keeping a permanent nest. If other Pokémon approach it as it sleeps, this Pokémon will never fight—it will just move somewhere else.

001-100

101-200

201-300

301-400

401-442

443-500

501-600

701-800

801-898

Prim Pokémon

POKÉDEX NO.	301
TYPE	Normal
ABILITY	Cute Charm, Normalize
HEIGHT	3'07"
WEIGHT	71.9 lbs

Description

Delcatty prefers to live an unfettered existence in which it can do as it pleases at its own pace. Because this Pokémon eats and sleeps whenever it decides, its daily routines are completely random.

Special Moves

Attract, Fake Out, Double Slap

Evolution

SKITTY

DELCATTY

SABLEYE

Darkness Pokémon	

POKÉDEX NO.	**302**

TYPE	Dark, Ghost
ABILITY	Keen Eye, Stall
HEIGHT	1'08"
WEIGHT	24.3 lbs

It feeds on gemstone crystals. In darkness, its eyes sparkle with the glitter of jewels.

Description

This Pokémon is feared. When its gemstone eyes begin to glow with a sinister shine, it's believed that Sableye will steal people's spirits away.

Special Moves

Shadow Claw, Confuse Ray, Foul Play

Evolution

SABLEYE

Does not evolve

MEGA SABLEYE

It blocks any and all attacks with its giant-sized gemstone. However, the stone's a heavy burden, and it limits Mega Sableye's movements.

SABLEYE

001-100
101-200
201-300
301-400
401-442
443-500
501-600
701-800
801-898

Darkness Pokémon

POKÉDEX NO.	**302**
TYPE	Dark, Ghost
ABILITY	Magic Bounce
HEIGHT	1'08"
WEIGHT	354.9 lbs

Description

Bathed in the energy of Mega Evolution, the gemstone on its chest expands, rips through its skin, and falls out.

Special Moves

Shadow Ball, Mean Look, Fury Swipes

MAWILE

Deceiver Pokémon

POKÉDEX NO.	**303**

TYPE	Steel, Fairy
ABILITY	Intimidate, Hyper Cutter
HEIGHT	2'00"
WEIGHT	25.4 lbs

It chomps with its gaping mouth. Its huge jaws are actually steel horns that have been transformed.

Description

It uses its docile-looking face to lull foes into complacency, then bites with its huge, relentless jaws.

Special Moves

Iron Head, Play Rough, Crunch

Evolution

MAWILE

Does not evolve

MEGA MAWILE

It has an extremely vicious disposition.
It grips prey in its two sets of jaws and
tears them apart with raw power.

MAWILE

001-100
101-200
201-300
301-400
401-442
443-500
501-600
701-800
801-898

Deceiver Pokémon

POKÉDEX NO.	**303**
TYPE	Steel, Fairy
ABILITY	Huge Power
HEIGHT	3'03"
WEIGHT	51.8 lbs

Description

Its two sets of jaws thrash
about violently as if they each
have a will of their own. One
gnash from them can turn a
boulder to dust.

Special Moves

Iron Head, Play Rough,
Fairy Wind

ARON

When Aron evolves, its steel armor peels off. In ancient times, people would collect Aron's shed armor and make good use of it in their daily lives.

Iron Armor Pokémon	
POKÉDEX NO.	**304**
TYPE	Steel, Rock
ABILITY	Rock Head, Sturdy
HEIGHT	1'04"
WEIGHT	132.3 lbs

Description

It eats iron ore—and sometimes railroad tracks—to build up the steel armor that protects its body.

Special Moves

Rock Slide, Metal Claw, Iron Defense

Evolution

ARON → LAIRON → AGGRON

LAIRON

During territorial disputes, Lairon fight by slamming into each other. Close inspection of their steel armor reveals scratches and dents.

Iron Armor Pokémon

POKÉDEX NO.	305
TYPE	Steel, Rock
ABILITY	Rock Head, Sturdy
HEIGHT	2'11"
WEIGHT	264.6 lbs

Description

Lairon live in mountains brimming with spring water and iron ore, so these Pokémon often came into conflict with humans in the past.

Special Moves

Iron Tail, Double-Edge, Take Down

001-100
101-200
201-300
301-400
401-442
443-500
501-600
701-800
801-898

Evolution

ARON → LAIRON → AGGRON

AGGRON

Long ago, there was a king who wore a helmet meant to resemble the head of an Aggron. He was trying to channel the Pokémon's strength.

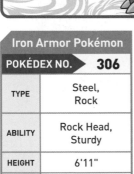

Iron Armor Pokémon	
POKÉDEX NO.	**306**
TYPE	Steel, Rock
ABILITY	Rock Head, Sturdy
HEIGHT	6'11"
WEIGHT	793.7 lbs

Description

Aggron claims an entire mountain as its own territory. It mercilessly beats up anything that violates its environment. This Pokémon vigilantly patrols its territory at all times.

Special Moves

Metal Burst, Heavy Slam, Protect

Evolution

ARON → LAIRON → AGGRON

MEGA AGGRON

Aggron has a horn sharp enough to perforate thick iron sheets. It brings down its opponents by ramming into them horn first.

001-100
101-200
201-300
301-400
401-442
443-500
501-600
701-800
801-898

AGGRON

Iron Armor Pokémon	
POKÉDEX NO.	**306**
TYPE	Steel
ABILITY	Filter
HEIGHT	7'03"
WEIGHT	870.8 lbs

Description

Aggron is protective of its environment. If its mountain is ravaged by a landslide or a fire, this Pokémon will haul topsoil to the area, plant trees, and beautifully restore its own territory.

Special Moves

Metal Burst, Iron Head, Double-Edge

MEDITITE

Meditate Pokémon	
POKÉDEX NO.	**307**
TYPE	Fighting, Psychic
ABILITY	Pure Power
HEIGHT	2'00"
WEIGHT	24.7 lbs

Meditite undertakes rigorous mental training deep in the mountains. However, whenever it meditates, this Pokémon always loses its concentration and focus. As a result, its training never ends.

Description

Meditite heightens its inner energy through meditation. It survives on just one berry a day. Minimal eating is another aspect of this Pokémon's training.

Special Moves

Confusion, High Jump Kick, Meditate

Evolution

MEDITITE → MEDICHAM

MEDICHAM

Meditate Pokémon

POKÉDEX NO.	308
TYPE	Fighting, Psychic
ABILITY	Pure Power
HEIGHT	4'03"
WEIGHT	69.4 lbs

It is said that through meditation, Medicham heightens energy inside its body and sharpens its sixth sense. This Pokémon hides its presence by merging itself with fields and mountains.

Description

Through the power of meditation, Medicham developed its sixth sense. It gained the ability to use psychokinetic powers. This Pokémon is known to meditate for a whole month without eating.

Special Moves

Force Palm, Hidden Power, Meditate

Evolution

MEDITITE   MEDICHAM

001-100
101-200
201-300
301-400
401-442
443-500
501-600
701-800
801-098

MEGA MEDICHAM

MEDICHAM

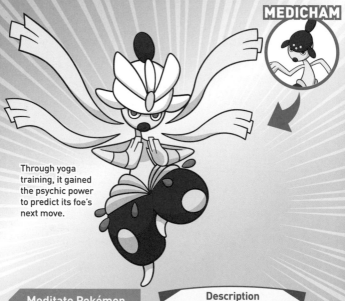

Through yoga training, it gained the psychic power to predict its foe's next move.

Meditate Pokémon

POKÉDEX NO.	**308**
TYPE	Fighting, Psychic
ABILITY	Pure Power
HEIGHT	4'03"
WEIGHT	69.4 lbs

Description

It elegantly avoids attacks with dance-like steps, then launches a devastating blow in the same motion.

Special Moves

Power Trick, Zen Headbutt, Meditate

ELECTRIKE

Friction between the air and its fur produces static electricity. When Electrike runs, it makes a crackling sound.

001-100
101-200
201-300
301-400
401-442
443-500
501-600
701-800
801-898

Lightning Pokémon

POKÉDEX NO.	309
TYPE	Electric
ABILITY	Static, Lightning Rod
HEIGHT	2'00"
WEIGHT	33.5 lbs

Description

It stores static electricity in its fur for discharging. It gives off sparks if a storm approaches.

Special Moves

Thunder Wave, Wild Charge, Charge

Evolution

ELECTRIKE → MANECTRIC

MANECTRIC

It rarely appears before people. It is said to nest where lightning has fallen.

Discharge Pokémon	
POKÉDEX NO.	**310**
TYPE	Electric
ABILITY	Static, Lightning Rod
HEIGHT	4'11"
WEIGHT	88.6 lbs

Description

It stimulates its own muscles with electricity, so it can move quickly. It eases its soreness with electricity, too, so it can recover quickly as well.

Special Moves

Thunder, Electric Terrain, Shock Wave

Evolution

ELECTRIKE

MANECTRIC

MEGA MANECTRIC

Too much electricity has built up in its body, irritating Manectric. Its explosive speed is equal to that of a lightning bolt.

MANECTRIC

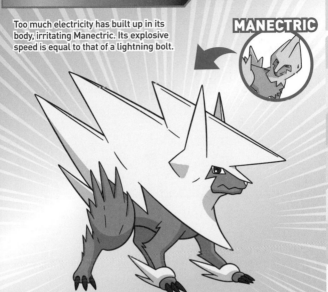

001-
100

101-
200

201-
300

301-
400

401-
442

443-
500

501-
600

701-
800

801-
898

Discharge Pokémon

POKÉDEX NO.	**310**
TYPE	Electric
ABILITY	Intimidate
HEIGHT	5'11"
WEIGHT	97.0 lbs

Description

Mega Evolution fills its body with a tremendous amount of electricity, but il's too much for Manectric to fully control.

Special Moves

Thunder Fang, Wild Charge, Electric Terrain

395

PLUSLE

Cheering Pokémon

POKÉDEX NO.	311
TYPE	Electric
ABILITY	Plus
HEIGHT	1'04"
WEIGHT	9.3 lbs

It cheers on friends with pom-poms made of sparks. It drains power from telephone poles.

Description

Plusle always acts as a cheerleader for its partners. Whenever a teammate puts out a good effort in battle, this Pokémon shorts out its body to create the crackling noises of sparks to show its joy.

Special Moves

Play Nice, Nuzzle, Spark

Evolution

PLUSLE

Does not evolve

MINUN

Cheering Pokémon

POKÉDEX NO.	**312**
TYPE	Electric
ABILITY	Minus
HEIGHT	1'04"
WEIGHT	9.3 lbs

001-100
101-200
201-300
301-400
401-442
443-500
501-600
701-800
801-898

Exposure to electricity from Minun and Plusle promotes blood circulation and relaxes muscles.

Description

Minun is more concerned about cheering on its partners than its own safety. It shorts out the electricity in its body to create brilliant showers of sparks to cheer on its teammates.

Special Moves

Play Nice, Baton Pass, Electro Ball

Evolution

MINUN

Does not evolve

VOLBEAT

Firefly Pokémon

POKÉDEX NO.	313
TYPE	Bug
ABILITY	Swarm, Illuminate
HEIGHT	2'04"
WEIGHT	39.0 lbs

Volbeat's tail glows like a lightbulb. With other Volbeat, it uses its tail to draw geometric shapes in the night sky.

Description

With the arrival of night, Volbeat emits light from its tail. It communicates with others by adjusting the intensity and flashing of its light. This Pokémon is attracted by the sweet aroma of Illumise.*

Special Moves

Flash, Bug Buzz, Tail Glow

Evolution

VOLBEAT

Does not evolve

*Illumise: A Pokémon you'll find on page 399.

ILLUMISE

Illumise leads a flight of illuminated Volbeat to draw signs in the night sky. This Pokémon is said to earn greater respect from its peers by composing more complex designs in the sky.

Firefly Pokémon	
POKÉDEX NO.	**314**
TYPE	Bug
ABILITY	Tinted Lens, Oblivious
HEIGHT	2'00"
WEIGHT	39.0 lbs

Description

Illumise attracts a swarm of Volbeat* using a sweet fragrance. Once the Volbeat have gathered, this Pokémon leads the lit-up swarm in drawing geometric designs on the canvas of the night sky.

Special Moves

Struggle Bug, Moonlight, Wish

Evolution

ILLUMISE

Does not evolve

*Volbeat: A Pokémon you'll find on page 398.

001-100
101-200
201-300
301-400
401-442
443-500
501-600
701-800
801-898

ROSELIA

Thorn Pokémon

POKÉDEX NO.	315
TYPE	Grass, Poison
ABILITY	Poison Point, Natural Cure
HEIGHT	1'00"
WEIGHT	4.4 lbs

Description

Its flowers give off a relaxing fragrance. The stronger its aroma, the healthier the Roselia is.

It uses the different poisons in each hand separately when it attacks.

Special Moves

Poison Sting, Magical Leaf, Petal Dance

Evolution

BUDEW ➡ ROSELIA ➡ ROSERADE

GULPIN

Stomach Pokémon

POKÉDEX NO.	**316**
TYPE	Poison
ABILITY	Liquid Ooze, Sticky Hold
HEIGHT	1'04"
WEIGHT	22.7 lbs

001-100
101-200
201-300
301-400
401-442
443-500
501-600
701-800
801-898

Description

Virtually all of Gulpin's body is its stomach. As a result, it can swallow something its own size. This Pokémon's stomach contains a special fluid that digests anything.

Special Moves

Swallow, Stockpile, Sludge

While it is digesting, vile, overpowering gases are expelled.

Evolution

GULPIN ➡ SWALOT

SWALOT

When Swalot spots prey, it spurts out a hideously toxic fluid from its pores and sprays the target. Once the prey has weakened, this Pokémon gulps it down whole with its cavernous mouth.

Poison Bag Pokémon	
POKÉDEX NO.	**317**
TYPE	Poison
ABILITY	Liquid Ooze, Sticky Hold
HEIGHT	5'07"
WEIGHT	176.4 lbs

Description

Swalot has no teeth, so what it eats, it swallows whole, no matter what. Its cavernous mouth yawns widely. An automobile tire could easily fit inside this Pokémon's mouth.

Special Moves

Body Slam, Venom Drench, Stockpile

Evolution

GULPIN → SWALOT

CARVANHA

It won't attack while it's alone—not even if it spots prey. Instead, it waits for other Carvanha to join it, and then the Pokémon attack as a group.

Savage Pokémon	
POKÉDEX NO.	**318**
TYPE	Water, Dark
ABILITY	Rough Skin
HEIGHT	2'07"
WEIGHT	45.9 lbs

Description

These Pokémon have sharp fangs and powerful jaws. Sailors avoid Carvanha dens at all costs.

Special Moves

Aqua Jet, Bite, Agility

Evolution

CARVANHA → SHARPEDO

001-100
101-200
201-300
301-400
401-442
443-500
501-600
701-800
801-898

SHARPEDO

As soon as it catches the scent of prey, Sharpedo will jet seawater from its backside, hurtling toward the target to attack at 75 mph.

Brutal Pokémon	
POKÉDEX NO.	**319**
TYPE	Water, Dark
ABILITY	Rough Skin
HEIGHT	5'11"
WEIGHT	195.8 lbs

Description

This Pokémon is known as the Bully of the Sea. Any ship entering the waters Sharpedo calls home will be attacked—no exceptions.

Special Moves

Liquidation, Ice Fang, Crunch

Evolution

CARVANHA → SHARPEDO

404

MEGA SHARPEDO

SHARPEDO

The moment it charges into its opponent, sharp spikes pop out of Sharpedo's head, leaving its opponent with deep wounds.

001-100

101-200

201-300

301-400

401-442

443-500

501-600

701-800

801-898

Brutal Pokémon	
POKÉDEX NO.	**319**
TYPE	Water, Dark
ABILITY	Strong Jaw
HEIGHT	8'02"
WEIGHT	287.3 lbs

Description

The yellow patterns it bears are old scars. The energy from Mega Evolution runs through them, causing it sharp pain and suffering.

Special Moves

Aqua Jet, Skull Bash, Poison Fang

405

WAILMER

Ball Whale Pokémon

POKÉDEX NO.	**320**
TYPE	Water
ABILITY	Oblivious, Water Veil
HEIGHT	6'07"
WEIGHT	286.6 lbs

Description

When it sucks in a large volume of seawater, it becomes like a big, bouncy ball. It eats a ton of food daily.

It swims along with its mouth open and swallows down seawater with its food. It sprays excess water out of its nostrils.

Special Moves

Body Slam, Dive, Water Pulse

Evolution

WAILMER → WAILORD

WAILORD

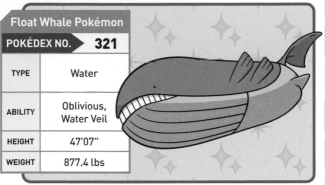

Float Whale Pokémon

POKÉDEX NO.	**321**
TYPE	Water
ABILITY	Oblivious, Water Veil
HEIGHT	47'07"
WEIGHT	877.4 lbs

Its immense size is the reason for its popularity. Wailord watching is a favorite sightseeing activity in various parts of the world.

Description

It can sometimes knock out opponents with the shock created by breaching and crashing its big body onto the water.

Special Moves

Heavy Slam, Hydro Pump, Water Spout

Evolution

WAILMER

WAILORD

001-100
101-200
201-300
301-400
401-442
443-500
501-600
701-800
801-890

NUMEL

Numel is extremely dull witted—it doesn't notice being hit. However, it can't stand hunger for even a second. This Pokémon's body is a seething cauldron of boiling magma.

Numb Pokémon	
POKÉDEX NO.	322
TYPE	Fire, Ground
ABILITY	Oblivious, Simple
HEIGHT	2'04"
WEIGHT	52.9 lbs

Description

Numel stores magma of almost 2,200 degrees Fahrenheit within its body. If it gets wet, the magma cools and hardens. In that event, the Pokémon's body grows heavy, and its movements become sluggish.

Special Moves

Earth Power, Take Down, Flame Burst

Evolution

NUMEL → CAMERUPT

CAMERUPT

If angered, the humps on its back erupt in a shower of molten lava. It lives in the craters of volcanoes.

Eruption Pokémon

POKÉDEX NO.	323
TYPE	Fire, Ground
ABILITY	Magma Armor, Solid Rock
HEIGHT	6'03"
WEIGHT	485.0 lbs

Description

The humps on Camerupt's back are formed by a transformation of its bones. They sometimes blast out molten magma. This Pokémon apparently erupts often when it is enraged.

Special Moves

Rock Slide, Lava Plume, Magnitude

Evolution

 ➡

NUMEL   CAMERUPT

001-100
101-200
201-300
301-400
401-442
443-500
501-600
701-800
801-898

MEGA CAMERUPT

If magma builds up in its body, it shudders, then erupts violently.

CAMERUPT

Eruption Pokémon	
POKÉDEX NO.	**323**
TYPE	Fire, Ground
ABILITY	Sheer Force
HEIGHT	8'02"
WEIGHT	706.6 lbs

Description

Camerupt has a volcano inside its body. Magma of 18,000 degrees Fahrenheit courses through its body. Occasionally, the humps on this Pokémon's back erupt, spewing the superheated magma.

Special Moves

Earth Power, Flame Burst, Magnitude

TORKOAL

You can find abandoned coal mines full of them. They dig tirelessly in search of coal.

Coal Pokémon	
POKÉDEX NO.	**324**
TYPE	Fire
ABILITY	White Smoke, Drought
HEIGHT	1'08"
WEIGHT	177.3 lbs

Description

It burns coal inside its shell for energy. It blows out black soot if it is endangered.

Special Moves

Flamethrower, Heat Wave, Flame Wheel

Evolution

TORKOAL

Does not evolve

001-100
101-200
201-300
301-400
401-442
443-500
501-600
701-800
801-898

SPOINK

Spoink keeps a pearl on top of its head. The pearl functions to amplify this Pokémon's psychokinetic powers. It is therefore on a constant search for a bigger pearl.

Bounce Pokémon	
POKÉDEX NO.	**325**
TYPE	Psychic
ABILITY	Own Tempo, Thick Fat
HEIGHT	2'04"
WEIGHT	67.5 lbs

Description

Spoink bounces around on its tail. The shock of its bouncing makes its heart pump. As a result, this Pokémon cannot afford to stop bouncing—if it stops, its heart will also stop.

Special Moves

Splash, Psybeam, Zen Headbutt

Evolution

SPOINK → GRUMPIG

GRUMPIG

Grumpig uses the black pearls on its body to wield its fantastic powers. When it is doing so, it dances bizarrely. This Pokémon's black pearls are valuable as works of art.

Manipulate Pokémon	
POKÉDEX NO.	**326**
TYPE	Psychic
ABILITY	Own Tempo, Thick Fat
HEIGHT	2'11"
WEIGHT	157.6 lbs

Description

Grumpig uses the black pearls on its body to amplify its psychic power waves for gaining total control over its foe. When this Pokémon uses its special power, its snorting breath grows labored.

Special Moves

Teeter Dance, Psyshock, Rest

Evolution

SPOINK → GRUMPIG

001-100
101-200
201-300
301-400
401-442
443-500
601-600
701-800
801-898

SPINDA

Spot Panda Pokémon	
POKÉDEX NO.	**327**
TYPE	Normal
ABILITY	Tangled Feet, Own Tempo
HEIGHT	3'07"
WEIGHT	11.0 lbs

Its steps are shaky and stumbling. Walking for a long time makes it feel sick.

Description

Each Spinda's spot pattern is different. With its stumbling movements, it evades opponents' attacks brilliantly!

Special Moves

Dizzy Punch, Teeter Dance, Copy Cat

Evolution — Does not evolve

SPINDA

001-100
101-200
201-300
301-400
401-442
443-500
501-600
701-800
801-898

TRAPINCH

Its nest is a sloped, bowl-like pit in the desert. Once something has fallen in, there is no escape.

Ant Pit Pokémon	
POKÉDEX NO.	**328**
TYPE	Ground
ABILITY	Arena Trap, Hyper Cutter
HEIGHT	2'04"
WEIGHT	33.1 lbs

Description

Its jaws are strong enough to crush rocks but so heavy that it can't get up if it flips over. Sandile seize those moments as their chance.

Special Moves

Sand Attack, Dig, Earth Power

Evolution

TRAPINCH →  VIBRAVA → FLYGON

VIBRAVA

To help make its wings grow, it dissolves quantities of prey in its digestive juices and guzzles them down every day.

Vibration Pokémon	
POKÉDEX NO.	**329**
TYPE	Ground, Dragon
ABILITY	Levitate
HEIGHT	3'07"
WEIGHT	33.7 lbs

Description

The ultrasonic waves it generates by rubbing its two wings together cause severe headaches.

Special Moves

Dragon Breath, Bulldoze, Bug Buzz

Evolution

TRAPINCH   VIBRAVA   FLYGON

FLYGON

Mystic Pokémon

POKÉDEX NO.	**330**
TYPE	Ground, Dragon
ABILITY	Levitate
HEIGHT	6'07"
WEIGHT	180.8 lbs

Description

This Pokémon hides in the heart of sandstorms it creates and seldom appears where people can see it.

It is nicknamed the Desert Spirit because the flapping of its wings sounds like a woman singing.

Special Moves

Dragon Claw, Earthquake, Dragon Rush

Evolution

 → →

TRAPINCH　　　　VIBRAVA　　　　FLYGON

001-100
101-200
201-300
301-400
401-442
443-500
501-600
701-800
801-898

CACNEA

The more arid and harsh the environment, the more pretty and fragrant a flower Cacnea grows. This Pokémon battles by wildly swinging its thorny arms.

Cactus Pokémon	
POKÉDEX NO.	**331**
TYPE	Grass
ABILITY	Sand Veil
HEIGHT	1'04"
WEIGHT	113.1 lbs

Description

Cacnea lives in arid locations such as deserts. It releases a strong aroma from its flower to attract prey. When prey comes near, this Pokémon shoots sharp thorns from its body to bring the victim down.

Special Moves

Poison Sting, Growth, Leech Seed

Evolution

CACNEA → CACTURNE

CACTURNE

During the daytime, Cacturne remains unmoving so that it does not lose any moisture to the harsh desert sun. This Pokémon becomes active at night when the temperature drops.

Scarecrow Pokémon	
POKÉDEX NO.	**332**
TYPE	Grass, Dark
ABILITY	Sand Veil
HEIGHT	4'03"
WEIGHT	170.6 lbs

Description

If a traveler is going through a desert in the thick of night, Cacturne will follow in a ragtag group. The Pokémon are biding their time, waiting for the traveler to tire and become incapable of moving.

Special Moves

Needle Arm, Spiky Shield, Spikes

Evolution

CACNEA

CACTURNE

001-100
101-200
201-300
301-400
401-442
443-500
501-600
701-800
801-898

SWABLU

Since Swablu looks like a cumulus cloud, foes can have a hard time finding it. Apparently its wings turned white over many generations.

Cotton Bird Pokémon	
POKÉDEX NO.	**333**
TYPE	Normal, Flying
ABILITY	Natural Cure
HEIGHT	1'04"
WEIGHT	2.6 lbs

Description

Its cottony wings are full of air, making them light and fluffy to the touch. Swablu takes diligent care of its wings.

Special Moves

Dragon Breath, Sing, Disarming Voice

Evolution

SWABLU → ALTARIA

ALTARIA

001-
100

101-
200

201-
300

301-
400

401-
442

443-
500

501-
600

701-
800

801-
898

Humming Pokémon

POKÉDEX NO.	**334**
TYPE	Dragon, Flying
ABILITY	Natural Cure
HEIGHT	3'07"
WEIGHT	45.4 lbs

As it flies in a calm and relaxed manner, Altaria performs a humming song that would enrapture any audience.

Description

This Pokémon has a kind disposition, but if it's provoked, it will threaten opponents with shrill cries before attacking them without mercy.

Special Moves

Dragon Pulse,
Sky Attack, Fury Attack

Evolution

SWABLU → ALTARIA

MEGA ALTARIA

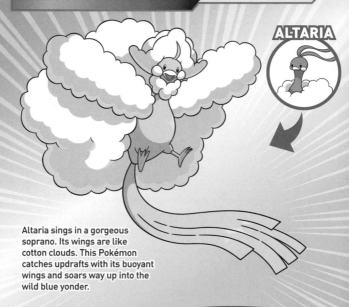

ALTARIA

Altaria sings in a gorgeous soprano. Its wings are like cotton clouds. This Pokémon catches updrafts with its buoyant wings and soars way up into the wild blue yonder.

Humming Pokémon	
POKÉDEX NO.	**334**
TYPE	Dragon, Fairy
ABILITY	Pixilate
HEIGHT	4'11"
WEIGHT	45.4 lbs

Description

Altaria dances and wheels through the sky among billowing, cotton-like clouds. By singing melodies in its crystal-clear voice, this Pokémon makes its listeners experience dreamy wonderment.

Special Moves

Dragon Breath, Moonblast, Cotton Guard

ZANGOOSE

Zangoose usually stays on all fours, but when angered, it gets up on its hind legs and extends its claws. This Pokémon shares a bitter rivalry with Seviper that dates back over generations.

Cat Ferret Pokémon	
POKÉDEX NO.	**335**
TYPE	Normal
ABILITY	Immunity
HEIGHT	4'03"
WEIGHT	88.8 lbs

Description

Memories of battling its archrival Seviper* are etched into every cell of Zangoose's body. This Pokémon adroitly dodges attacks with incredible agility.

Special Moves

Swords Dance, Crush Claw, Pursuit

Evolution

ZANGOOSE

Does not evolve

*Seviper: A Pokémon you'll find on page 424.

SEVIPER

Seviper's swordlike tail serves two purposes—it slashes foes and douses them with secreted poison.

Fang Snake Pokémon

POKÉDEX NO.	336
TYPE	Poison
ABILITY	Shed Skin
HEIGHT	8'10"
WEIGHT	115.7 lbs

Description

Seviper shares a generations-long feud with Zangoose.* The scars on its body are evidence of vicious battles. This Pokémon attacks using its sword-edged tail.

Special Moves

Coil, Poison Fang, Glare

Evolution

SEVIPER

Does not evolve

*Zangoose: A Pokémon you'll find on page 423.

LUNATONE

It was discovered at the site of a meteor strike 40 years ago. Its stare can lull its foes to sleep.

Meteorite Pokémon

POKÉDEX NO.	337
TYPE	Rock, Psychic
ABILITY	Levitate
HEIGHT	3'03"
WEIGHT	370.4 lbs

Description

The phase of the moon apparently has some effect on its power. It's active on the night of a full moon.

Special Moves

Moonlight, Cosmic Power, Future Sight

Evolution

LUNATONE

Does not evolve

001-100
101-200
201-300
301-400
401-442
443-500
501-600
701-800
801-898

SOLROCK

Solar energy is the source of its power, so it is strong during the daytime. When it spins, its body shines.

Meteorite Pokémon	
POKÉDEX NO.	**338**
TYPE	Rock, Psychic
ABILITY	Levitate
HEIGHT	3'11"
WEIGHT	339.5 lbs

Description

Solrock is a new species of Pokémon that is said to have fallen from space. It floats in the air and moves silently. In battle, this Pokémon releases intensely bright light.

Special Moves

Morning Sun, Cosmic Power, Explosion

Evolution

SOLROCK

Does not evolve

BARBOACH

001-100
101-200
201-300
301-400
401-442
443-500
501-600
701-800
801-890

It probes muddy riverbeds with its two long whiskers. A slimy film protects its body.

Whiskers Pokémon	
POKÉDEX NO.	**339**
TYPE	Water, Ground
ABILITY	Oblivious, Anticipation
HEIGHT	1'04"
WEIGHT	4.2 lbs

Description

Its slimy body is hard to grasp. In one region, it is said to have been born from hardened mud.

Special Moves

Mud-Slap, Water Gun, Future Sight

Evolution

BARBOACH → WHISCASH

427

WHISCASH

It claims a large swamp for itself. If a foe comes near it, it sets off tremors by thrashing around.

Whiskers Pokémon	
POKÉDEX NO.	**340**
TYPE	Water, Ground
ABILITY	Oblivious, Anticipation
HEIGHT	2'11"
WEIGHT	52.0 lbs

Description

It makes its nest at the bottom of swamps. It will eat anything—if it is alive, Whiscash will eat it.

Special Moves

Earthquake, Aqua Tail, Zen Headbutt

Evolution

BARBOACH → WHISCASH

CORPHISH

Ruffian Pokémon

POKÉDEX NO.	341

TYPE	Water
ABILITY	Shell Armor, Hyper Cutter
HEIGHT	2'00"
WEIGHT	25.4 lbs

Description

It can adapt very well to its environment. Feebas and Corphish are about the only Pokémon to live in stagnant ditches.

It was originally a Pokémon from afar that escaped to the wild. It can adapt to the dirtiest water.

Special Moves

Protect, Water Gun, Razor Shell

Evolution

CORPHISH

CRAWDAUNT

001-100
101-200
201-300
301-400
401-442
443-500
501-600
701-800
801-898

CRAWDAUNT

A brutish Pokémon that loves to battle. It will crash itself into any foe that approaches its nest.

Rogue Pokémon	
POKÉDEX NO.	**342**
TYPE	Water, Dark
ABILITY	Shell Armor, Hyper Cutter
HEIGHT	3'07"
WEIGHT	72.3 lbs

Description

A rough customer that wildly flails its giant claws. It is said to be extremely hard to raise.

Special Moves

Crabhammer, Guillotine, Night Slash

Evolution

 →

CORPHISH   CRAWDAUNT

BALTOY

It was discovered in ancient ruins. While moving, it constantly spins. It stands on one foot even when asleep.

Clay Doll Pokémon	
POKÉDEX NO.	**343**
TYPE	Ground, Psychic
ABILITY	Levitate
HEIGHT	1'08"
WEIGHT	47.4 lbs

Description

It moves while spinning around on its single foot. Some Baltoy have been seen spinning on their heads.

Special Moves

Ancient Power, Confusion, Extrasensory

001-100
101-200
201-300
301-400
401-442
443-500
501-600
701-800
801-898

Evolution

BALTOY → CLAYDOL

CLAYDOL

This mysterious Pokémon started life as an ancient clay figurine made over 20,000 years ago.

Clay Doll Pokémon	
POKÉDEX NO.	**344**
TYPE	Ground, Psychic
ABILITY	Levitate
HEIGHT	4'11"
WEIGHT	238.1 lbs

Description

If it gets wet, its body melts. When rain starts to fall, it wraps its whole body up with its psychic powers to protect itself.

Special Moves

Hyper Beam, Teleport, Explosion

Evolution

BALTOY

CLAYDOL

LILEEP

Lileep clings to rocks on the seabed. When prey comes close, this Pokémon entangles it with petallike tentacles.

Sea Lily Pokémon

POKÉDEX NO.	**345**
TYPE	Rock, Grass
ABILITY	Suction Cups
HEIGHT	3'03"
WEIGHT	52.5 lbs

Description

This Pokémon was restored from a fossil. Lileep once lived in warm seas that existed approximately 100 million years ago.

Special Moves

Wrap, Ancient Power, Mega Drain

Evolution

LILEEP → CRADILY

CRADILY

It has short legs and can't walk very fast, but its neck and tentacles can extend to over three times their usual length to nab distant prey.

Barnacle Pokémon	
POKÉDEX NO.	**346**
TYPE	Rock, Grass
ABILITY	Suction Cups
HEIGHT	4'11"
WEIGHT	133.2 lbs

Description

Once Cradily catches prey in its tentacles, it digests them whole and absorbs their nutrients.

Special Moves

Energy Ball, Giga Drain, Swallow

Evolution

LILEEP → CRADILY

434

ANORITH

Anorith can swim swiftly by pulling its eight wings through the water like oars on a boat. This Pokémon is an ancestor of modern bug Pokémon.

Old Shrimp Pokémon	
POKÉDEX NO.	**347**
TYPE	Rock, Bug
ABILITY	Battle Armor
HEIGHT	2'04"
WEIGHT	27.6 lbs

Description

This Pokémon was restored from a fossil. Anorith lived in the ocean about 100 million years ago, hunting with its pair of claws.

Special Moves

Harden, Metal Claw, Water Gun

Evolution

ANORITH → ARMALDO

001-100
101-200
201-300
301-400
401-442
443-500
501-600
701-800
801-898

ARMALDO

Though it lives on land, it's also a good swimmer. It dives into the ocean in search of prey, using its sharp claws to take down its quarry.

Plate Pokémon

POKÉDEX NO.	348
TYPE	Rock, Bug
ABILITY	Battle Armor
HEIGHT	4'11"
WEIGHT	150.4 lbs

Description

After evolution, this Pokémon emerged onto land. Its lower body has become stronger, and blows from its tail are devastating.

Special Moves

Brine, X-Scissor, Crush Claw

Evolution

ANORITH → ARMALDO

FEEBAS

Although unattractive and unpopular, this Pokémon's marvelous vitality has made it a subject of research.

001-100
101-200
201-300
301-400
401-442
443-500
501-600
701-800
801-898

Fish Pokémon	
POKÉDEX NO.	**349**
TYPE	Water
ABILITY	Oblivious, Swift Swim
HEIGHT	2'00"
WEIGHT	16.3 lbs

Description

It is a shabby and ugly Pokémon. However, it is very hardy and can survive on little water.

Special Moves

Splash, Tackle, Flail

Evolution

FEEBAS

MILOTIC

MILOTIC

Tender Pokémon

POKÉDEX NO.	**350**
TYPE	Water
ABILITY	Marvel Scale, Competitive
HEIGHT	20'04"
WEIGHT	357.1 lbs

Description

Milotic has provided inspiration to many artists. It has even been referred to as the most beautiful Pokémon of all.

It's said that a glimpse of a Milotic and its beauty will calm any hostile emotions you're feeling.

Special Moves

Dragon Tail, Twister, Recover

Evolution

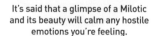

FEEBAS → MILOTIC

CASTFORM

The rougher the conditions get, the rougher Castform's disposition!

Weather Pokémon

POKÉDEX NO.	351
TYPE	Normal
ABILITY	Forecast
HEIGHT	1'00"
WEIGHT	1.8 lbs

Description

Although its form changes with the weather, that is apparently the result of a chemical reaction and not the result of its own free will.

Special Moves

Weather Ball, Hurricane, Water Gun

Evolution

CASTFORM

Does not evolve

001-
100

101-
200

201-
300

301-
400

401-
442

443-
500

501-
600

701-
800

801-
898

CASTFORM

RAINY FORM

Castform changes to this form when rain hits it. Its body is soft and slightly swollen with water.

Weather Pokémon	
POKÉDEX NO.	**351**
TYPE	Water
ABILITY	Forecast
HEIGHT	1'00"
WEIGHT	1.8 lbs

Description

This is Castform's form when pelted by rain. In an experiment where it was placed in a shower, this Pokémon didn't change to this form.

Special Moves

Hydro Pump, Rain Dance, Weather Ball

Evolution

CASTFORM
[RAINY FORM]

Does not evolve

CASTFORM

SUNNY FORM

Castform changes to this form when it basks in bright sunlight. When you touch its glowing skin, it feels all dried out!

Weather Pokémon	
POKÉDEX NO.	351
TYPE	Fire
ABILITY	Forecast
HEIGHT	1'00"
WEIGHT	1.8 lbs

Description

This is the form Castform takes on bright days. In an experiment where Castform was placed in front of a heater, it didn't change to this form.

Special Moves

Fire Blast, Sunny Day, Weather Ball

Evolution

CASTFORM
(SUNNY FORM)

Does not evolve

001-100
101-200
201-300
301-400
401-442
443-500
501-600
701-800
801-898

CASTFORM

SNOWY FORM

This is Castform's form when caught in a hailstorm. Its whole body is chilled, and its skin is partially frozen!

Weather Pokémon

POKÉDEX NO.	351
TYPE	Ice
ABILITY	Forecast
HEIGHT	1'00"
WEIGHT	1.8 lbs

Description

This is the form Castform takes when hit by hail. In an experiment where it was placed in a freezer, it didn't change to this form.

Special Moves

Powder Snow, Blizzard, Weather Ball

Evolution

CASTFORM
(SNOWY FORM)

Does not evolve

KECLEON

Color Swap Pokémon

POKÉDEX NO.	**352**
TYPE	Normal
ABILITY	Color Change
HEIGHT	3'03"
WEIGHT	48.5 lbs

001-100

101-200

201-300

301-400

401-442

443-500

501-600

701-800

801-898

Description

It changes its hue to blend into its surroundings. If no one takes notice of it for too long, it will pout and never reveal itself.

Its color changes for concealment and also when its mood or health changes. The darker the color, the healthier it is.

Special Moves

Feint Attack, Feint, Fury Swipes

Evolution

KECLEON

Does not evolve

443

SHUPPET

Puppet Pokémon	
POKÉDEX NO.	**353**
TYPE	Ghost
ABILITY	Insomnia, Frisk
HEIGHT	2'00"
WEIGHT	5.1 lbs

It eats up emotions like malice, jealousy, and resentment, so many people are grateful for its presence.

Description

There's a proverb that says, "Shun the house where Shuppet gather in the growing dusk."

Special Moves

Shadow Ball, Phantom Force, Shadow Sneak

Evolution

SHUPPET → BANETTE

BANETTE

Marionette Pokémon

POKÉDEX NO.	**354**	
TYPE	Ghost	
ABILITY	Insomnia, Frisk	
HEIGHT	3'07"	
WEIGHT	27.6 lbs	

001–100

101–200

201–300

301–400

401–442

443–500

501–600

701–800

801–898

Resentment at being cast off made it spring into being. Some say that treating it well will satisfy it, and it will once more become a stuffed toy.

Description

It's a stuffed toy that was thrown away and became possessed, ever searching for the one who threw it away so it can exact its revenge.

Special Moves

Night Shade, Phantom Force, Trick

Evolution

 ➡

SHUPPET   **BANETTE**

MEGA BANETTE

Mega Evolution increases its vindictiveness, and the cursing power that was held back by its zipper comes spilling out.

BANETTE

Marionette Pokémon	
POKÉDEX NO.	**354**
TYPE	Ghost
ABILITY	Prankster
HEIGHT	3'11"
WEIGHT	28.7 lbs

Description

Extraordinary energy amplifies its cursing power to such an extent that it can't help but curse its own Trainer.

Special Moves

Phantom Force, Shadow Ball, Night Shade

DUSKULL

Requiem Pokémon	
POKÉDEX NO.	**355**
TYPE	Ghost
ABILITY	Levitate
HEIGHT	2'07"
WEIGHT	33.1 lbs

Description

If it finds bad children who won't listen to their parents, it will spirit them away—or so it's said.

Making itself invisible, it silently sneaks up to prey. It has the ability to slip through thick walls.

Special Moves

Will-O-Wisp, Confuse Ray, Mean Look

Evolution

DUSKULL   DUSCLOPS   DUSKNOIR

001-100
101-200
201-300
301-400
401-442
443-500
501-600
701-800
801-898

DUSCLOPS

Its body is entirely hollow. When it opens its mouth, it sucks everything in as if it were a black hole.

Beckon Pokémon

POKÉDEX NO.	356
TYPE	Ghost
ABILITY	Pressure
HEIGHT	5'03"
WEIGHT	67.5 lbs

Description

It seeks drifting will-o'-the-wisps and sucks them into its empty body. What happens inside is a mystery.

Special Moves

Shadow Punch, Future Sight, Shadow Sneak

Evolution

DUSKULL → DUSCLOPS → DUSKNOIR

TROPIUS

Fruit Pokémon

POKÉDEX NO.	**357**
TYPE	Grass, Flying
ABILITY	Chlorophyll, Solar Power
HEIGHT	6'07"
WEIGHT	220.5 lbs

Description

The bunches of fruit growing around the necks of Tropius in Alola are especially sweet compared to those in other regions.

Bunches of delicious fruit grow around its neck. In warm areas, many ranches raise Tropius.

Special Moves

Leaf Storm, Solar Beam, Stomp

Evolution

TROPIUS

Does not evolve

001–100
101–200
201–300
301–400
401–442
443–500
501–600
701–800
801–898

CHIMECHO

Chimecho makes its cries echo inside its hollow body. When this Pokémon becomes enraged, its cries result in ultrasonic waves that have the power to knock foes flying.

Wind Chime Pokémon

POKÉDEX NO.	358
TYPE	Psychic
ABILITY	Levitate
HEIGHT	2'00"
WEIGHT	2.2 lbs

Description

In high winds, Chimecho cries as it hangs from a tree branch or the eaves of a building using the suction cup on its head. This Pokémon plucks berries with its long tail and eats them.

Special Moves

Heal Bell, Psywave, Take Down

Evolution

CHINGLING → CHIMECHO

ABSOL

Swift as the wind, Absol races through fields and mountains. Its curved, bow-like horn is acutely sensitive to the warning signs of natural disasters.

001-100
101-200
201-300
301-400
401-442
443-500
501-600
701-800
801-898

Disaster Pokémon

POKÉDEX NO.	359
TYPE	Dark
ABILITY	Pressure, Super Luck
HEIGHT	3'11"
WEIGHT	103.6 lbs

Description

Because of this Pokémon's ability to detect danger, people mistook Absol as a bringer of doom.

Special Moves

Knock Off, Double Team, Swords Dance

Evolution

ABSOL

Does not evolve

MEGA ABSOL

ABSOL

Normally, it dislikes fighting, so it really hates changing to this form for battles.

Disaster Pokémon	
POKÉDEX NO.	**359**
TYPE	Dark
ABILITY	Magic Bounce
HEIGHT	3'11"
WEIGHT	108.0 lbs

Description

It converts the energy from Mega Evolution into an intimidating aura.* Fainthearted people expire from shock at the sight of it.

Special Moves

Psycho Cut, Razor Wind, Perish Song

*Aura: An energy-like power rising out of the body.

WYNAUT

Bright Pokémon

POKÉDEX NO.	360
TYPE	Psychic
ABILITY	Shadow Tag
HEIGHT	2'00"
WEIGHT	30.9 lbs

It tends to move in a pack with others. They cluster in a tight group to sleep in a cave.

Description

Wynaut can always be seen with a big, happy smile on its face. Look at its tail to determine if it is angry. When angered, this Pokémon will be slapping the ground with its tail.

Special Moves

Counter, Safeguard, Encore

Evolution

 ➡

WYNAUT   WOBBUFFET

001-100
101-200
201-300
301-400
401-442
443-500
501-600
701-800
801-898

SNORUNT

Snow Hat Pokémon

POKÉDEX NO.	361

TYPE	Ice
ABILITY	Inner Focus, Ice Body
HEIGHT	2'04"
WEIGHT	37.0 lbs

It's said that if they are seen at midnight, they'll cause heavy snow. They eat snow and ice to survive.

Description

It can only survive in cold areas. It bounces happily around, even in environments as cold as −150 degrees Fahrenheit.

Special Moves

Powder Snow, Double Team, Icy Wind

Evolution

SNORUNT → GLALIE FROSLASS

GLALIE

It has a body of ice that won't melt, even with fire. It can instantly freeze moisture in the atmosphere.

Face Pokémon

POKÉDEX NO.	362
TYPE	Ice
ABILITY	Inner Focus, Ice Body
HEIGHT	4'11"
WEIGHT	565.5 lbs

Description

Its actual body is a rock that isn't particularly hard. Glalie absorbs moisture from the air and drapes itself in an armor of ice.

Special Moves

Sheer Cold, Freeze-Dry, Blizzard

Evolution

SNORUNT → GLALIE

001-100
101-200
201-300
301-400
401-442
443-500
501-600
701-800
801-898

MEGA GLALIE

GLALIE

When it spews stupendously cold air from its broken mouth, the entire area around it gets whited out.*

Face Pokémon

POKÉDEX NO.	**362**
TYPE	Ice
ABILITY	Refrigerate
HEIGHT	6'11"
WEIGHT	772.1 lbs

Description

The power of Mega Evolution was so strong that it smashed Glalie's jaw. Its inability to eat well leaves Glalie irritated.

Special Moves

Freeze-Dry, Sheer Cold, Frost Breath

*White out: When geographical formations are obscured by the tremendous snowfall.

SPHEAL

Clap Pokémon	
POKÉDEX NO.	**363**
TYPE	Ice, Water
ABILITY	Thick Fat, Ice Body
HEIGHT	2'07"
WEIGHT	87.1 lbs

001-100
101-200
201-300
301-400
401-442
443-500
501-600
701-800
801-898

Description

As it drifts among the waves, Spheal probes the sea. As soon as it spots prey, it informs the Walrein in its herd.

This Pokémon's body is covered in blubber and is impressively round. It's faster for Spheal to roll around than walk.

Special Moves

Surf, Water Gun, Defense Curl

Evolution

SPHEAL → SEALEO → WALREIN

SEALEO

Sealeo live on top of drift ice. They go swimming when they're on the hunt, seeking out their prey by scent.

Ball Roll Pokémon

POKÉDEX NO.	364
TYPE	Ice, Water
ABILITY	Thick Fat, Ice Body
HEIGHT	3'07"
WEIGHT	193.1 lbs

Description

This Pokémon has a habit of spinning round things on its nose, whether those things are Poké Balls or Spheal.

Special Moves

Aurora Beam, Water Gun, Body Slam

Evolution

SPHEAL → SEALEO → WALREIN

WALREIN

Walrein's tusks keep growing throughout its life. Tusks broken in battle will grow back to their usual impressive size in a year.

Ice Break Pokémon	
POKÉDEX NO.	**365**
TYPE	Ice, Water
ABILITY	Thick Fat, Ice Body
HEIGHT	4'07"
WEIGHT	332.0 lbs

Description

Walrein form herds of 20 to 30 individuals. When a threat appears, the herd's leader will protect the group with its life.

Special Moves

Sheer Cold, Blizzard, Ice Fang

Evolution

SPHEAL → SEALEO → WALREIN

001-100
101-200
201-300
301-400
401-442
443-500
501-600
701-800
801-898

CLAMPERL

Clamperl's pearls are exceedingly precious. They can be more than 10 times as costly as Shellder's* pearls.

Bivalve Pokémon

POKÉDEX NO.	366
TYPE	Water
ABILITY	Shell Armor
HEIGHT	1'04"
WEIGHT	115.7 lbs

Description

Despite its appearance, it's carnivorous. It clamps down on its prey with both sides of its shell and doesn't let go until they stop moving.

Special Moves

Water Gun, Whirlpool, Clamp

Evolution

CLAMPERL HUNTAIL GOREBYSS

*Shellder: A Pokémon you'll find on page 137.

HUNTAIL

Deep seas are their habitat. According to tradition, when Huntail wash up onshore, something unfortunate will happen.

Deep Sea Pokémon

POKÉDEX NO.	**367**
TYPE	Water
ABILITY	Swift Swim
HEIGHT	5'07"
WEIGHT	59.5 lbs

Description

It's not the strongest swimmer. It wags its tail to lure in its prey and then gulps them down as soon as they get close.

Special Moves

Hydro Pump, Dive, Coil

Evolution

 →

CLAMPERL   HUNTAIL

001-100
101-200
201-300
301-400
401-442
443-500
501-600
701-800
801-898

GOREBYSS

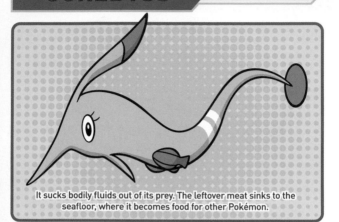

It sucks bodily fluids out of its prey. The leftover meat sinks to the seafloor, where it becomes food for other Pokémon.

South Sea Pokémon

POKÉDEX NO.	368
TYPE	Water
ABILITY	Swift Swim
HEIGHT	5'11"
WEIGHT	49.8 lbs

Description

The color of its body changes with the water temperature. The coloration of Gorebyss in Alola is almost blindingly vivid.

Special Moves

Draining Kiss, Water Sport, Aqua Tail

Evolution

CLAMPERL → GOREBYSS

RELICANTH

Rock-hard scales and oil-filled swim bladders allow this Pokémon to survive the intense water pressure of the deep sea.

Longevity Pokémon

POKÉDEX NO.	369
TYPE	Water, Rock
ABILITY	Rock Head, Swift Swim
HEIGHT	3'03"
WEIGHT	51.6 lbs

Description

This Pokémon was discovered during deep-sea exploration. Its appearance hasn't changed in 100 million years, so it's called a living fossil.

Special Moves

Ancient Power, Double-Edge, Take Down

Evolution

RELICANTH

Does not evolve

001-100
101-200
201-300
301-400
401-442
443-500
501-600
701-800
801-898

LUVDISC

Luvdisc makes its home in coral reefs in warm seas. It especially likes sleeping in the space between Corsola's* branches.

Rendezvous Pokémon	
POKÉDEX NO.	370
TYPE	Water
ABILITY	Swift Swim
HEIGHT	2'00"
WEIGHT	19.2 lbs

Description

There was an era when it was overfished due to the rumor that having one of its heart-shaped scales would enable you to find a sweetheart.

Special Moves

Heart Stamp, Sweet Kiss, Charm

Evolution

LUVDISC

Does not evolve

*Corsola: A Pokémon you'll find on page 293.

BAGON

Bagon is a solitary Pokémon that doesn't form groups with others of its kind. It also has a head hard enough to cleave a boulder in one strike.

Rock Head Pokémon	
POKÉDEX NO.	**371**
TYPE	Dragon
ABILITY	Rock Head
HEIGHT	2'00"
WEIGHT	92.8 lbs

Description

Bagon jumps off cliffs every day, trying to grow stronger so that someday it will be able to fly.

Special Moves

Ember, Crunch, Double-Edge

001-100
101-200
201-300
301-400
401-442
443-500
501-600
701-800
801-898

Evolution

BAGON SHELGON SALAMENCE

SHELGON

This Pokémon has covered its body in a hard shell that has the same composition as bone. Shelgon stores energy for evolution.

Endurance Pokémon

POKÉDEX NO.	372
TYPE	Dragon
ABILITY	Rock Head
HEIGHT	3'07"
WEIGHT	243.6 lbs

Description

Shelgon ignores its hunger entirely, never eating any food. Apparently, Shelgon will evolve once all its energy stores are used up.

Special Moves

Dragon Claw, Zen Headbutt, Outrage

Evolution

BAGON → SHELGON → SALAMENCE

SALAMENCE

Dragon Pokémon

POKÉDEX NO.	**373**

TYPE	Dragon, Flying
ABILITY	Intimidate
HEIGHT	4'11"
WEIGHT	226.2 lbs

Description

Salamence is an unusual Pokémon in that it was able to evolve a body with wings just by constantly wishing to be able to fly.

While basking in the joy of flight generally keeps this Pokémon in high spirits, Salamence turns into an uncontrollable menace if something angers it.

Special Moves

Fly, Flamethrower, Outrage

001-100
101-200
201-300
301-400
401-442
443-500
501-600
701-800
801-898

Evolution

BAGON SHELGON SALAMENCE

MEGA SALAMENCE

It puts its forelegs inside its shell to streamline itself for flight. Salamence flies at high speeds over all kinds of topographical features.

SALAMENCE

Dragon Pokémon	
POKÉDEX NO.	**373**
TYPE	Dragon, Flying
ABILITY	Aerilate
HEIGHT	5'11"
WEIGHT	248.2 lbs

Description

The stress of its two proud wings becoming misshapen and stuck together because of strong energy makes it go on a rampage.

Special Moves

Flamethrower, Dragon Tail, Dragon Claw

BELDUM

The cells in this Pokémon's body are composed of magnetic material. Instead of blood, magnetic forces flow through Beldum's body.

Iron Ball Pokémon

POKÉDEX NO.	374
TYPE	Steel, Psychic
ABILITY	Clear Body
HEIGHT	2'00"
WEIGHT	209.9 lbs

Description

From its rear, Beldum emits a magnetic force that rapidly pulls opponents in. They get skewered on Beldum's sharp claws.

Special Moves

Tackle

001-100
101-200
201-300
301-400
401-442
443-500
501-600
701-800
801-898

Evolution

BELDUM → METANG → METAGROSS

METANG

Using magnetic forces to stay aloft, this Pokémon flies at high speeds, weaving through harsh mountain terrain in pursuit of prey.

Iron Claw Pokémon

POKÉDEX NO.	375
TYPE	Steel, Psychic
ABILITY	Clear Body
HEIGHT	3'11"
WEIGHT	446.4 lbs

Description

Two Beldum have become stuck together via their own magnetic forces. With two brains, the resulting Metang has doubled psychic powers.

Special Moves

Confusion, Metal Claw, Agility

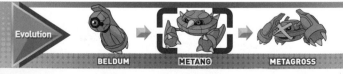

Evolution

BELDUM → METANG → METAGROSS

METAGROSS

Iron Leg Pokémon

POKÉDEX NO.	**376**
TYPE	Steel, Psychic
ABILITY	Clear Body
HEIGHT	5'03"
WEIGHT	1212.5 lbs

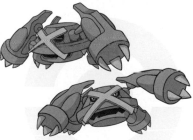

Because the magnetic powers of these Pokémon get stronger in freezing temperatures, Metagross living on snowy mountains are full of energy.

Description

Metagross is the result of the fusion of two Metang. This Pokémon defeats its opponents through use of its supercomputer-level brain.

Special Moves

Bullet Punch, Hammer Arm, Iron Defense

Evolution

BELDUM ➡ METANG ➡ METAGROSS

001-100
101-200
201-300
301-400
401-442
443-500
501-600
701-800
801-898

MEGA METAGROSS

When it knows it can't win, it digs the claws on its legs into its opponent and starts the countdown to a big explosion.

METAGROSS

Iron Leg Pokémon	
POKÉDEX NO.	**376**
TYPE	Steel, Psychic
ABILITY	Tough Claws
HEIGHT	8'02"
WEIGHT	2078.7 lbs

Description

Its intellect surpasses its previous level, resulting in battles so cruel, they'll make you want to cover your eyes.

Special Moves

Bullet Punch, Meteor Mash, Hyper Beam

REGIROCK

Rock Peak Pokémon

POKÉDEX NO.	**377**
TYPE	Rock
ABILITY	Clear Body
HEIGHT	5'07"
WEIGHT	507.1 lbs

Cutting-edge technology was used to study the internals of this Pokémon's rock body, but nothing was found—not even a brain or a heart.

Description

Every bit of Regirock's body is made of stone. As parts of its body erode, this Pokémon sticks rocks to itself to repair what's been lost.

Special Moves

Rock Throw, Charge Beam, Superpower

Evolution

REGIROCK

Does not evolve

001-100
101-200
201-300
301-400
401-442
443-500
501-600
701-600
801-898

REGICE

Iceberg Pokémon	
POKÉDEX NO.	**378**
TYPE	Ice
ABILITY	Clear Body
HEIGHT	5'11"
WEIGHT	385.8 lbs

This Pokémon's body is made of solid ice. It's said that Regice was born beneath thick ice in the ice age.

Description

With cold air that can reach temperatures as low as –328 degrees Fahrenheit, Regice instantly freezes any creature that approaches it.

Special Moves

Icy Wind, Ice Beam, Blizzard

Evolution — Does not evolve

REGICE

REGISTEEL

Iron Pokémon

POKÉDEX NO.	**379**
TYPE	Steel
ABILITY	Clear Body
HEIGHT	6'03"
WEIGHT	451.9 lbs

It's rumored that this Pokémon was born deep underground in the planet's mantle and that it emerged onto the surface 10,000 years ago.

Description

Registeel's body is made of a strange material that is flexible enough to stretch and shrink but also more durable than any metal.

Special Moves

Metal Claw, Iron Head, Zap Cannon

Evolution

REGISTEEL

Does not evolve

001-100
101-200
201-300
301-442
443-500
501-600
701-800
801-898

LATIAS

Eon Pokémon

POKÉDEX NO.	**380**
TYPE	Dragon, Psychic
ABILITY	Levitate
HEIGHT	4'07"
WEIGHT	88.2 lbs

Latias is highly intelligent and capable of understanding human speech. It is covered in a glass-like down. The Pokémon enfolds its body with its down and refracts light to alter its appearance.

Description

Latias is highly sensitive to the emotions of people. If it senses any hostility, this Pokémon ruffles the feathers all over its body and cries shrilly to intimidate the foe.

Special Moves

Mist Ball, Psychic, Wish

Evolution Does not evolve

LATIAS

MEGA LATIAS

001-
100

101-
200

201-
300

301-
400

401-
442

443-
500

501-
600

701-
800

801-
898

LATIAS

They make a small herd with several members. They rarely make contact with people or other Pokémon. They disappear if they sense enemies.

Eon Pokémon	
POKÉDEX NO.	**380**
TYPE	Dragon, Psychic
ABILITY	Levitate
HEIGHT	5'11"
WEIGHT	114.6 lbs

Description

It can telepathically communicate with people. It changes its appearance using its down, which refracts light.

Special Moves

Mist Ball, Dragon Pulse, Psywave

LATIOS

Eon Pokémon

POKÉDEX NO.	**381**
TYPE	Dragon, Psychic
ABILITY	Levitate
HEIGHT	6'07"
WEIGHT	132.3 lbs

Latios has the ability to make others see an image of what it has seen or imagines in its head. This Pokémon is intelligent and understands human speech.

Description

Latios will only open its heart to a Trainer with a compassionate spirit. This Pokémon can fly faster than a jet plane by folding its forelegs to minimize air resistance.

Special Moves

Luster Purge, Simple Beam, Tailwind

Evolution

LATIOS

Does not evolve

MEGA LATIOS

It understands human speech and is highly intelligent. It is a tender Pokémon that dislikes fighting.

LATIOS

Eon Pokémon

POKÉDEX NO.	**381**
TYPE	Dragon, Psychic
ABILITY	Levitate
HEIGHT	7'07"
WEIGHT	154.3 lbs

Description

A highly intelligent Pokémon. By folding back its wings in flight, it can overtake jet planes.

Special Moves

Luster Purge, Dragon Breath, Psychic

001-100
101-200
201-300
301-400
401-442
443-500
501-600
701-800
801-898

KYOGRE

Sea Basin Pokémon

POKÉDEX NO.	**382**

TYPE	Water
ABILITY	Drizzle
HEIGHT	14'09"
WEIGHT	776.0 lbs

It is said to have widened the seas by causing downpours. It had been asleep in a marine trench.

Description

Kyogre is said to be the personification of the sea itself. Legends tell of its many clashes against Groudon, as each sought to gain the power of nature.

Special Moves

Water Spout, Hydro Pump, Water Pulse

Evolution Does not evolve

KYOGRE

PRIMAL KYOGRE

A mythical Pokémon said to have swelled the seas with rain and tidal waves. It battled with Groudon.

GROUDON

001-100

101-200

201-300

301-400

401-442

443-500

501-600

701-800

801-898

Sea Basin Pokémon

POKÉDEX NO.	**382**
TYPE	Water
ABILITY	Primordial Sea
HEIGHT	32'02"
WEIGHT	948.0 lbs

Description

Through Primal Reversion and with nature's full power, It will take back its true form. It can summon storms that cause the sea levels to rise.

Special Moves

Origin Pulse, Sheer Cold, Hydro Pump

GROUDON

Continent Pokémon

POKÉDEX NO.	**383**
TYPE	Ground
ABILITY	Drought
HEIGHT	11'06"
WEIGHT	2094.4 lbs

This Legendary Pokémon is said to represent the land. It went to sleep after dueling Kyogre.

Description

Groudon is said to be the personification of the land itself. Legends tell of its many clashes against Kyogre, as each sought to gain the power of nature.

Special Moves

Eruption, Earth Power, Hammer Arm

Evolution Does not evolve

GROUDON

PRIMAL GROUDON

GROUDON

Said to have expanded the lands by evaporating water with raging heat. It battled titanically with Kyogre.

001-100
101-200
201-300
301-400
401-442
443-500
501-600
701-800
801-898

Continent Pokémon

POKÉDEX NO.	**383**
TYPE	Ground, Fire
ABILITY	Desolate Land
HEIGHT	16'05"
WEIGHT	2204.0 lbs

Description

Through Primal Reversion and with nature's full power, it will take back its true form. It can cause magma to erupt and expand the landmass of the world.

Special Moves

Precipice Blades, Mud Shot, Earth Power

RAYQUAZA

Sky High Pokémon

POKÉDEX NO.	384
TYPE	Dragon, Flying
ABILITY	Air Lock
HEIGHT	23'00"
WEIGHT	455.3 lbs

It lives in the ozone layer far above the clouds and cannot be seen from the ground.

Description

Rayquaza is said to have lived for hundreds of millions of years. Legends remain of how it put to rest the clash between Kyogre and Groudon.

Special Moves

Dragon Ascent, Dragon Dance, Twister

Evolution Does not evolve

RAYQUAZA

MEGA RAYQUAZA

001-100

101-200

201-300

301-400

401-442

443-500

501-600

701-800

801-898

RAYQUAZA

It flies in the ozone layer, way up high in the sky. Until recently, no one had ever seen it.

Sky High Pokémon	
POKÉDEX NO.	**384**
TYPE	Dragon, Flying
ABILITY	Delta Stream
HEIGHT	35'05"
WEIGHT	864.2 lbs

Description

It flies forever through the ozone layer, consuming meteoroids for sustenance. The many meteoroids in its body provide the energy it needs to Mega Evolve.

Special Moves

Outrage, Hyper Voice, Hyper Beam

JIRACHI

Wish Pokémon	
POKÉDEX NO.	**385**
TYPE	Steel, Psychic
ABILITY	Serene Grace
HEIGHT	1'00"
WEIGHT	2.4 lbs

Once every 1,000 years, the singing of a pure voice will rouse this Pokémon from its near-perpetual slumber. It wakes for only seven days.

Description

It's believed that when this Pokémon wakes from its 1,000-year slumber, it will grant any wishes written on the notes attached to its head.

Special Moves

Doom Desire, Healing Wish, Confusion

Evolution   Does not evolve

JIRACHI

DEOXYS

001-100
101-200
201-300
301-400
401-442
443-500
501-600
701-800
801-898

NORMAL FORME

DNA Pokémon

POKÉDEX NO.	**386**
TYPE	Psychic
ABILITY	Pressure
HEIGHT	5'07"
WEIGHT	134.0 lbs

Description

The DNA of a space virus underwent a sudden mutation upon exposure to a laser beam and resulted in Deoxys. The crystalline organ on this Pokémon's chest appears to be its brain.

Special Moves

Psycho Boost, Cosmic Power, Teleport

It is highly intelligent and wields psychokinetic powers. This Pokémon shoots lasers from the crystalline organ on its chest.

Evolution

DEOXYS
(NORMAL FORME)

Does not evolve

DEOXYS

ATTACK FORME

DNA Pokémon	
POKÉDEX NO.	**386**
TYPE	Psychic
ABILITY	Pressure
HEIGHT	5'07"
WEIGHT	134.0 lbs

It is highly intelligent and wields psychokinetic powers. This Pokémon shoots lasers from the crystalline organ on its chest.

Description

The DNA of a space virus underwent a sudden mutation upon exposure to a laser beam and resulted in Deoxys. The crystalline organ on this Pokémon's chest appears to be its brain.

Special Moves

Psycho Boost, Hyper Beam, Pursuit

Evolution   Does not evolve

DEOXYS
[ATTACK FORME]

DEOXYS

001-100
101-200
201-300
301-400
401-442
443-500
501-600
701-800
801-898

DEFENSE FORME

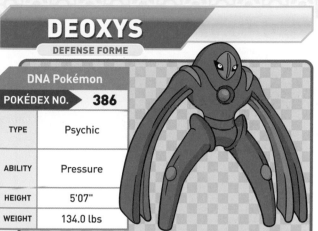

DNA Pokémon

POKÉDEX NO.	**386**
TYPE	Psychic
ABILITY	Pressure
HEIGHT	5'07"
WEIGHT	134.0 lbs

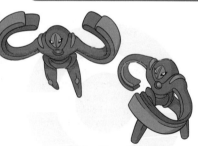

It is highly intelligent and wields psychokinetic powers. This Pokémon shoots lasers from the crystalline organ on its chest.

Description

The DNA of a space virus underwent a sudden mutation upon exposure to a laser beam and resulted in Deoxys. The crystalline organ on this Pokémon's chest appears to be its brain.

Special Moves

Psycho Boost, Recover, Iron Defense

Evolution

DEOXYS
(DEFENSE FORME)

Does not evolve

489

DEOXYS

SPEED FORME

DNA Pokémon	
POKÉDEX NO.	**386**
TYPE	Psychic
ABILITY	Pressure
HEIGHT	5'07"
WEIGHT	134.0 lbs

It is highly intelligent and wields psychokinetic powers. This Pokémon shoots lasers from the crystalline organ on its chest.

Description

The DNA of a space virus underwent a sudden mutation upon exposure to a laser beam and resulted in Deoxys. The crystalline organ on this Pokémon's chest appears to be its brain.

Special Moves

Psycho Boost, Extreme Speed, Agility

Evolution

Does not evolve

DEOXYS
(SPEED FORME)

TURTWIG

Tiny Leaf Pokémon

POKÉDEX NO.	387
TYPE	Grass
ABILITY	Overgrow
HEIGHT	1'04"
WEIGHT	22.5 lbs

001-100
101-200
201-300
301-400
401-442
443-500
501-600
701-800
801-898

Description

It undertakes photosynthesis within its body, making oxygen. The leaf on its head wilts if it is thirsty.

Photosynthesis occurs across its body under the sun. The shell on its back is actually hardened soil.

Special Moves

Razor Leaf, Absorb, Tackle

Evolution

TURTWIG → GROTLE → TORTERRA

491

GROTLE

It lives along water in forests. In the daytime, it leaves the forest to sunbathe its treed shell.

Grove Pokémon	
POKÉDEX NO.	**388**
TYPE	Grass
ABILITY	Overgrow
HEIGHT	3'07"
WEIGHT	213.8 lbs

Description

It knows where pure water wells up. It carries fellow Pokémon there on its back.

Special Moves

Mega Drain, Leech Seed, Bite

Evolution

TURTWIG → GROTLE → TORTERRA

TORTERRA

001-100
101-200
201-300
301-400
401-442
443-500
501-600
701-800
801-898

Continent Pokémon

POKÉDEX NO.	**389**
TYPE	Grass, Ground
ABILITY	Overgrow
HEIGHT	7'03"
WEIGHT	683.4 lbs

Ancient people imagined that beneath the ground, a gigantic Torterra dwelled.

Description

Small Pokémon occasionally gather on its unmoving back to begin building their nests.

Special Moves

Leaf Storm, Wood Hammer, Earthquake

Evolution

TURTWIG

GROTLE

TORTERRA

493

CHIMCHAR

Chimp Pokémon

POKÉDEX NO.	**390**
TYPE	Fire
ABILITY	Blaze
HEIGHT	1'08"
WEIGHT	13.7 lbs

It is very agile. Before going to sleep, it extinguishes the flame on its tail to prevent fires.

Description

The gas made in its belly burns from its rear end. The fire burns weakly when it feels sick.

Special Moves

Ember, Fury Swipes, Acrobatics

Evolution

CHIMCHAR → MONFERNO → INFERNAPE

MONFERNO

001-100
101-200
201-300
301-400
401-442
443-500
501-600
701-800
801-898

Playful Pokémon	
POKÉDEX NO.	**391**
TYPE	Fire, Fighting
ABILITY	Blaze
HEIGHT	2'11"
WEIGHT	48.5 lbs

Description

It skillfully controls the intensity of the fire on its tail to keep its foes at an ideal distance.

It uses ceilings and walls to launch aerial attacks. Its fiery tail is but one weapon.

Special Moves

Mach Punch, Fire Spin, Feint

Evolution

CHIMCHAR → MONFERNO → INFERNAPE

INFERNAPE

Flame Pokémon

POKÉDEX NO.	392

TYPE	Fire, Fighting
ABILITY	Blaze
HEIGHT	3'11"
WEIGHT	121.3 lbs

It tosses its enemies around with agility. It uses all its limbs to fight in its own unique style.

Description

Its crown of fire is indicative of its fiery nature. It is beaten by none in terms of quickness.

Special Moves

Flare Blitz, Close Combat, Feint

Evolution

CHIMCHAR → MONFERNO → INFERNAPE

PIPLUP

001-100
101-200
201-300
301-400
401-442
443-500
501-600
701-800
801-898

Penguin Pokémon

POKÉDEX NO.	393
TYPE	Water
ABILITY	Torrent
HEIGHT	1'04"
WEIGHT	11.5 lbs

Because it is very proud, it hates accepting food from people. Its thick down guards it from cold.

Description

It doesn't like to be taken care of. It's difficult to bond with since it won't listen to its Trainer.

Special Moves

Pound, Bubble Beam, Water Sport

Evolution

PIPLUP → PRINPLUP → EMPOLEON

PRINPLUP

Its wings deliver wicked blows that can snap even the thickest of trees.

Penguin Pokémon	
POKÉDEX NO.	**394**
TYPE	Water
ABILITY	Torrent
HEIGHT	2'07"
WEIGHT	50.7 lbs

Description

It lives alone, away from others. Apparently, every one of them believes it is the most important.

Special Moves

Metal Claw, Bubble Beam, Fury Attack

Evolution

PIPLUP → PRINPLUP → EMPOLEON

EMPOLEON

Emperor Pokémon

POKÉDEX NO.	**395**	
TYPE	Water, Steel	
ABILITY	Torrent	
HEIGHT	5'07"	
WEIGHT	186.3 lbs	

001-100
101-200
201-300
301-400
401-442
443-500
501-600
701-800
801-898

Description

It swims as fast as a jet boat. The edges of its wings are sharp and can slice apart drifting ice.

The three horns that extend from its beak attest to its power. The leader has the biggest horns.

Special Moves

Aqua Jet, Hydro Pump, Whirlpool

Evolution

PIPLUP   PRINPLUP   EMPOLEON

STARLY

Starling Pokémon

POKÉDEX NO.	396
TYPE	Normal, Flying
ABILITY	Keen Eye
HEIGHT	1'00"
WEIGHT	4.4 lbs

Description

They flock around mountains and fields, chasing after bug Pokémon. Their singing is noisy and annoying.

They flock in great numbers. Though small, they flap their wings with great power.

Special Moves

Wing Attack, Whirlwind, Quick Attack

Evolution

STARLY → STARAVIA → STARAPTOR

500

STARAVIA

001-100
101-200
201-300
301-400
401-442
443-500
501-600
701-800
801-898

Starling Pokémon	
POKÉDEX NO.	**397**
TYPE	Normal, Flying
ABILITY	Intimidate
HEIGHT	2'00"
WEIGHT	34.2 lbs

Description

Recognizing their own weakness, they always live in a group. When alone, a Staravia cries noisily.

They maintain huge flocks, although fierce scuffles break out between various ones.

Special Moves

Agility, Aerial Ace, Take Down

Evolution

STARLY → STARAVIA → STARAPTOR

STARAPTOR

When Staravia evolve into Staraptor, they leave the flock to live alone. They have sturdy wings.

Predator Pokémon	
POKÉDEX NO.	398
TYPE	Normal, Flying
ABILITY	Intimidate
HEIGHT	3'11"
WEIGHT	54.9 lbs

Description

The muscles in its wings and legs are strong. It can easily fly while gripping a small Pokémon.

Special Moves

Close Combat, Brave Bird, Final Gambit

Evolution

STARLY STARAVIA STARAPTOR

BIDOOF

Plump Mouse Pokémon

POKÉDEX NO.	▶ **399**
TYPE	Normal
ABILITY	Simple, Unaware
HEIGHT	1'08"
WEIGHT	44.1 lbs

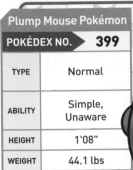

It constantly gnaws on logs and rocks to whittle down its front teeth. It nests alongside water.

Description

With nerves of steel, nothing can perturb it. It is more agile and active than it appears

Special Moves

Tackle, Crunch, Super Fang

Evolution

BIDOOF → BIBAREL

001-100
101-200
201-300
301-400
401-442
443-500
501-600
701-800
801-898

BIBAREL

Beaver Pokémon

POKÉDEX NO.	400	
TYPE	Normal, Water	
ABILITY	Simple, Unaware	
HEIGHT	3'03"	
WEIGHT	69.4 lbs	

Description

It busily makes its nest with stacks of branches and roots it has cut up with its sharp incisors.

It makes its nest by damming streams with bark and mud. It is known as an industrious worker.

Special Moves

Hyper Fang, Water Gun, Crunch

Evolution

BIDOOF → BIBAREL

KRICKETOT

When its antennae hit each other, it sounds like the music of a xylophone.

Cricket Pokémon	
POKÉDEX NO.	**401**
TYPE	Bug
ABILITY	Shed Skin
HEIGHT	1'00"
WEIGHT	4.9 lbs

Description

It chats with others using the sounds of its colliding antennae. These sounds are fall hallmarks.

Special Moves

Growl, Bug Bite, Struggle Bug

Evolution

KRICKETOT → KRICKETUNE

001-100
101-200
201-300
401-442
443-500
501-600
701-800
801-898

KRICKETUNE

Cricket Pokémon

POKÉDEX NO.	402
TYPE	Bug
ABILITY	Swarm
HEIGHT	3'03"
WEIGHT	56.2 lbs

It signals its emotions with its melodies. Scientists are studying these melodic patterns.

Description

It crosses its knifelike arms in front of its chest when it cries. It can compose melodies ad lib.

Special Moves

Fury Cutter, X-Scissor, Fell Stinger

Evolution

KRICKETOT KRICKETUNE

SHINX

001-100
101-200
201-300
401-442
443-500
501-600
701-800
801-898

Flash Pokémon

POKÉDEX NO.	**403**
TYPE	Electric
ABILITY	Intimidate, Rivalry
HEIGHT	1'08"
WEIGHT	20.9 lbs

This Pokémon generates electricity by contracting its muscles. Excited trembling is a sign that Shinx is generating a tremendous amount of electricity.

Description

Electricity makes this Pokémon's fur glow. Shinx sends signals to others of its kind by shaking the tip of its tail while the tail tip is shining brightly.

Special Moves

Thunder Shock, Thunder Wave, Crunch

Evolution

SHINX → LUXIO → LUXRAY

LUXIO

Upon encountering an opponent, this Pokémon prepares for battle by extending its claws, which can put out 1,000,000 volts of electricity.

Spark Pokémon	
POKÉDEX NO.	**404**
TYPE	Electric
ABILITY	Intimidate, Rivalry
HEIGHT	2'11"
WEIGHT	67.2 lbs

Description

By joining its tail with that of another Luxio, this Pokémon can receive some of the other Luxio's electricity and power up its own electric blasts.

Special Moves

Volt Switch, Spark, Charge

Evolution

SHINX → LUXIO → LUXRAY

LUXRAY

Seeing through solid objects uses up a lot of Luxray's electricity, so the Pokémon sleeps for long periods of time to store up energy.

Gleam Eyes Pokémon	
POKÉDEX NO.	**405**
TYPE	Electric
ABILITY	Intimidate, Rivalry
HEIGHT	4'07"
WEIGHT	92.6 lbs

Description

Luxray can see through solid objects. It will instantly spot prey trying to hide behind walls, even if the walls are thick.

Special Moves

Volt Switch, Wild Charge, Discharge

Evolution

SHINX → LUXIO → LUXRAY

001-100

101-200

201-300

401-442

443-500

501-600

701-800

801-898

BUDEW

This Pokémon is highly sensitive to temperature changes. When its bud starts to open, that means spring is right around the corner.

Bud Pokémon

POKÉDEX NO.	406
TYPE	Grass, Poison
ABILITY	Poison Point, Natural Cure
HEIGHT	0'08"
WEIGHT	2.6 lbs

Description

The pollen it releases contains poison. If this Pokémon is raised on clean water, the poison's toxicity is increased.

Special Moves

Stun Spore, Growth, Worry Seed

Evolution

BUDEW → ROSELIA → ROSERADE

ROSERADE

The poison in its right hand is quick acting.* The poison in its left hand is slow acting.** Both are life threatening.

001-100

101-200

201-300

401-442

443-500

501-600

701-800

801-898

Bouquet Pokémon	
POKÉDEX NO.	**407**
TYPE	Grass, Poison
ABILITY	Poison Point, Natural Cure
HEIGHT	2'11"
WEIGHT	32.0 lbs

Description

After captivating opponents with its sweet scent, it lashes them with its thorny whips.

Special Moves

Petal Blizzard, Petal Dance, Toxic

Evolution

BUDEW → ROSELIA → ROSERADE

*Quick acting: Quick to take effect. **Slow acting: Slow to take effect.

CRANIDOS

A primeval Pokémon, it possesses a hard and sturdy skull, lacking any intelligence within.

Head Butt Pokémon	
POKÉDEX NO.	**408**
TYPE	Rock
ABILITY	Mold Breaker
HEIGHT	2'11"
WEIGHT	69.4 lbs

Description

Its hard skull is its distinguishing feature. It snapped trees by headbutting them, and then it fed on their ripe berries.

Special Moves

Head Smash, Zen Headbutt, Take Down

Evolution

CRANIDOS ➡ RAMPARDOS

RAMPARDOS

Head Butt Pokémon

POKÉDEX NO.	409
TYPE	Rock
ABILITY	Mold Breaker
HEIGHT	5'03"
WEIGHT	226.0 lbs

In ancient times, people would dig up fossils of this Pokémon and use its skull, which is harder than steel, to make helmets.

Description

This ancient Pokémon used headbutts skillfully. Its brain was really small, so some theories suggest that its stupidity led to its extinction.

Special Moves

Ancient Power, Endeavor, Focus Energy

001-100
101-200
201-300
401-442
501-600
701-800
801-898

Evolution

CRANIDOS

RAMPARDOS

SHIELDON

Shield Pokémon

POKÉDEX NO.	410

TYPE	Rock, Steel
ABILITY	Sturdy
HEIGHT	1'08"
WEIGHT	125.7 lbs

Although its fossils can be found in layers of primeval rock, nothing but its face has ever been discovered.

Description

A mild-mannered, herbivorous Pokémon, it used its face to dig up tree roots to eat. The skin on its face was plenty tough.

Special Moves

Ancient Power, Iron Defense, Iron Head

Evolution

SHIELDON ➡ BASTIODON

BASTIODON

This Pokémon is from roughly 100 million years ago. Its terrifyingly tough face is harder than steel.

Shield Pokémon	
POKÉDEX NO.	**411**
TYPE	Rock, Steel
ABILITY	Sturdy
HEIGHT	4'03"
WEIGHT	329.6 lbs

Description

The bones of its face are huge and hard, so they were mistaken for its spine until after this Pokémon was successfully restored.

Special Moves

Heavy Slam, Metal Burst, Take Down

Evolution

SHIELDON → BASTIODON

001-100
101-200
201-300
401-442
443-500
501-600
701-800
801-898

BURMY

Plant Cloak

Trash Cloak

Sandy Cloak

If its cloak is broken in battle, it quickly remakes the cloak with materials nearby.

Bagworm Pokémon

POKÉDEX NO.	412
TYPE	Bug
ABILITY	Shed Skin
HEIGHT	0'08"
WEIGHT	7.5 lbs

Description

To shelter itself from cold, wintry winds, it covers itself with a cloak made of twigs and leaves.

Special Moves

Tackle, Bug Bite, Hidden Power

Evolution

BURMY

WORMADAM
(FEMALE ONLY)

MOTHIM
(MALE ONLY)

WORMADAM

001-100
101-200
201-300
401-442
443-500
501-600
701-800
801-898

Plant Cloak   Trash Cloak   Sandy Cloak

Bagworm Pokémon

POKÉDEX NO.	413

Plant Cloak	
TYPE	Bug, Grass
Trash Cloak	
TYPE	Bug, Steel
Sandy Cloak	
TYPE	Bug, Ground
ABILITY	Anticipation
HEIGHT	1'08"
WEIGHT	14.3 lbs

Its appearance changes depending on where it evolved. The materials on hand become a part of its body.

Description

When Burmy evolved, its cloak became a part of this Pokémon's body. The cloak is never shed.

Special Moves

Quiver Dance, Bug Buzz, Flail

Evolution

BURMY

WORMADAM
[FEMALE ONLY]

517

MOTHIM

It loves the honey of flowers and steals honey collected by Combee.*

Moth Pokémon	
POKÉDEX NO.	**414**
TYPE	Bug, Flying
ABILITY	Swarm
HEIGHT	2'11"
WEIGHT	51.4 lbs

Description

It flutters around at night and steals honey from the Combee hive.

Special Moves

Quiver Dance, Psychic, Poison Powder

Evolution

BURMY
(MALE ONLY)

MOTHIM

COMBEE

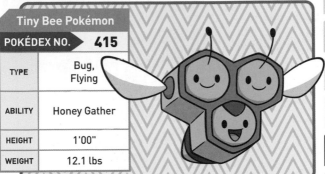

Tiny Bee Pokémon

POKÉDEX NO.	**415**
TYPE	Bug, Flying
ABILITY	Honey Gather
HEIGHT	1'00"
WEIGHT	12.1 lbs

001-100

101-200

201-300

401-442

443-500

501-600

601-700

701-800

801-898

The members of the trio spend all their time together. Each one has a slightly different taste in nectar.

Description

It ceaselessly gathers nectar from sunrise to sundown, all for the sake of Vespiquen and the swarm.

Special Moves

Gust, Sweet Scent, Struggle Bug

Evolution

COMBEE → VESPIQUEN (FEMALE ONLY)

VESPIQUEN

Vespiquen that give off more pheromones* have larger swarms of Combee attendants.

Beehive Pokémon	
POKÉDEX NO.	**416**
TYPE	Bug, Flying
ABILITY	Pressure
HEIGHT	3'11"
WEIGHT	84.9 lbs

Description

It skillfully commands its grubs in battles with its enemies. The grubs are willing to risk their lives to defend Vespiquen.

Special Moves

Attack Order, Defend Order, Slash

Evolution

COMBEE
(FEMALE ONLY)

VESPIQUEN

*Pheromone: A substance animals use toward other individuals of the same species. The reactive behavior of the others will differ depending on the type of pheromone they received.

PACHIRISU

EleSquirrel Pokémon

POKÉDEX NO.	**417**
TYPE	Electric
ABILITY	Run Away, Pickup
HEIGHT	1'04"
WEIGHT	8.6 lbs

001-100

101-200

201-300

401-442

443-500

501-600

701-800

801-898

Description

A pair may be seen rubbing their cheek pouches together in an effort to share stored electricity.

It makes fur balls that crackle with static electricity. It stores them with berries in tree holes.

Special Moves

Super Fang, Electro Ball, Charm

Evolution

PACHIRISU

Does not evolve

BUIZEL

Sea Weasel Pokémon

POKÉDEX NO.	418

TYPE	Water
ABILITY	Swift Swim
HEIGHT	2'04"
WEIGHT	65.0 lbs

It swims by rotating its two
tails like a screw. When it dives,
its flotation sac collapses.

Description

It inflates the flotation
sac around its neck and
pokes its head out of
the water to see what
is going on.

Special Moves

Water Gun, Swift,
Water Sport

Evolution

BUIZEL → FLOATZEL

FLOATZEL

001-100

101-200

201-300

401-442

443-500

501-600

601-700

701-800

801-898

It floats using its well-developed flotation sac. It assists in the rescues of drowning peuple.

Sea Weasel Pokémon	
POKÉDEX NO.	**419**
TYPE	Water
ABILITY	Swift Swim
HEIGHT	3'07"
WEIGHT	73.9 lbs

Description

Its flotation sac developed as a result of pursuing aquatic prey. Floatzel carries people as if it were a rubber raft.

Special Moves

Hydro Pump, Aqua Tail, Razor Wind

Evolution

BUIZEL

FLOATZEL

CHERUBI

Cherry Pokémon

POKÉDEX NO.	**420**
TYPE	Grass
ABILITY	Chlorophyll
HEIGHT	1'04"
WEIGHT	7.3 lbs

It evolves by sucking the energy out of the small ball where it has been storing nutrients.

It nimbly dashes about to avoid getting pecked by bird Pokémon that would love to make off with its small, nutrient-rich storage ball.

Special Moves

Morning Sun, Magical Leaf, Leafage

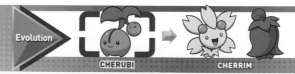

Evolution

CHERUBI → CHERRIM

CHERRIM

Blossom Pokémon

001-100
101-200
201-300
401-442
443-500
501-600
701-800
801-898

POKÉDEX NO.	421
TYPE	Grass
ABILITY	Flower Gift
HEIGHT	1'08"
WEIGHT	20.5 lbs

Sunshine Form

Overcast Form

As a bud, it barely moves. It sits still, placidly waiting for sunlight to appear.

Description

After absorbing plenty of sunlight, Cherrim takes this form. It's full of energy while it's like this, and its liveliness will go on until sundown.

Special Moves

Flower Shield, Petal Blizzard, Sunny Day

Evolution

CHERUBI ➡ CHERRIM

SHELLOS

WEST SEA

This Pokémon's habitat shapes its physique. According to some theories, life in warm ocean waters causes this variation to develop.

Sea Slug Pokémon

POKÉDEX NO.	422
TYPE	Water
ABILITY	Sticky Hold, Storm Drain
HEIGHT	1'00"
WEIGHT	13.9 lbs

Description

Subjecting this Pokémon to a strong force causes it to secrete a strange purple fluid. Though harmless, the fluid is awfully sticky.

Special Moves

Water Gun, Muddy Water, Body Slam

Evolution

SHELLOS
(WEST SEA)

GASTRODON
(WEST SEA)

SHELLOS

EAST SEA

Its appearance changes depending on the environment. One theory suggests that living in cold seas causes Shellos to take on this form.

001-100
101-200
201-300
401-442
443-500
501-600
701-800
801-898

Sea Slug Pokémon

POKÉDEX NO.	422
TYPE	Water
ABILITY	Sticky Hold, Storm Drain
HEIGHT	1'00"
WEIGHT	13.9 lbs

Description

There's speculation that its appearance is determined by what it eats, but the truth remains elusive.

Special Moves

Water Gun, Muddy Water, Body Slam

Evolution

 →

SHELLOS (EAST SEA)   GASTRODON (EAST SEA)

GASTRODON

WEST SEA

The softness of its body helps disperse the force of impacts, so although its body is uncommonly squishy, it's also surprisingly resilient.

Sea Slug Pokémon

POKÉDEX NO.	**423**
TYPE	Water, Ground
ABILITY	Sticky Hold, Storm Drain
HEIGHT	2'11"
WEIGHT	65.9 lbs

Description

Its search for food sometimes leads it onto land, where it leaves behind a sticky trail of slime as it passes through.

Special Moves

Water Pulse, Earth Power, Rain Dance

Evolution

SHELLOS
(WEST SEA)

GASTRODON
(WEST SEA)

GASTRODON

001-100

101-200

201-300

401-442

443-500

501-600

701-800

801-898

EAST SEA

It secretes a purple fluid to deter enemies. This fluid isn't poisonous—instead, it's super sticky, and once it sticks, it's very hard to unstick.

Sea Slug Pokémon	
POKÉDEX NO.	**423**
TYPE	Water, Ground
ABILITY	Sticky Hold, Storm Drain
HEIGHT	2'11"
WEIGHT	65.9 lbs

Description

Its body is covered in a sticky slime. It's very susceptible to dehydration, so it can't spend too much time on land.

Special Moves

Water Pulse, Earth Power, Rain Dance

Evolution

SHELLOS
(EAST SEA)

GASTRODON
(EAST SEA)

AMBIPOM

Long Tail Pokémon

POKÉDEX NO.	424

TYPE	Normal
ABILITY	Pickup, Technician
HEIGHT	3'11"
WEIGHT	44.8 lbs

Description

In their search for comfortable trees, they get into territorial disputes with groups of Passimian.* They win about half the time.

It uses its tails for everything. If it wraps both of its tails around you and gives you a squeeze, that's proof it really likes you.

Special Moves

Double Hit, Fury Swipes, Tickle

Evolution

AIPOM → AMBIPOM

*Passimian: A Pokémon you'll find in volume 2.

DRIFLOON

Balloon Pokémon

POKÉDEX NO.	**425**
TYPE	Ghost, Flying
ABILITY	Aftermath, Unburden
HEIGHT	1'04"
WEIGHT	2.6 lbs

The gathering of many souls gave rise to this Pokémon. During humid seasons, they seem to appear in abundance.

Description

Perhaps seeking company, it approaches children. However, it often quickly runs away again when the children play too roughly with it.

Special Moves

Shadow Ball, Gust, Destiny Bond

001-100
101-200
201-300
401-442
443-500
501-600
701-800
801-898

Evolution

DRIFLOON → DRIFBLIM

DRIFBLIM

Blimp Pokémon

POKÉDEX NO.	**426**
TYPE	Ghost, Flying
ABILITY	Aftermath, Unburden
HEIGHT	3'11"
WEIGHT	33.1 lbs

It grabs people and Pokémon and carries them off somewhere. Where do they go? Nobody knows.

Description

Some say this Pokémon is a collection of souls burdened with regrets, silently drifting through the dusk.

Special Moves

Phantom Force, Strength Sap, Self-Destruct

Evolution

DRIFLOON ➡ DRIFBLIM

BUNEARY

001-100
101-200
201-300
401-442
443-500
501-600
701-800
801-898

Rabbit Pokémon	
POKÉDEX NO.	**427**
TYPE	Normal
ABILITY	Run Away, Klutz
HEIGHT	1'04"
WEIGHT	12.1 lbs

If both of Buneary's ears are rolled up, something is wrong with its body or mind. It's a sure sign the Pokémon is in need of care.

Description

Buneary can attack by rolling up its ears and then striking with the force created by unrolling them. This attack becomes stronger with training.

Special Moves

Double Kick, Quick Attack, Baby-Doll Eyes

Evolution

BUNEARY → LOPUNNY

LOPUNNY

Once the hot seasons are over, Lopunny's coat will be replaced with fur that holds a lot of insulating air in preparation for colder weather.

Rabbit Pokémon

POKÉDEX NO.	428
TYPE	Normal
ABILITY	Cute Charm, Klutz
HEIGHT	3'11"
WEIGHT	73.4 lbs

Description

Lopunny is constantly monitoring its surroundings. If dangers approaches, this Pokémon responds with super-destructive kicks.

Special Moves

High Jump Kick, Entrainment, Bounce

Evolution

  →

BUNEARY LOPUNNY

MEGA LOPUNNY

LOPUNNY

001-100
101-200
201-300
401-442
443-500
501-600
701-800
801-898

Mega Evolution awakens its combative instincts. It has shed any fur that got in the way of its attacks.

Rabbit Pokémon	
POKÉDEX NO.	**428**
TYPE	Normal, Fighting
ABILITY	Scrappy
HEIGHT	4'03"
WEIGHT	62.4 lbs

Description

It swings its ears like whips and strikes its enemies with them. It has an intensely combative disposition.

Special Moves

Dizzy Punch, High Jump Kick, Agility

535

MISMAGIUS

Magical Pokémon

POKÉDEX NO.	**429**
TYPE	Ghost
ABILITY	Levitate
HEIGHT	2'11"
WEIGHT	9.7 lbs

Its muttered curses can cause awful headaches or terrifying visions that torment others.

Description

Feared for its wrath and the curses it spreads, this Pokémon will also, on a whim, cast spells that help people.

Special Moves

Mystical Fire, Phantom Force, Spite

Evolution

MISDREAVUS → MISMAGIUS

HONCHKROW

Its goons take care of most of the fighting for it. The only time it dirties its own hands is in delivering the final blow to finish off an opponent.

Big Boss Pokémon	
POKÉDEX NO.	**430**
TYPE	Dark, Flying
ABILITY	Insomnia, Super Luck
HEIGHT	2'11"
WEIGHT	60.2 lbs

Description

It will absolutely not forgive failure from or betrayal by its goons. It has no choice in this if it wants to maintain the order of the flock.

Special Moves

Night Slash, Wing Attack, Dark Pulse

Evolution

MURKROW → HONCHKROW

001-100
101-200
201-300
401-442
443-500
501-600
701-800
801-898

GLAMEOW

Catty Pokémon	
POKÉDEX NO.	**431**
TYPE	Normal
ABILITY	Limber, Own Tempo
HEIGHT	1'08"
WEIGHT	8.6 lbs

When it's happy, Glameow demonstrates beautiful movements of its tail, like a dancing ribbon.

Description

It claws if displeased and purrs when affectionate. Its fickleness is very popular among some.

Special Moves

Fake Out, Play Rough, Fury Swipes

Evolution

GLAMEOW → PURUGLY

PURUGLY

It will claim another Pokémon's nest as its own if it finds a nest sufficiently comfortable.

001-100
101-200
201-300
401-442
443-500
501-600
701-800
801-898

Tiger Cat Pokémon	
POKÉDEX NO.	432
TYPE	Normal
ABILITY	Own Tempo, Thick Fat
HEIGHT	3'03"
WEIGHT	96.6 lbs

Description

To make itself appear intimidatingly beefy, it tightly cinches its waist with its twin tails.

Special Moves

Body Slam, Hypnosis, Feint Attack

Evolution

GLAMEOW

PURUGLY

539

CHINGLING

Bell Pokémon	
POKÉDEX NO.	**433**
TYPE	Psychic
ABILITY	Levitate
HEIGHT	0'08"
WEIGHT	1.3 lbs

There is an orb inside its mouth. When it hops, the orb bounces all over and makes a ringing sound.

Description

Each time it hops, it makes a ringing sound. It deafens foes by emitting high-frequency cries.

Special Moves

Wrap, Astonish, Entrainment

Evolution

 ➡

CHINGLING   CHIMECHO

001–100

101–200

201–300

401–442

443–500

501–600

701–800

801–898

STUNKY

If it lifts its tail and points its rear at you, beware. It's about to spray you with a fluid stinky enough to make you faint.

Skunk Pokémon

POKÉDEX NO.	**434**
TYPE	Poison, Dark
ABILITY	Stench, Aftermath
HEIGHT	1'04"
WEIGHT	42.3 lbs

Description

From its rear, it sprays a foul-smelling liquid at opponents. It aims for their faces, and it can hit them from over 16 feet away.

Special Moves

Poison Gas, Venoshock, Explosion

Evolution

STUNKY   SKUNTANK

SKUNTANK

It digs holes in the ground to make its nest. The stench of the fluid it lets fly from the tip of its tail is extremely potent.

Skunk Pokémon	
POKÉDEX NO.	**435**
TYPE	Poison, Dark
ABILITY	Stench, Aftermath
HEIGHT	3'03"
WEIGHT	83.8 lbs

Description

In its belly, it reserves stinky fluid that it shoots from its tail during battle. As this Pokémon's diet varies, so does the stench of its fluid.

Special Moves

Flamethrower, Venom Drench, Toxic

Evolution

STUNKY

SKUNTANK

BRONZOR

They are found in ancient tombs. The patterns on their backs are said to be imbued with mysterious power.

Bronze Pokémon

POKÉDEX NO.	436
TYPE	Steel, Psychic
ABILITY	Levitate, Heatproof
HEIGHT	1'08"
WEIGHT	133.4 lbs

Description

Polishing Bronzor to a shine makes its surface reflect the truth, according to common lore. Be that as it may, Bronzor hates being polished.

Special Moves

Confusion, Safeguard, Hypnosis

Evolution

BRONZOR   BRONZONG

BRONZONG

Some believe it to be a deity that summons rain clouds. When angered, it lets out a warning cry that rings out like the tolling of a bell.

Bronze Bell Pokémon	
POKÉDEX NO.	**437**
TYPE	Steel, Psychic
ABILITY	Levitate, Heatproof
HEIGHT	4'03"
WEIGHT	412.3 lbs

Description

Ancient people believed that petitioning Bronzong for rain was the way to make crops grow.

Special Moves

Gyro Ball, Heavy Slam, Iron Defense

Evolution

BRONZOR → BRONZONG

BONSLY

001-100
101-200
201-300
401-442
443-500
501-600
701-800
801-898

Bonsai Pokémon

POKÉDEX NO.	438
TYPE	Rock
ABILITY	Rock Head, Sturdy
HEIGHT	1'08"
WEIGHT	33.1 lbs

Description

It expels both sweat and tears from its eyes. The sweat is a little salty, while the tears have a slight bitterness.

This Pokémon lives in dry, rocky areas. As its green spheres dry out, their dull luster increases.

Special Moves

Fake Tears, Rock Tomb, Double-Edge

Evolution

BONSLY → SUDOWOODO

MIME JR.

Mime Pokémon	
POKÉDEX NO.	**439**
TYPE	Psychic, Fairy
ABILITY	Soundproof, Filter
HEIGHT	2'00"
WEIGHT	28.7 lbs

It looks for a Mr. Rime that's a good dancer and carefully copies the Mr. Rime's steps like an apprentice.

Description

It mimics everyone it sees, but it puts extra effort into copying the graceful dance steps of Mr. Rime as practice.

Special Moves

Copy Cat, Psybeam, Psychic

Evolution

MIME JR.

MR. MIME

MR. MIME (GALARIAN FORM)

MR. RIME

HAPPINY

Playhouse Pokémon

POKÉDEX NO.	**440**
TYPE	Normal
ABILITY	Natural Cure, Serene Grace
HEIGHT	2'00"
WEIGHT	53.8 lbs

Happiny's willing to lend its precious round stone to those it's friendly with, but if the stone isn't returned, Happiny will cry and throw a tantrum.

Description

Mimicking Chansey, Happiny will place an egg-shaped stone in its belly pouch. Happiny will treasure this stone.

Special Moves

Copy Cat, Minimize, Sweet Kiss

001-100
101-200
201-300
401-442
443-500
501-600
701-800
801-898

Evolution

HAPPINY → CHANSEY → BLISSEY

CHATOT

Music Note Pokémon

POKÉDEX NO.	**441**
TYPE	Normal, Flying
ABILITY	Keen Eye, Tangled Feet
HEIGHT	1'08"
WEIGHT	4.2 lbs

It can learn and speak human words. If they gather, they all learn the same saying.

Description

It mimics the cries of other Pokémon to trick them into thinking it's one of them. This way they won't attack it.

Special Moves

Hyper Voice, Confide, Sing

Evolution

CHATOT

Does not evolve

SPIRITOMB

All Spiritomb's mischief and misdeeds compelled a traveler to use a mysterious spell to bind Spiritomb to an odd keystone.

001-100

101-200

201-300

401-442

443-500

501-600

701-800

801-898

Forbidden Pokémon

POKÉDEX NO.	442
TYPE	Ghost, Dark
ABILITY	Pressure
HEIGHT	3'03"
WEIGHT	238.1 lbs

Description

Exactly 108 spirits gathered to become this Pokémon. Apparently there are some ill-natured spirits in the mix.

Special Moves

Confuse Ray, Shadow Ball, Dream Eater

Evolution

Does not evolve

SPIRITOMB

POKÉ BALL GUIDE

There are many kinds of Poké Balls that can be used against wild Pokémon. Each ball has a different effect!

POKÉ BALL

A ball used to capture a wild Pokémon.

GREAT BALL

A ball that has a better chance of capturing a Pokémon than a Poké Ball.

ULTRA BALL

A ball that has a greater chance of capturing a Pokémon than a Great Ball.

MASTER BALL

An amazing ball that will catch any wild Pokémon without fail.

PREMIER BALL

A rare ball made in commemoration of some event.

CHERISH BALL

A very rare ball made in commemoration of some event.

HEAL BALL

A remedial ball that eliminates any status conditions and heals the captured Pokémon's wounds.

NET BALL

A ball that works well on Water- and Bug-type Pokémon.

DUSK BALL

A ball that makes it easier to capture Pokémon at night and inside caves.

NEST BALL

A ball that works better on lower-level Pokémon.

QUICK BALL

A ball that has a high catch rate if you use it at the beginning of a battle.

TIMER BALL

A ball that is more effective the more turns you spend in battle.

REPEAT BALL

A ball that is more effective on Pokémon you've caught before.

DIVE BALL

A ball that is effective on Pokémon that live underwater.

LUXURY BALL

A ball that makes the captured Pokémon grow more friendly.

SAFARI BALL

A special ball that is only used in the Safari Zone.

BEAST BALL

A unique ball that has a better catch rate for capturing an Ultra Beast.

LURE BALL

A Poké Ball for catching Pokémon hooked by a rod when fishing.

LEVEL BALL

A ball for catching Pokémon that are of a lower level than your own Pokémon.

MOON BALL

A ball that is effective against Pokémon that evolve with the Moon Stone.

HEAVY BALL

A Poké Ball for catching very heavy Pokémon.

FAST BALL

A ball effective for catching fast Pokémon.

FRIEND BALL

A Poké Ball that makes the captured Pokémon more friendly.

LOVE BALL

A ball that is effective at catching Pokémon that are the opposite gender of your Pokémon.

ALPHABETICAL INDEX

Use this index to locate your favorite Pokémon from each volume!
The index is listed alphabetically by the Pokémon's name, with the
volume number and page number next to it.

NAME	VOL.	PAGE	NAME	VOL.	PAGE	NAME	VOL.	PAGE
Shaymin	2	69	Smeargle	1	308	Sunflora	1	259
Shedinja	1	372	Smoochum	1	311	Sunkern	1	258
Shelgon	1	466	Sneasel	1	286	Surskit	1	363
Shellder	1	137	Snivy	2	75	Swablu	1	420
Shellos	1	526	Snom	2	511	Swadloon	2	122
Shelmet	2	204	Snorlax	1	203	Swalot	1	402
Shieldon	1	514	Snorunt	1	454	Swampert	1	336
Shiftry	1	354	Snover	2	28	Swanna	2	169
Shiinotic	2	366	Snubbull	1	278	Swellow	1	356
Shinx	1	507	Sobble	2	435	Swinub	1	291
Shroomish	1	365	Solgaleo	2	404	Swirlix	2	284
Shuckle	1	283	Solosis	2	165	Swoobat	2	108
Shuppet	1	444	Solrock	1	426	Sylveon	2	300
Sigilyph	2	147	Spearow	1	42	Taillow	1	355
Silcoon	1	345	Spectrier	2	546	Talonflame	2	259
Silicobra	2	469	Spewpa	2	261	Tangela	1	167
Silvally	2	383	Spheal	1	457	Tangrowth	2	35
Simipour	2	96	Spinarak	1	233	Tapu Bulu	2	400
Simisage	2	92	Spinda	1	414	Tapu Fini	2	401
Simisear	2	94	Spiritomb	1	549	Tapu Koko	2	398
Sinistea	2	486	Spoink	1	412	Tapu Lele	2	399
Sirfetch'd	2	501	Spritzee	2	282	Tauros	1	184
Sizzlipede	2	481	Squirtle	1	21	Teddiursa	1	287
Skarmory	1	299	Stakataka	2	421	Tentacool	1	108
Skiddo	2	269	Stantler	1	307	Tentacruel	1	109
Skiploom	1	255	Staraptor	1	502	Tepig	2	78
Skitty	1	380	Staravia	1	501	Terrakion	2	228
Skorupi	2	20	Starly	1	500	Thievul	2	450
Skrelp	2	290	Starmie	1	175	Throh	2	119
Skuntank	1	542	Staryu	1	174	Thundurus	2	232
Skwovet	2	439	Steelix	1	276	Thwackey	2	428
Slaking	1	369	Steenee	2	372	Timburr	2	113
Slakoth	1	367	Stonjourner	2	513	Tirtouga	2	151
Sliggoo	2	305	Stoutland	2	88	Togedemaru	2	389
Slowbro	1	122	Stufful	2	369	Togekiss	2	38
Slowking	1	266	Stunfisk	2	206	Togepi	1	241
Slowpoke	1	120	Stunky	1	541	Togetic	1	242
Slugma	1	289	Sudowoodo	1	252	Torchic	1	330
Slurpuff	2	285	Suicune	1	318	Torkoal	1	411

The Complete Pokémon Pocket Guide
Volume 1

VIZ Media Edition

Original Japanese edition published by SHOGAKUKAN.
English translation rights in United States of America, Canada,
the United Kingdom, Ireland, Australia, and New Zealand
arranged with SHOGAKUKAN.

Editing/Writing (Original Japanese Edition): Takuma Kaede
Translation (VIZ Media Edition): Tetsuichiro Miyaki
English Adaptation (VIZ Media Edition): Christine Hunter
Design (Original Japanese Edition): Yuriko Naito, Yu Ishimoto
Design (VIZ Media Edition): Paul Padurariu
Editor (VIZ Media Edition): Joel Enos

Special thanks to Trish Ledoux and Wendy Hoover at The Pokémon
Company International.

The stories, characters, and incidents mentioned in this publication
are entirely fictional.

Library of Congress Cataloging-in-Publication data available.

Printed in China

Published by VIZ Media, LLC
P.O. Box 77010
San Francisco, CA 94107

10 9 8 7 6 5 4 3 2 1
First printing, April 2024

VIZ MEDIA
viz.com

PARENTAL ADVISORY
POKÉMON: THE COMPLETE POKÉMON
POCKET GUIDE is rated A and is suitable
for readers of all ages.